Pamela Browning

LOVER'S LEAP

Harlequin Books

TORONTO • NEW YORK • LONDON
AMSTERDAM • PARIS • SYDNEY • HAMBURG
STOCKHOLM • ATHENS • TOKYO • MILAN
MADRID • WARSAW • BUDAPEST • AUCKLAND

ISBN 0-373-16632-X

LOVER'S LEAP

This edition published by arrangement with Harlequin Books S.A.

® and TM are trademarks of the publisher. Trademarks indicated with ® are registered in the United States Patent and Trademark Office, the Canadian Trade Marks Office and in other countries.

Printed in U.S.A.

Prologue

On the Little Deer River, more than one hundred and fifty years ago...

Tsani raced through the mist-shrouded forest, a Cherokee brave at the height of his manhood. In the distance he heard the baying of Old Man Garvey's dogs; they had been set on Tsani's trail after he'd escaped the shed where he'd been held captive. Tsani knew now that he had been a fool to try to reason with Garvey, had been stupid to think he could appease the man who wanted Margaret, his Margaret, in marriage.

Thorns tore at Tsani's clothes, wet branches slapped across his face, mud sucked at his moccasins. Or maybe it wasn't thorns or branches or mud that were holding him back—perhaps it was the mischievous Yunwi Tsundsi, the Little People of Cherokee legend. Maybe the Little People didn't want him to reach the river where his woman waited. Maybe they didn't want the two of them to escape to a better life.

The dogs grew closer, and Tsani ran even faster, his heart pounding like a drum. Sweat poured down his face, stung his eyes. He shoved aside fallen branches, sidestepped logs, leaped a boulder and fell. His ankle twisted under him, sending shooting pains up his leg. After wasting a few precious moments during which he lay stunned, his face pressed into a pile of damp leaves, he struggled to his feet, all sense of direction lost.

Then he heard it, the rush of the falls, and he knew that Long Man, the name by which the Cherokee called the Little Deer River, was nearby. Tsani crashed through a thicket and emerged onto the jutting promontory of land overhanging the stream. True to their plan, Margaret was waiting below in his canoe. She was a woman of uncommon beauty; her long golden hair trailed through the drifting mist like wayward rays of sun. The river was too high, higher than they had thought, and Tsani saw with horror that she was in danger of being swept into the rapids above the falls.

The dogs grew closer, closer, and Margaret struggled to hold the canoe against the current. He called her name, but she couldn't hear him over the din of rushing water. Frantic now, Tsani knew that with his injured ankle, he would never make it down the steep riverbank with its crumbling rock face before the dogs caught him and ripped him to shreds.

He glanced over his shoulder, heard the panting of the dogs as they broke through the underbrush, knew that if he didn't get away, any hope for happiness with Margaret was doomed.

I love you, Margaret, he told her silently, and then he stepped to the edge of the precipice and jumped.

Chapter One

If Maggie Macintyre thought anything when the man dropped out of the sky, it was that an oversize and possibly demented bird was dive-bombing from the cliff above. But she barely had time to think in that split second before he landed in the stern and swamped the canoe.

"What—?" she managed to gasp before she was precipitously tossed into the churning waters of the Little Deer River. The man, who looked as surprised as she was, slid under the water along with the canoe.

She felt him beside her in the current, his arms and legs tangling with hers as she struggled upward toward the bright surface. When Maggie came up gasping for air, she found herself staring into the darkest eyes she had ever seen, and they belonged to a man with bronzed skin and long wet black hair that swirled around his shoulders. The eyes blinked once, and strong arms curved around her to hold her up.

"Can you swim?" shouted the man over the rush of the water, and instead of answering, Maggie twisted out of his embrace and kicked toward shore. She regretted not wearing a life jacket; it was hanging on a hook back at the cabin. Fortunately, she was a competent swimmer.

Nevertheless she was out of breath when she grabbed a tree limb protruding from the steep bank and heaved herself up onto a rock ledge. The man was close behind her, his body slick and shiny as he slid effortlessly out of the water.

"Are you all right?" he asked, but she was watching in dismay as her new canoe surfaced and careened crazily toward the noisy rapids, bumping against boulders as it went. She had spent too much money on that canoe, and now it was gone. She knew it would never survive its inevitable trip over the falls.

"I said," repeated her companion, "are you all right?"

"No," Maggie snapped in outright disgust. "And what ever possessed you to jump into my canoe? Of all the stupid things to do, that is possibly—no, *probably*—the stupidest." She was pleased when he winced under her glare.

He tossed a stray strand of hair out of his eyes. "You wouldn't believe why I did it," he said.

"So you did jump? You didn't fall? You weren't pushed?"

"Oh, I jumped, all right," he said. He was clearly paying too much attention to the way her wet silk blouse outlined her breasts.

Maggie rounded her shoulders in an attempt at concealment. Not that this did much good; her breasts were swollen and tender, the nipples puckered with the chill of the damp air. When he still didn't have the good manners to look away, she scooted as far back on the ledge as she could and drew her knees up to her chest.

"It was a new canoe. I bought it only two days ago," she said forlornly. She shivered.

''You're cold,'' he said. He hunkered down on his haunches and peered into her face. His eyes were jet-black and anxious.

Maggie closed her own eyes to block him from her vision. Maybe if she pretended that this wasn't happening, it would all go away. She had certainly not intended to rush headlong into yet another Awful Predicament when she started out in her canoe. All she'd had in mind was a leisurely paddle downstream and back. She'd thought that her time on the river would be an opportunity to think. To plan. To curse Kip Baker, the guy who had run out on her, and to indulge in a good therapeutic cry if she felt like it. Right now she certainly felt like crying, but it wasn't because of Kip Baker. It was because of being dumped into the drink by this man in a loincloth.

A loincloth? Was the man really wearing a loincloth? She opened one eye slightly and peeked through the slit. Yes. He *was* wearing a loincloth. And that was all.

''Look, we'd better get you home. I'll see you safely there. You can't sit around in wet clothes.'' His eyes were remarkably watchful, and she detected a certain expectancy.

''At least I'm wearing clothes to sit around in,'' she retorted, opening the other eye and attempting to stare him down.

He ignored both the remark and the stare and stood up, pulling her with him. ''Come along. We'd better get moving before the sun goes down.''

Maggie yanked her hand away. It had not escaped her that he hadn't expressed one iota of apology about the loss of her canoe. ''I'm not going anywhere with you. I don't know who you are. I don't know why you're running around in the woods half-naked. I don't know why you jumped in my canoe, and I don't know why I'm having this conversation. Goodbye, Mr. —"

"Jennings. Tate Jennings." He drew himself up to his full height, which was considerably over six feet, and she had to admit, however grudgingly, that he was a perfect physical specimen. At least her friend Bronwyn would think so. *She* didn't. Maggie liked her men a lot more civilized. More urbane. More *clothed*. At least at the outset. She certainly didn't find anything attractive about this wild man with wet hair slicked back like an otter's and eyes that were hungry for more than she had to give. Now his eyes were studying her face, his gaze lingering on her lips and delving deep into her eyes as if—

As if they were lovers. For a moment, Maggie had the eerie feeling that she had known more than the sensation of this man's eyes upon her, that she had intimate knowledge of his body and heart and soul. But that was ridiculous. She didn't even know him.

"And your name?" His voice was low and melodious.

"Maggie Macintyre," she said crossly.

"Margaret," he said with a kind of wonder, and his expression softened his otherwise sharp features.

"Yes. But no one calls me that."

"Perhaps I shall. It suits you." The words implied a future relationship, which was impossible considering what Bronwyn had termed Maggie's Awful Predicament, not to mention the unlikelihood of her having anything to do with this guy. He was looking at her in such a familiar way that she wondered briefly if she had met him somewhere before. It was possible that at one of the many parties she'd attended in Atlanta their paths had crossed, or maybe in college, or even before that. Certainly she would remember him, though. Wouldn't she?

Maggie felt herself starting to blush under his thorough scrutiny, and she turned away, her heart beating fast. She told herself that she was reacting to this man in a highly inappropriate way. She knew her emotions were in a turmoil because of her Awful Predicament, but she shouldn't be imagining things.

It was time to cut this short. "Well, it was definitely *not* nice meeting you, Mr. Jennings," she said brusquely. With a curt nod in his direction, she stuffed her hands into the wet pockets of her jeans, and, keeping her head down, started up the bank toward the rock path, her sneakers squishing with every step.

The fog that had taken the river by stealth clung to the tree trunks and swirled like smoke in the hollows; damp leaves clung to her shoes. It was May in the Great Smoky Mountains, the quiet time before the tourists arrive. Maggie usually came to the cabin during the hot Atlanta summers; she had been unprepared for the almost daily afternoon thundershowers of spring, the sudden damp fogs that descended without warning and the towering silence of the forest. She was getting used to it, though. She even liked it at times.

"I can't let you find your way home alone," said a voice behind her, and she whirled to face Tate Jennings. He had walked so silently that she hadn't even been aware that he had followed her.

"Mr. Jennings—"

"Tate."

"Haven't you done enough damage for one day? What do you intend to do next? Lose me in the woods? Abandon me to the bears? Oh, there's no end to the harm I can expect if I entrust myself to you, Tate Jennings. Kindly cease and desist. I'll find my way home." She marched away, only to catch her foot in a vine and go sprawling across the path.

"The Tsagasi are at it again," he said, walking around in front of her and bending down.

His hand, strong and sinewy, was in front of her face. She didn't want him to help her up; she only wanted him to go away. He did not give any indication that he was prepared to do so, however.

Maggie shook her head to clear it. "What Tsagasi?" she said wearily.

"One of the tribes of Little People of the Cherokee. When someone trips and falls, we say that the Tsagasi tripped him or her."

"Your Tsagasi looks and feels a lot like a kudzu vine," she said, kicking her foot free of its tendrils. Her eyes were at the moment trained on Tate Jennings' feet, and her gaze rose to his knees before she realized that she really didn't want to look at the loincloth at such close range. She availed herself of his hand and hauled herself up.

When she dared to look full into his face, Tate Jennings smiled an amused smile. She found herself staring at the chiseled cleft in his chin and quickly looked away, but not before she saw a spark flare in his eyes. He knew she had been admiring him, and she was embarrassed. Why was she so fascinated by him, anyway? She couldn't have explained it to anyone; not to him, and certainly not to herself.

"The Little People are Indians between one and three feet tall. They like to laugh and have fun. There are a couple of varieties including Tsagasi and Yunwi Tsunsdi, and some like to play tricks on humans," he said easily.

Maggie was aware that the Cherokees' Qualla Boundary, their tribal-owned land, was nearby, and it suddenly occurred to her that this wearer of the loincloth, this man of the abundant black locks, was an actor who must have wandered away from the outdoor drama there. Whoever and whatever he was, she was definitely not in the mood to hear farfetched tales of Indian mythology.

"I'm part Irish," she said dismissively. "I've heard of Little People before."

"Good. Then you'll know that you can't be too careful when they're in a mood to confound, confuse and calamitize."

"Calamitize?" she said, staring up at him.

"Cause a calamity," he said. He had a characteristic way of tilting his head slightly to one side when he answered a question. "In case the Little People are so inclined," he continued, "I'm going to follow you home."

"Yes, indeed," she said stiffly. "I've certainly been calamitized enough today."

That shut him up, and he fell into step behind her as she stood up and started along the path again. This time in case any of those pesky Tsagoomahs or whatever they were called happened to be around, she took care to watch where she was going as she placed one foot in front of another.

It was a long walk home, and she'd have to cross the river. That was going to be a problem; should she try to swim across at the narrowest place where the swirling water made such a crossing dangerous, or should she ford the river at a wider point where the rocks were hazardous?

"I think it's safer at the widest point," said Tate, who was close behind her. "I've crossed the river many times, and it's easier to deal with the rocks there than with the current at the narrow place. The river's especially high now because of the spring rains."

Maggie stopped in her tracks. "I never said anything about crossing the river. How did you know that's what I need to do? Do you know where I live?"

Tate's face remained impassive. "Perhaps," he said.

Her eyes narrowed. "Have you been watching me? Who are you?"

"I told you who I am. I haven't been watching you. But I have been living in these woods, and I'm familiar with the river. We don't want to ford it in the dark, so will you please hurry up?"

"I thought you were an actor in the drama," she said uncertainly. "I thought you were taking a rehearsal break."

"A rehearsal—? You thought I was playing a part in the play the Cherokees put on for tourists near here?"

"Yes. I figured you were going for a walk maybe, I don't know."

He laughed. "I doubt that this year's actors have even started rehearsals yet. I am half Cherokee, though. I do live in these woods."

Okay, so he wasn't what she'd thought he was. So exactly who and what was he? Perhaps Maggie should have been scared of him and of this situation. No one knew where she was, and no one expected her back home at a certain time. No one would come looking for her if she didn't show up. But for some reason, this half-clad man inspired confidence. She couldn't figure out why. Maybe it was the confident set of his shoulders, or his take-charge manner, or maybe—and this was what worried her most of all—it was another misjudgment on her part. Lately she'd really gone overboard with misjudgments.

Nevertheless, she did what Tate said and made herself move. There was nothing else she could do.

It was rough going in these parts with the undergrowth so close to the steep riverbank that they had to claw their way through it in places. Sometimes they had to climb over rocks, and other times they had to crawl through narrow passageways between boulders. In places, tangles of kudzu vine, that scourge of the South that gobbled up everything in its path, made their passage next to impossible, and they had to tear at the vines with their hands to clear the way.

When the terrain finally flattened out, they found themselves walking side by side. A thin stream of sunlight had managed to slice through the fog; it slanted across Tate Jennings' face, casting his features into sharp relief. Maggie decided that although she had probably never met him before, he definitely resembled someone she knew.

Maggie eyed Tate warily. "Have you, um, lived in the woods long?"

"A little over five months. I'm reclaiming my Cherokee heritage," he said in a wry tone of voice.

She shot him a curious glance. "You sound like you're mocking yourself," she said.

He shrugged. "Yes and no. I took leave from my public relations job to live in the woods as a six-month experiment."

This came as such a surprise that Maggie didn't reply until they had walked some distance.

"Isn't it dangerous?"

He seemed amused. "In the woods, you know what the hazards are and you learn how to deal with them. Cities are far more dangerous. Think about all the carjackings, burglaries, rapes, kidnappings—"

"I'd rather not," Maggie said hastily. Atlanta, where she lived, was a perfect example of a place where all of the above could happen and often did. She changed the subject.

"I suppose you live in some sort of house? With modern conveniences?" she ventured.

He laughed. "The stars provide a roof over my head. The river and ponds and forest supply my food."

Maggie indulged in a ladylike snort. "You call that a six-month experiment? It sounds like six-month madness to me."

"Maybe so," he said, and she knew from his tone of voice that he didn't appreciate her scoffing at his way of life.

"I mean, don't you miss television? Ice cream? Cappuccino machines?"

"I'd be lying if I said I didn't, at least at first. I still have my apartment in town, and I check in there every once in a while. But I don't *need* it. I like making do with less."

"You never said why you wanted to take off into the woods in the first place," she pointed out.

He seemed reluctant. "Personal reasons," he said.

"That's not much of an answer."

"All right. I'm employed as head public relations honcho for Consolidated Development Corporation. My father died recently, and I asked for some time off as I was entitled to do under company policy."

Maggie knew of the Consolidated Development Corporation, or Conso, as it was called locally. Conso was an international company that specialized in developing resorts. One Atlanta paper had called Conso a "boon to the Great Smokies, an engine of economic development." Its executives, who had developed several successful retirement communities in Florida, were some of the most prominent movers and shakers in the South.

"That's a high-powered job," Maggie said. As a woman who fully appreciated the material things in life, she couldn't imagine walking away from such a secure position to live in the woods. Maybe he was putting her on, but she didn't think so. He seemed totally serious.

"I've been assured that my job will be waiting for me when my six months' leave is over. If..." He looked for a moment as if he had been going to say something but had thought better of it, and now his mouth was clamped shut.

"You think you won't go back?" she asked sharply.

"I think we'd better walk single file. Keep an eye out for copperheads. They tend to coil on rocks when the ground gets soggy." He moved into the lead, and Maggie, who realized that he had effectively put an end to the discussion, switched to the train of thought that he had so abruptly thrust upon her. She was terrified of snakes, and she thought she'd gladly trade a good old carjacking for a coiled copperhead any day. She concentrated on planting her feet exactly where Tate put his.

Not that he seemed to think he was in danger. Each nimble and silent step that Tate Jennings took seemed calculated, calibrated for the terrain, and he walked soundlessly. He moved fluidly, with no wasted motion. Maggie strained to emulate him but found it impossible. In her wake, twigs snapped, leaves rustled, birds squawked, and the whole woods burst into a cacophony of sound to mark her passing.

"Did you learn that after you came to live in the woods?" she called out to him.

"Learn what?"

"How to walk like an Indian."

"I told you I'm part Cherokee."

"So it's inborn? That silent stalking?"

To her surprise, he laughed. "Maybe so," was all he said.

As he forged the way through thickets of oaks and mountain laurel, Maggie became mesmerized by the slim turn of his ankles, the burgeoning muscles of his calves, the strong hard contours of his thighs and the way they met the curve of his bare buttocks. She was seized by a primitive reaction that seemed to originate somewhere apart from her emotions; she told herself to ignore it. Didn't she have enough problems right now without adding a sexual dimension to them? But at one point when Tate slowed down and she caught up, it was all she could do not to reach out and touch that smooth bronze skin.

He swiveled his head, a smile on his lips. "Anything wrong?" he said.

If he really could read her thoughts, she was in deep trouble. She shook her head. She thought he slanted a knowing look at her out of the edges of his eyes, but he didn't say anything else.

When they came to the place where Tate had said they should cross the river, he said, "I wish we had a rope. Then I'd go across by myself to secure it, and you could hold on to it as you came over."

"*I* wish we had a canoe," said Maggie.

His eyes flared. "Throwing it up to me won't bring the canoe back," he told her.

"What will? Those Little People of yours?"

"I doubt it." He bit the words off sharply.

"I still want to know why you jumped off that cliff, Tate Jennings. It was a fool thing to do."

"All right, maybe under normal circumstances it would be, but I had my reasons, which, if you insist, I'll explain later. Now are we going to stand here all day and argue, or are we going to cross the river?" He was angry, she could tell from his tone of voice, but by this time, Maggie was satisfied with even so grudging a promise of explanation for his foolhardiness. Having accomplished that, she now felt free to turn her attention to the crossing of the Little Deer River.

"How would you suggest we go about this?" she said, staring at the mist rising from the river. She didn't like the looks of the increasingly muddy water, which seemed to be rising by the minute.

"Give me your hand. It's safer if we hold on to each other."

Reluctantly Maggie extended her hand, and Tate enveloped it in his warm grip.

"We'd better do it this way," he said, moving his hand upward to grasp her wrist, and she did the same with his although her fingers were too small to encircle it.

"Hold on tight," he cautioned, and she nodded mutely.

"Ready?"

She nodded again, and he waded into the river. Gingerly she followed him until the water surged around her chest.

"Don't worry, I've crossed here lots of times," he said reassuringly. His voice was amplified by the fog and echoed eerily off the rocky banks. *Lots of times... lots of times... lots of times.* Maggie made herself feel her way carefully along the river bottom, sliding her sneakers up and down the curves of the rocks. The water was cold and fresh with torrents from the abundant spring rains.

Tate seemed unaffected by the temperature of the water; he plunged ahead, glancing back at her occasionally as she navigated in his wake. "Careful—there's a big rock here," he said once, and she skirted it carefully. Another time she lost her footing, gasping as the water rose to her neck. She was only five feet four inches tall, and she worried that the water was too deep here for her to make it safely across.

Tate hauled her toward him with a viselike grip and supported her in the circle of his arm until her feet found the bottom again. "This is the deepest point," Tate said reassuringly, answering her question before she even had a chance to ask it, and he held on to her tightly until she could proceed.

"Only a few more steps," he said when they had nearly reached the shore.

"Do those Tsagoblins of yours live in rivers?" she asked him through teeth that clattered like castanets. "Is it their idea of fun to pull people underwater?"

"Oh, there are Little People who live everywhere," he said, looking back at her with a twinkle in his eyes, but she ignored the twinkle and racked her brain for something sarcastic to say. Before she could think of anything, they had reached the shore, and Tate helped her out of the water.

"Sit down for a minute," he ordered, gesturing at a convenient flat rock, and she did, lowering herself on shaky legs. She felt exhausted.

"Your lips are blue," Tate said, sitting down beside her. Water ran off his body in rivulets, but he didn't seem cold at all.

She stuck out her hand so he could see it. "My hands are blue, too. I think I'm turning into a Smurf," she said.

"You, uh, have a clever way of putting things," he said. "How much farther is it to your place?"

"A mile. M-maybe more." Her teeth were striking against each other so hard that she was sure the enamel was rattling right off.

"You can't go on like this. We'd better get you warm," said Tate.

"So what are you g-going to do? Rub two sticks together and start a fire?"

He looked at her as if he'd like to snap back a retort, which, considering the sarcasm that dripped from her every word, she could understand.

"There's another way," he said, and before she could object, he drew her gently into his arms and held her close.

She pushed him away. "Are you out of your mind? I can't let you—"

"It's a survival tactic. In the absence of a fire or a blanket, of course you can do this," he said comfortably, pushing her head down so it rested against his smooth chest. She held herself aloof at first, then relaxed. Here she was being cradled in the arms of a fellow who seemed convinced of the existence of an Indian tribe of Little People and who was wearing only a loincloth. Her best friend Bronwyn, if she were in Maggie's place, would be laughing her head off at the absurdity of all of it. Maggie didn't dare laugh. She wasn't sure how Tate would take it.

Her cheek exactly fit the hollow between Tate's solid pectoral muscles, and his heart beat slowly and steadily beneath her ear. Below that, his bare stomach was tight and fit. Below that—she bit back a giggle. One part of her wondered, if Tate Jennings would jump into her canoe, what on earth would he do next?

"Feeling better?" he murmured after she stopped shivering, and she said, "Um-hmm." She did not, because of the laughter that seemed to be forming into a lump in her throat, trust herself to say actual words.

"Let's move," he said, and for one regretful—and possibly stupid—moment, Maggie wished he wouldn't take his arms away. Once he did, she wondered suddenly how he had made her feel so warm and so safe. Safe was not a feeling with which she felt familiar lately.

Here the path along the riverbank was wide enough for them to walk abreast. At the moment a companionable feeling existed between them, much to Maggie's surprise, and she liked it. She had felt so alone ever since Kip left, and being alone was an unaccustomed condition for her after two years of being one half of a couple.

"You wouldn't have to be alone," Bronwyn had pointed out before Maggie left Atlanta. "You could move in with me."

But Maggie hadn't wanted that; if she had moved into Bronwyn's noisy apartment, she wouldn't have been able to think about what she was going to do with her life. And Bronwyn was her boss at the advertising agency, so there would have been no getting away from the constant barrage of advice that was Bronwyn's way of offering support. No, Maggie had thought it best to retreat to the cabin on the lower slope of Flat Top Mountain that had belonged to her family for generations, there to contemplate the changes in her life. And in her body.

"Is it only my questions that you don't like to answer, or do you ignore everyone?" asked Tate, and Maggie realized that he'd been talking and she hadn't even heard him.

"I'm sorry, I wasn't paying attention. I haven't been around other people much lately, so I may have lost the knack of conversation," Maggie explained. The excuse sounded lame even to her.

"I've been living alone in these woods for five months now, but I still hear people when they talk," he pointed out.

"That makes us different, doesn't it?"

He muttered something under his breath, and she strode quickly ahead.

"We're almost there," she said when she saw the gray cedar shingles of the cabin roof through a lacy screen of dogwoods. "This place has never looked so inviting. I'll be glad to get into dry clothes."

Tate's voice held a trace of laughter. "That's not a problem for me."

Maggie rolled her eyes, but he didn't see. She moved ahead rapidly now that she was walking on familiar ground, eager to reach the cabin. At the door, she adopted a matter-of-fact air before she turned to him. "Okay, I'm safely home, and you can leave. What are you going to do about my canoe?"

"Do?" he said.

"About replacing it. It's the least you can do, considering that you're the one who is responsible for losing it."

"Perhaps it will be found safe and sound below the falls tomorrow. I'll ask the local people to look for it."

She couldn't believe the irresponsibility of the man. A gentleman, she thought with rapidly rising indignation, would have offered to buy her a new canoe.

"I thought you wanted to put on dry clothes," he said.

She did. She would. Thoroughly exasperated by this time, she pushed the cabin door open and stepped wearily inside. As always, she felt comforted to be there; the place had a way of reaching out and enfolding her, welcoming her home.

"We'll continue this discussion after I've changed," she said. When Tate hesitated uncertainly on the doorstep, she felt compelled to say, albeit ungraciously, "Come on in. You might as well. Aren't you cold?"

"Only wet," he said. By this time, his hair was beginning to dry into a long, flowing mane. When he shook his head, it separated into silky black strands that slid across his bare shoulders. For some reason, the movement and sheen of it fascinated her.

She decided to take pity on him. "Do you want to put on something dry?" she said. She cast a skeptical and cautious glance at the loincloth.

"I don't have any other clothes with me," he reminded her.

"If you wish, you can put on any of the clothes you find in the box in the utility room. They're about your size. I don't suppose you drink tea, do you?"

"Every now and then," he said.

"Well, go in the kitchen and put the teakettle on. The utility room and a half bathroom are off the kitchen. There's no shower, but you can wash off in the sink if you like. I'll be out in a minute.'' She went into the bedroom and shut the door before she realized how foolish she had been.

She had just invited a half-naked man whom she didn't even know into her cabin, which at present was supposed to be her safe refuge from the world. Bronwyn would say she was crazy.

Well, maybe she was. It wasn't something she could categorically deny. If she'd been normal, she'd still be in Atlanta spinning out sparkling ad copy for unappreciative clients. Come to think of it, she thought ruefully, if she was normal, she'd find a job that she liked better. But she'd developed expensive tastes in the seven years since she'd graduated from college, and there wasn't anyone else she could depend on to support her upscale life-style. Especially now.

Maggie peeled out of her wet clothes and stared for a moment at the expensive silk shirt. It was ruined. She tossed it and the designer jeans on a convenient chair before heading for the closet. The full-length mirror on the bathroom door reflected her image as she passed.

Her hands moved protectively to cup the slight curve of her abdomen. She'd had a close call today; she could have been swept into the rapids past Lover's Leap and over the falls. It wasn't something she liked to think about, especially now that she was harboring a new life inside her— a new life that had become infinitely precious to her in the past couple of weeks.

I'm going to have a baby, she told herself for the umpteenth time, but this time it was with a sense of amazement rather than despair. Maybe the hormones of early pregnancy were doing a number on her or maybe she was temporarily insane, but the idea of a cute little dumpling of a baby was actually pleasant. Well, mostly pleasant, if she didn't linger on thoughts of labor and delivery, which more or less terrified her. But there were a lot of babies being born everywhere, and most women had more than one. Maybe giving birth was not the ordeal that it had been cracked up to be.

And after the birth of the baby, which she now imagined dressed in a pale aqua ruffly something with a matching cap—well, how could she think about an event that wouldn't happen until six and a half months from now? The baby was on its way, and she would give birth to it. Okay, so she'd temporarily lose her figure, as Bronwyn had pointed out. And it would be hard to rear a child all by herself. But it wasn't as if other single mothers didn't do it. It wasn't as if other women hadn't found themselves in this Awful Predicament. It wasn't as if she were planning to try something completely new.

It only felt like it.

Chapter Two

Tate knew what Maggie Macintyre wanted, and he was going to give it to her. Eventually.

Sure, he'd buy her a new canoe. But there was no doubt whatsoever in his mind that as soon as she knew that he intended to do it, she'd insist that he leave. So why not make this last as long as possible?

For a moment after entering the cabin, he stood in front of the door and got his bearings. Being indoors now seemed, after five months in the woods, slightly claustrophobic. He had never realized before his stint in the outdoors how confining houses were. Walls. Roofs. Windows that kept the outside out and the inside in. It seemed unnatural to be able to look through the glass but not be able to smell or touch what was on the other side.

One thing that the cabin did, however, was give him a clue about its occupant. Letters addressed to Margaret Macintyre sat on the low table beside the door, and a pair of expensive but sturdy hiking boots seemed to have been kicked off haphazardly near the hearth, where they lay at odd angles.

Suddenly he had the distinct sense of someone near. "Maggie?" he said, whirling around, but the bedroom door was still closed. Maggie hadn't mentioned whether anyone lived with her.

No one appeared, but he continued to feel as if someone else were in the room, especially when he heard a few random notes of music being played. The instrument was a plucked mountain dulcimer, if he wasn't mistaken. He had attended a mountain crafts fair here shortly after moving to Scot's Cove; there he had listened to someone strumming such an instrument, which resembled a zither and was played with a wood plectrum. Now he listened closely. The music faded, which was when he decided that he was imagining things. Or had river water sloshing around in his ears. Or something.

He saw the box of clothes that Maggie had mentioned piled high inside the open utility room door, and he thought that he might as well put on something that would make her feel more comfortable around him. He didn't want her to ask him to leave. He wasn't quite sure how he'd achieve an objective that hadn't made itself completely clear to him yet, he only knew that it had something to do with his destiny. He still had no earthly idea how he was going to explain why he'd jumped into her canoe other than to say that this seemingly rash action was connected in some mysterious way to the dream he'd had last night.

After a spate of concerted digging through the clothes that Maggie had offered, Tate lit upon a pair of shorts and a short-sleeved shirt and put them on. He caught sight of himself in the mirror over the bathroom sink and grinned. The clothes made him look a bit more like his old self, but he didn't feel like his old self, and that was good.

Tate found the teakettle sitting on the stove. When he went to fill it, water roared out of the spigot so forcefully that it splashed out of the kettle's spout. Chagrined, he adjusted the flow, but at that moment, a faucet seemed like a particularly worthwhile gadget. Imagine turning a handle and having water spurt out! In the old days, he had taken faucets for granted.

The dishes stacked in the sink were dirty. He rummaged in the back of the kitchen cabinets until he found two clean cups, and he set them out on the kitchen counter. Then, with nothing else to do but wait for Maggie to reappear, he stuffed his damp deerskin loincloth in one pocket and prowled around the cabin.

The main section was a solid little house constructed of hickory logs and chinked with clay, probably built more than a century ago. This served as the present-day living room; one end had been partitioned off into the bedroom. Later and more modern add-ons were a dining room, the kitchen, and the half bath off the utility room. There was an indefinably warm and cheerful feeling about the cabin, a pleasant ambience at odds with Maggie's offhand and reluctant hospitality.

He liked the way the cabin was furnished in varied textures and strong colors—it was comfortably country without being too cute. Which was more than he could say about those rambling monstrosities that his colleagues at Conso were building in the former wilderness once known as Indian Ridge and now renamed Cherokee Acres. Their interior designers tended toward quaint bent-twig furniture strewn with sunbonnet-girl quilts, which were apparently supposed to convey a rustic atmosphere. They didn't.

Speaking of quilts, several pieced cotton squares were draped across the arm of a rocking chair in one corner. Tate bent for a closer look, and at that moment, the bedroom door opened and Maggie came out.

"Is the tea ready?" she asked, and he decided not to mention the mysterious dulcimer music. Judging from her tone of voice, she was still plenty hacked at him, and he supposed he couldn't blame her. It wasn't every day that a guy jumped out of the sky and scuttled a new canoe.

"I haven't heard the teakettle whistle," he said, forgetting about the music and the quilt pieces and zoning in on her.

"I broke the whistle on purpose when I realized that the last thing I wanted to hear when I'm ready for a little rest and relaxation was the screech of that kettle," she said, and although he heartily agreed with Maggie's low opinion of whistling teakettles, he didn't reply. All he could do—all he wanted to do—was look at her.

Maggie Macintyre had transformed herself from waterlogged waif into one beautiful woman. She had changed into a long floaty skirt that swirled around her legs, sensuously outlining the contours of her hips and abdomen and revealing glimpses of slim ankles and tiny feet. Above the skirt she wore a loose-fitting sort of pullover, something light and filmy and looking as if it were made of woven cobwebs. But her clothes were the least of it; it was her hair, now only slightly damp and falling in shimmering curtains from a center part, that he liked best. However, he changed his mind about that when he looked into her eyes, which were water gray and edged in long, tangled lashes.

She spared a brief glance at the shorts and shirt he had put on before brushing past him into the kitchen. For one spellbound moment he thought that their bodies might touch, but they did not. All he felt was the silken whisper of the hem of her skirt as it brushed his leg.

There was no doubt in Tate's mind that Maggie Macintyre was the woman of last night's dream, in which she had come to him gently in the dark as he slept, had pressed her supple body against the hard muscled contours of his, had wound her fingertips through his flowing locks. When, in the gray light of dawn, he had turned to her for comfort, his dream woman had been gone. *Margaret,* he'd thought as he woke up. *She is called Margaret.* He hadn't the slightest idea how he'd known her name.

Thus it had seemed no less than a miracle today when he'd spotted Maggie from the promontory as she was paddling on the river below. He'd had a sense that for an instant time stood still, ceased to exist, but he made himself pull back from the sensation and forced himself to concentrate on the woman navigating the river below. He knew this woman, knew her intimately. He had thought she wasn't real.

But she was real, and she was supposed to be his. And so, with a sense of the rightness of it all, he had jumped. He didn't know why, only that it was something that he was meant to do. And at the moment, he didn't regret doing it. He didn't regret it at all.

He was glad that Maggie wasn't aware of his thoughts as she tossed a couple of tea bags into a pot and deftly poured boiling water over them. "Do you live here with some- one?" he asked, not only because of the strange feeling he'd had that someone was watching earlier but because he wanted to get a conversation going.

"No," she said with a withering look that invited no fur- ther questions.

Okay, so he'd bombed out. He was trying to think of something else to say when she spoke up.

"I'm starved," she said, opening the refrigerator and peering inside. She took out a bowl of spaghetti and eyed it speculatively. "There's enough for two here if you want some."

Tate hadn't expected an invitation. On top of that, he hadn't eaten spaghetti for five months. His mouth watered at the thought of it.

"Well?" Maggie said. "Are you in the mood for spa- ghetti? I've got to eat something."

"Sure," he said, but it wasn't strictly the offer of food that interested him. He wanted more than anything to sit down across the table from her, to look deep into those remarkable eyes, to listen to her clear lilting speaking voice as it tripped up and down the scale; he truly had never heard such a lovely voice.

"I could make a salad if you'd like," she was saying. "This is my dinnertime." She shoved the spaghetti into the microwave oven and punched the timer.

"Whatever," he said, not wishing to appear too eager. When she took a head of lettuce, a cucumber and a tomato out of the refrigerator, he leaned against the counter, his arms folded across his chest.

"If you think the kitchen is a mess, I'm not apologizing," she said as she cut lettuce into a large bowl. "I haven't felt like cleaning it up, that's all."

"You don't need to apologize to me, in any case," he pointed out.

"That's a good point. It's you who should be apologizing. To me." She skewered him with a look and measured oil and vinegar into a cup.

"All right, I do apologize for what happened to your canoe. But how else were we going to—"

"Going to what?" she asked.

"Meet," he said.

She dumped the dressing over the salad greens and very deliberately drew a deep breath. She exhaled slowly and swiveled her head to look at him. "What makes you think that I wanted to meet you or anyone else?" she said in a dangerously low tone.

"I—well, I didn't think about that," he admitted.

The microwave bell dinged, and Maggie whirled around to take out the spaghetti. "See if you can find a couple of forks in that drawer," she said, gesturing toward the one on which his hip rested as she bore the spaghetti into the dining room.

He looked, but there were no clean eating utensils in that drawer or any other. He found a bottle of dishwashing detergent under the sink and washed two of the forks he found in the sink. He also washed two knives and two spoons. By that time, Maggie had returned.

"Okay, everything's ready," she said. He followed her into the dining room and saw that she had set two colorful plates on the oak gateleg dining table. She took the silverware from him and portioned it out.

The spaghetti steamed invitingly, and Tate's taste buds, which were now accustomed to dinners that more often than not consisted of whatever fish he happened to catch and grilled over the coals of an open fire, perked up at the prospect of tangy, tomatoey meat sauce topped with parmesan cheese.

"Sit down," she said, and he pulled out the chair and hesitated. "Go ahead. You're not wearing that leather thingamajig you had on, so you don't have to worry about splinters."

"That leather thingamajig," he said, "is part of my heritage."

"So is taking scalps," she said darkly.

Tate had grown up in the white man's world, and digging remarks had no effect on him anymore. "Are you trying to insult me?" he said mildly. Actually, he hoped she was. It would give them something to talk about.

She looked slightly less sure of herself. "No. Of course not. I'm just curious."

"I can imagine," he said, sitting down.

"When you're wearing the thingamajig—"

"Say 'loincloth.' Lots of famous people have worn one. Tarzan, for instance."

"When you're wearing it, don't you get stung by yellow jackets? Isn't sunburn a problem? And why don't you have scratches from brambles?"

He relaxed and helped himself to the spaghetti, shooting her a grin calculated to put her at ease. "I've never had a yellow jacket sting. As for sunburn, the shade of the forest prevents that. Brambles? In the old days when we Cherokees met up with a harmful plant like poison ivy, we talked to it and made it our friend in hopes that it wouldn't hurt us. I tried it with brambles, too. There—does that answer all your questions?"

She looked slightly taken aback. That tongue-in-cheek bit about the brambles had probably done that. "Not quite, but it's a start," she said, and Tate wondered what that meant.

"My turn to ask questions," he said. She raised her eyebrows, but he plunged ahead anyway. "How long have you lived here?" he asked.

"I arrived a week ago, but I've summered here forever. I usually rent the place out for most of the summer now since my job more often than not keeps me busy in Atlanta. This is the ancestral home of the Macintyres, who were part of the Scotch-Irish group that settled these mountains back in the 1700s." She pushed the saltshaker toward him.

"So, are you here on a vacation?"

"Sort of. Please pass the salad."

He wished she'd elaborate on her answers. "I should think you'd bring someone with you for company," he said.

She looked at him for a moment. "You might say that I have," she said and sipped pensively from her teacup.

"But you said—"

"Let's drop it, okay?"

He set his fork down. "Look, if my questions are too personal, I'm perfectly willing to talk about something else. Lovely rain we've been having, isn't it? Have you read any good books lately? How great an effect do you think the Atlanta Olympics will have on tourism in the mountains?" He also thought for a moment of asking if she had ever sensed something strange and eerie about this ancestral home of the Macintyres, but the thought fled when the expression on her face became even more forbidding.

Maggie banged her teacup down in its saucer so hard that tea splashed over the sides. She passed a hand over her eyes and drew a deep breath. "Oh, for Pete's sake," she said. "I knew I shouldn't have asked you to stay. I'm not fit company for anyone these days."

"I wouldn't say that," he said slowly, trying to get a handle on the situation. He had thought things were going well, that she was opening up to him, and now he had the sense that she was in full retreat. One thing was for sure: he didn't feel welcome now that her face had that pinched, shuttered look. Something was bothering her, something more serious than the loss of a canoe.

He made his decision swiftly. "I'll go," he said. He stood up and flung his napkin down before heading for the door.

A clock ticked somewhere, and birds fluttered noisily in the rafters as they settled down for the night. A purple haze hung over the distinctive humped shape of Breadloaf Mountain. Soon it would be dark.

"Wait," Maggie said. "Wait."

Something in her tone of voice gave him pause. What was it? Desperation? Misery? A little of both, perhaps, and something more as well. *Loneliness,* he thought in a burst of insight. Maggie Macintyre was lonely and terrified of being that way. Tate knew because he had so often been lonely himself.

"I really don't want you to leave," she said.

Tate went back to the table and sat down. "All right," he said evenly.

"The truth is that I came up here to think things over. To figure out what to *do* about my life."

"The first thing you should probably do is eat your spaghetti," he said. He picked up his own fork and dug in.

"By this time, you've probably figured out that there's a man involved," she said. She toyed with her food, not looking at him.

"I hadn't," he said, but his heart zoomed to his feet and back again.

"Well, there was. His name is Kip Baker, and he left me to go off to South America to photograph some god-awful beauty contest. He's a photographer, that's how he makes his living. For various reasons, I decided it was ultimatum time and said, 'Listen, Kip, if you go running off to South America, it's over,' and he said, 'I'm going,' and I said, 'Don't bother to come back if you do.' He went. I had three weeks of vacation coming, and I was planning to spend time at this cabin soon to get it ready to rent for the summer, so I came up here to get some serious thinking out of the way." She paused as if to catch her breath.

"Care to elaborate?"

"No. I just wanted to complain about Kip. And now I feel much better." She smiled at him, which was encouraging, and started to eat.

He watched her for a while, wondering how any guy in his right mind could leave Maggie Macintyre to go anywhere.

"So," he said cautiously, "are you figuring it all out?"

"A little. I've made a few major decisions, gotten acclimated, and remembered what I used to like about coming here when I was a kid. The nature aspect kind of grows on you, doesn't it?" This was said between mouthfuls.

"Yes, the mountains are a good place to do serious thinking. Maybe after a couple of weeks of peace and contentment, your problems will sort themselves out."

"Let's hope so. Would you care for more salad?" She held the bowl out toward him, and he shook his head, trying to get a handle on what made Maggie tick. She blew hot and cold at intervals; was she always like this?

The spaghetti was delicious. He complimented her on her cooking, and she blushed. "Kip used to say—" she began but stopped talking abruptly. "I've got to stop thinking about Kip, don't I?" she said.

He wanted to shout, Yes! He wanted to personally eradicate any reminder of the man from Maggie's brain. But he merely said, "It might be a good idea."

"Bronwyn said I should stop thinking about him. She's my best friend and my boss at the Mickle, Martyn, Baffin and Ousley Advertising Agency where I work." She stopped eating and frowned. "You must think I'm a raving lunatic," she said suddenly.

"Maybe a ravenous lunatic, considering the way you're digging into that spaghetti."

"To stop thinking about Kip, I should stop talking about him. To stop talking about him, I'd have to forget about the Awful Predicament I'm in, and that's impossible." Suddenly Maggie looked as if she'd said too much and clamped her mouth shut.

"He left you in an Awful Predicament?" Tate said with mild interest. Awful Predicaments held less fascination for him than the curve of her lips as she held them so tightly shut, and he wanted to reach out and touch a finger to them, and they would open and kiss his fingertip, and—

"Forget I ever said that," she said, and she got up from the table and took her plate into the kitchen. While she was gone and taking an inordinately long time doing whatever she was doing in there, Tate finished his meal, and when she came back he thought he detected a redness around her eyes that hadn't been there before.

"Well, that's dinner," she said abruptly. "If you don't mind, I have some things to do."

He was being asked to leave. Even he could figure that out, but he was confused. He'd thought they were getting along well. Had he offended her in some way?

He stood up uncertainly. There was nothing friendly about Maggie now, and she seemed disinclined to chat. He tried to think of something to say, but he failed utterly in the face of her stony expression.

"What are you going to do about my canoe?" she asked as he stood there wondering what he was supposed to do next.

Suddenly he didn't want to do anything next. He'd had enough. He wanted to be out of there. Gone was the wish to drag this out; he wasn't going to get anywhere with Maggie Macintyre. He had no doubt that she was the woman in his dream, but the dream had lied. There must be another Margaret somewhere, one with long flowing blond hair like this one, one who liked him.

"I'll replace the canoe," he said.

"It was a Coleman. I bought it at the Little Deer River Outfitters."

"I'll see that you get one as much like it as possible."

"Okay." A baffled look crossed her face, and then she cried, "Oh, no. Oh," and she clapped a hand over her mouth before bolting for the bedroom, her pale hair swinging against her back. She slammed the bedroom door behind her.

Tate, who had been about to walk out the front door, was taken by surprise. He heard the unmistakable sound of her being sick followed by water running from a faucet. He didn't know whether to stay or to go. Finally he decided to stay, pacing nervously back and forth on the living room rug and glancing anxiously now and then at the closed bedroom door. Was he responsible for her being sick because he had precipitated her being dumped into the river? Should he knock on the door and offer help? Should he call out to her? He didn't know.

When Maggie finally returned after several minutes' absence, she looked pale but composed.

"A slight stomach upset," she said tersely. "Nothing to worry about."

"Are you all right? Is there anything I can do?" Tate felt helpless and in the way.

She managed a thin smile. "Just replace my canoe so I'll have somewhere to go when I get cabin fever," she said.

He felt troubled about her. "If I can do anything to help you," he began uncertainly, knowing even as he spoke that the offer sounded shallow and insincere.

"I'd say you've done quite enough for one day." She delivered the words without humor.

"Anytime you want me to 'drop' by—" he said, hoping to get a smile out of her, but she wasn't having any of it.

"Sorry, but I'm not in the mood for jokes," she said.

"Yeah, well, I guess it was kind of a bust." He opened the door and looked back at her. Her face seemed haloed in the light from the lamp above the dining room table. She looked inexpressibly lovely and lonely. His heart went out to her, but at that moment she raised her chin and he caught a glimpse of the steeliness behind those pale gray eyes. It was a side of her that he hadn't seen before, and it surprised him. However, it didn't change his mind about leaving this place where things had gone so wrong and where he felt as if he weren't quite seeing things out of the corners of his eyes and not quite hearing things that were just out of range.

"Good night, Maggie Macintyre," he said softly.

"Good night," she said, and after he left, she closed the door with a definitive click.

At the edge of the woods, Tate looked back at the cabin. The light of Grandfather Moon seemed to wreath the clearing in magic, but it was not the right magic—not for him, and not for her.

I won't be coming back here, Tate thought as he slipped into the profound silence of the waiting forest. A soft voice whispered, *But you will,* and at that moment, he thought he saw a pale female figure flitting through the trees. When he looked over his shoulder at the cabin, Maggie was standing at the window looking out, and he decided that the figure he'd seen was only a wisp of the fog that often rose from the river.

As he made his way back up the mountain to his camp, Tate thought he could hear the Little Peoples' laughter ringing in his ears as they rolled down the hills in their hidden glens, and he shut it out, pushed it away. The night was clear, calm and cool. As the pungent scent of cedar and sweet wild honeysuckle filled Tate's nostrils, he inhaled deeply, becoming one with nature again. Ah, well, what did he need with a woman at this stage of his life? At thirty-two, he was desperately hoping to regain his spirituality. He wanted to clear himself of problems; he did not wish to take on those of Maggie Macintyre. The thing to do was to deaden his feelings. That shouldn't be so difficult. It was a skill that he had perfected long ago.

All he needed in order to be happy, he reminded himself, was a warm blanket and a full belly. But when he rolled himself in his blanket in front of his *asi,* or sleeping lodge, and tried to sleep, he couldn't stop thinking about how soft Maggie's skin had looked and how much he had wanted to touch it. And as he drifted off to sleep, the wind in the trees sighed *Margaret, Margaret, Margaret.*

MAGGIE FOUND THE NEST containing a single robin's egg on the windowsill the next morning after being awakened by dulcimer music so faint that she'd decided she'd been dreaming. In Atlanta she wouldn't have let it disturb her sleep; she would have pulled on the black satin sleep mask she kept in a bedside drawer and rolled over to catch a few more Zs.

That was impossible in the mountains, however. For one thing, she hadn't brought the sleep mask. For another, there were birds outside, and they made an awful racket with their infernal twittering and chirping. There was no sleeping late in the country.

Having resigned herself to this depressing truth, Maggie was walking around bleary-eyed in her nightgown drinking a glass of orange juice and eating a banana while she contemplated measures to make the birds shut up. When she saw the tiny pale blue robin's egg glistening in the first slanting rays of the sun, her first thought was that a bird had managed to get in the house. Her second thought was that this was ridiculous; it would have had to be a nest builder extraordinaire in order to complete construction overnight.

Suddenly the hair on the back of her neck stood up. Someone was watching her. She whipped around, knowing that whoever it was would be standing directly behind her, but no one was there.

Silly me, she thought sheepishly. *Maybe I have been by myself too long.*

She bent over to inspect the egg, which was a real robin's egg judging from the shape and delicacy of it. She set her glass down and poked at the egg with a fingernail. It wobbled slightly in the artfully woven nest. She was sure that the nest containing the egg had not been there yesterday morning when she had opened the window; she would have noticed. And she had stood at the window for a long time last night after Tate Jennings left, staring out at the forest that had so quickly enfolded him. Neither the bird's nest nor the egg had been there then.

It was a puzzlement. Like other things. Like Tate Jennings. Maggie still couldn't make any sense out of the man's dropping into her canoe yesterday.

The phone rang, startling Maggie out of her thoughts and drawing her away from the window. A ringing telephone was something new; yesterday, it hadn't been connected yet. She ran to answer it and wasn't the least bit surprised when the caller was Bronwyn.

"Maggie? Oh, I'm so relieved. I've been so worried! Why don't the phones work up there in the mountains? Why haven't you called?"

"I've been busy," Maggie said.

"How are you, anyway?" Bronwyn demanded.

"Pregnant," said Maggie, sitting down on the stool in front of the breakfast bar and propping her feet up on the one next to it.

"Oh, is that all? Gosh, Maggie, at least pregnant is better than comatose! I didn't know what had happened to you. You promised to call every couple of days or so, remember? I was ready to hop in my car and drive up there just to make sure you hadn't died or something."

Maggie was used to Bronwyn, but since she hadn't talked to her in a while, she'd forgotten how Bronwyn could carry on. Not that Maggie was any slouch in that department herself, but still.

"What have you been doing?" Bronwyn wanted to know.

"Well, apparently the phone company has hooked up the phone, which is a major breakthrough. And yesterday I met a half-naked man," she said.

Dead silence. "You're joking," said Bronwyn.

"I thought *he* was joking when he jumped into my canoe."

"You haven't mentioned why he was half-naked."

"He's a Cherokee who is reclaiming his native heritage. This requires that he run around in the woods wearing a loincloth."

"Maggie. Are you sure you're all right?"

"No."

"He didn't hurt you, did he?"

"Of course not. I invited him in for dinner, and after we ate, he left," Maggie said.

"A man wearing only a loincloth jumped into your canoe and you asked him in for dinner," Bronwyn repeated slowly.

"Well, I had all this spaghetti in the fridge, and it seemed like a good idea at the time."

"Maggie, my dear flibbertigibbet friend, are you making this up?"

"No. But I've thought of a great ad for men's underwear. 'Why *wear* briefs when it's more fun to *be* brief? Try our new formfitting loincloth. One size fits most.' How does that sound?"

Bronwyn snickered. "Like the same old Maggie. Too bad that our illustrious firm of Mickle, Martyn, Baffin and Ousley doesn't have an underwear account. When are you coming back, anyway?"

"I have another two weeks' vacation coming to me," Maggie reminded her.

"I know," said Bronwyn. "But aren't you planning a vacation in the south of France this year?"

"I was. With Kip."

"Oh. Right. Say, Maggie. Maybe this guy in the loincloth qualifies as your next main man."

"Sure, that's what I need, all right—an involvement with another man. Get real, Bronwyn."

"It was only a thought."

"Seriously, I've decided that I won't have a steady relationship for a long time. Maybe not ever. After what Kip did to me, I know better than to make that kind of commitment again," said Maggie.

"Hmm," Bronwyn said. A pause. "We miss you around the office, Maggie."

Maggie was loath to say so, but she didn't miss the hustle and bustle of the MMB&O office at all. The urban life-style she'd been living for the past few years was beginning to seem empty and pointless, and along with it, so was her job. This was not the time, however, to mention this to Bronwyn.

"Now that the phone here is working, I'll call you often," Maggie promised.

"I'm sure we've got a lot to talk over. Like what you're going to do about your Awful Predicament."

"I think I already know."

"Good! So do you want me to ask a representative of the adoption agency to call you? I'm sure—"

"No, that won't be necessary." Maggie had an idea that Bronwyn would go through the roof when she heard that she planned to keep her baby. Fortunately the matter became irrelevant when Bronwyn said quickly, "Uh-oh, got to go, Mags. I have an important call. It's that Irwin guy who's been stringing us along about those ads we're trying to sell him for his twine company."

"Twine company...stringing us along. Bronwyn, I think you're finally getting the hang of writing scintillating ad copy."

"I'll talk to you soon—if I don't get tied up."

"Right," Maggie said, and she was laughing as Bronwyn hung up.

Maggie stared at the receiver in her hand before slowly lowering it to its cradle. She was glad she hadn't had to tell Bronwyn about her decision.

Heartened by this conversation with her dearest friend, Maggie dressed in shorts and a pullover shirt and quickly cleaned up the kitchen. She'd only been here for a week, and the place was a mess. She'd told herself she needed to make more of an effort, but she really hadn't had the energy to do anything about it.

Well, she was through being depressed. This morning, she decided, she'd drive into Scot's Cove to buy groceries. She'd cook good, nutritious meals for herself and eat them by candlelight. She'd figure out how to hook up the TV antenna so she could watch her favorite programs and keep up with the news. She'd get more sleep. Her life had not ended when Kip walked out; perhaps it had just begun.

"Now where did I put my boots?" Maggie muttered to herself, finally spotting them where they'd fallen in front of the fireplace. When she sat down in her mother's old rocker to lace them, the quilt squares that she had folded over the arm of the chair fell to the floor.

She picked up a few of the pieces and laid them out on the coffee table. Each square was an appliquéd scene, the colors bright and cheerful. The first square depicted a cabin— this cabin, or at least the original section of it—and showed a family of three, a mother, a father, and a young girl. The mother was hanging clothes on a line strung between two saplings, and the girl was gazing into the distance toward what was clearly the distinctive shape of Breadloaf Mountain. The father was hoeing corn in the garden.

The quilt, never finished, had been her mother's pride and joy. "It's going to tell the story of Peg Macintyre, who is your namesake," Mom had told Maggie enthusiastically as she was cutting out the fabric. "Each square will show another scene in her life."

Maggie had yawned. "Why would anyone be interested in the life of a woman who lived a zillion years ago?" she'd asked, and her mother had tsk-tsked impatiently and said, "She didn't live quite a zillion years ago. Peg was born around 1820, and anyway, she's a local legend."

At the time, Maggie, who had just graduated from college, had been able to muster no interest in legends, local or otherwise, and she'd forgotten about her mother's ambitious project until she'd found the squares packed away in a box on the top of the bookshelves a few days ago. Her mother had never had the chance to finish the quilt. During the winter after she'd started the project, Mom had become sick and had died the following spring.

Maggie ran her fingers over the one of the quilt squares. To do so made her feel closer to her mother; that must be why she felt such a sense of well-being when she looked at them. If she had a needle and thread, Maggie could perhaps finish her mother's project as a kind of memorial to her. Suddenly, she felt compelled to do it. But why? She wasn't much of a seamstress.

Dulcimer music filled the air, a plaintive tune that tapered off into silence. *Just do it,* said a voice, and then she heard a peal of silvery laughter.

"Me?" Maggie said out loud. The word was a mere squeak, and she looked around the room for the person who had spoken to her. Her gaze fell on the robin's egg in the nest on the windowsill. It seemed to glow in the sunlight pouring through the windowpane, but when Maggie blinked her eyes, it was just an ordinary robin's egg reposing in a nest that was sitting on the windowsill. And no one was in the room with her.

The voice had been inside her head. So had the music. They couldn't have come from anywhere else.

Did pregnant women hear voices inside their heads? Was she going crazy?

Disconcerted, she waited to see if she heard anything else. But she didn't. Okay, so she was imagining things. No need to be frightened, no need to freak out over it.

Maggie stared down at the quilt pieces for a long moment before returning to the kitchen to get her shopping list.

"I'll buy sewing supplies so I can finish the quilt," she said out loud before she left, surprising herself. She couldn't have explained why she felt it necessary to speak the words to the empty room, and after she'd done it, she felt confused and more than a little ridiculous.

And she was more than grateful when no one answered.

Chapter Three

Maggie and her parents had been trading at Pinter's General Store and Sundries since before she could remember. All the local people shopped there; the place functioned as an informal town meeting hall. None of the old-timers in Scot's Cove felt comfortable in the new Piggly Wiggly supermarket out on the highway where the Conso executives' wives shopped, and there was a tacit understanding that locals were loyal to the general store.

Today, unlike most days, Maggie didn't see the usual group gathered around the old cast iron stove in the back. Today only the aged proprietor was there.

"There you are," declared an affable Jacob Pinter as he rang up Maggie's groceries, sewing supplies, a craft book about quilting and a pamphlet published by the local historical society. "That'll be $45.26."

Maggie counted the money into Jacob's hand. "You going to be here all summer?" he asked.

"Only for a couple more weeks."

"Going to rent your place for the season?"

"If I can find a tenant," she said. "It seems as if I can never count on the same people to rent the cabin for more than one season."

"Could be they don't like to be alone out there. The place is kind of isolated."

"Yes, but the cabin has all the modern amenities. It's comfortable, and I charge a reasonable rent. Let me know if you hear of anyone who needs a place, will you?"

"Sure," he said. He flicked his eyes toward the craft book, which was sticking out of one of the bags. "You interested in crafts?"

"I need something to do while I'm here. I thought I might finish the quilt my mother started a long time ago."

"I remember your mother when she was a little tike, your father too—and you as well. You've become a fine young woman." He thumped his finger against the historical society's pamphlet. "Glad to see you're interested in local history," he said.

"My parents' families were two of the first to settle Scot's Cove, so I thought I should learn something about the area. I never really appreciated my roots."

Jacob slammed the cash register drawer. "Yep, there's a lot of history in these parts. Sometimes when the mist floats up from the valley, you can almost see the shapes of the people who have gone before. Indians, settlers, traders, trappers—all must have had their own stories to tell. Say, Maggie, didn't you have some ancestor who had something to do with that Lover's Leap legend hereabouts?"

"Peg Macintyre. She fell in love with an Indian brave."

"So they say. I believe he came to a sad end. Was swept over Maidenhair Falls or something."

"I'm sure the story's in the pamphlet, so by the time I come in here next time, I'll be able to tell you all the details." Maggie hesitated, reluctant to leave.

"Mr. Pinter," she said.

"Jacob," he corrected her.

Maggie had a hard time calling this man, who seemed as old as the mountains themselves, by his given name. She had been calling him Mr. Pinter since before she could reach the countertop.

"Jacob, then," she said, and she was rewarded by his gap-toothed smile. "Jacob, do you know a man named Tate Jennings?"

"Tate Jennings," he said, chewing on the inside of his lip. "That's the fellow who lives up above your place on Flat Top Mountain near Stoker's Knob. Lives off the land."

"I met him yesterday."

"And what were you doing up by the Knob? That's a good walk from where your place is."

"He—he was near the river," Maggie said. She didn't want to relate how they had actually met. It was too bizarre.

"Eh? Well, that don't surprise me none. Tate Jennings ranges from one place to another from what I hear. Got a big piece of land up there, used to belong to his dad, who went someplace up north years ago and left the place to rot. Died not long ago. Was a big surprise to all of us when his father left it to young Tate. We never knew Phil Jennings had a son."

"You knew Tate's family?"

"In a way, though in later years there was only Phil, who mostly kept to himself. Phil Jennings was a full-blood Cherokee whose folks owned that land before the government moved the Indians to the territory out west."

Maggie knew of this shameful episode in American history when seventeen thousand Cherokees had been rounded up from the mountains at gunpoint by soldiers, thrown into concentration camps, and their homes burned prior to resettlement in the west. They had been forced to march to Oklahoma in winter, and four thousand of them had died along the way.

"Well, the Jennings family was one of maybe seventy households that didn't have to go to Oklahoma. About four hundred Cherokee had bought land outside the Cherokee Nation around here, and they weren't made to leave. Along with the Cherokees that escaped the soldiers and hid out in the woods, they eventually formed the eastern band of the Cherokee. Anyway, there's no buildings on the Jennings property now, nothing but woods and rocks."

"Tate has apparently established his camp there. He told me that he's on a leave of absence from Conso. He said he's manager of their public relations office."

"Yup, that's true. Used to be, there was hardly a week went by that you didn't see that young Jennings fellow with his face plastered all over the television giving money to this charity or that one on behalf of Conso, glad-handing with politicians and explaining to reporters how the company was going to dig out a flat place on the east side of Breadloaf Mountain and put hundreds of tiny mobile homes with septic tanks up there."

"Mobile homes? On Breadloaf Mountain?" She was aghast.

"That's what Conso intends to do."

"Oh, no." Maggie hadn't heard of this before. Breadloaf Mountain was a wilderness area adjacent to Cherokee land; she had a spectacular view of the mountain from her cabin. She remembered hiking up Breadloaf with her mother every summer, dabbling her hot feet in the trilling little brooks that ran so merrily down the mountainside, taking pictures of the sun setting behind it with her first Instamatic camera. She couldn't imagine those deeply forested slopes carved into a mobile home park.

"You can't slow progress, or so they say," Jacob said. "'Course, there's those who like to try." He removed his glasses and rubbed them clean with the wrinkled bandanna he took from his back pocket.

"You mean someone is trying to prevent it?"

"Oh, the Kalmia Conservation Coalition, for one. They've got a lot of people stirred up about what Conso plans to do to Breadloaf. Trouble is, it ain't easy to fight Conso. All the big guns are on their side."

A stout woman with two small rambunctious children came in, slamming the door behind her. "You got any spray starch?" she asked Jacob as the children galloped energetically around the counter.

"To your left," he told her, and Maggie gathered up her groceries thoughtfully. Jacob Pinter turned to shoo the kids away from the Tom's Peanuts display, but before Maggie left, he called out, "The Kalmia Conservation Coalition is the name of the group. There's a number you can call in the phone book if you're interested."

She wasn't interested in joining any coalition, Maggie thought as she loaded the grocery bags into the trunk of her sleek little BMW. But she hated the thought of Breadloaf Mountain's being sliced up into bite-size portions.

The external appearance of the quiet and unspoiled town of Scot's Cove, which she'd loved ever since she was a child, had been changed for the better by Conso, she noticed as she drove down the main street and saw fresh paint on the storefronts and flower-filled planters along the curbs. New lampposts had replaced the old, ugly ones, and cozy park benches had been placed amid newly planted greenery. Conso was building a ski resort and several condominium buildings on nearby Candlelight Mountain; this would expand the tourist season to winter as well as summer. These were positive things that the company had done for the area.

But she didn't think she'd ever reconcile herself to the idea of Breadloaf Mountain's development. The majestic east face of Breadloaf was visible through the trees as her car started up Flat Top Mountain. No rooftops broke the hazy symmetry of Breadloaf's wilderness slopes; no roads scarred the peak. The more she thought about the mobile home park, the more angry Maggie became. How dare Conso destroy Breadloaf Mountain? Because destroy it they would, if they persisted with their plans. By the time she reached the cabin, she was furious.

She carried her groceries inside and put them away, fuming all the while. As she was finishing, a knock sounded on the door, which was a surprise because she had no near neighbors and so far, no one had visited.

"Who is it?" she called curtly.

"Tate," was the reply.

She pulled aside the curtain on the window to see Tate Jennings standing outside. Today he was wearing jeans and a T-shirt, and he was carrying something, although she couldn't see what. It wasn't big enough to be her new canoe, she could tell that.

She didn't want to invite him in, so she released the bolt on the door and burst outside, embarrassed when she had to stop stock-still because there was nowhere to go.

"Most people in these parts don't lock their doors," he said, smiling down at her.

When she refused to smile back, his own smile faded. "I brought back the clothes I borrowed," he said as he handed her the bundle he carried. Silhouetted against the mountains beyond with his thick rebellious mane flung back, Tate's high forehead and prominent cheekbones were unmistakably Indian.

Maggie looked down at the shirt and shorts. They brought back unwelcome memories of Kip and the weekends they had spent here. "You could have kept them," she said.

"I thought the person to whom they belonged might want them back." He studied her, the expression in his eyes inscrutable.

"The person to whom they belonged may be slogging around in the Amazon jungle right now. For all I know, he might be wearing loincloths," she said.

"Oh. You didn't mention that the clothes belonged to your boyfriend," Tate said.

"My *ex*-boyfriend," she reminded him.

He nodded slowly as if he were thinking something over. "About last night..." he began, but then he stopped.

"Forget it. I'm not in the mood," she said. She shaded her eyes against the sun. "You know what I heard today? I heard that Conso is going to build a mobile home park on Breadloaf Mountain."

"It's true," Tate told her. "The development is called Balsam Heights."

"It's bad enough that they're building condominiums on Candlelight Mountain, but it already has a number of rental apartment buildings, so condos don't seem out of character there. But Breadloaf has always been a wilderness area, a place where we would go to enjoy the spectacular scenery. Why, from Breadloaf Mountain, you can see Candlelight Mountain and Flat Top Mountain and the Little Deer River and, on clear days, all the way to Georgia. I might get used to condominiums on Candlelight, but not, by God, to mobile homes on Breadloaf."

"Top management at Conso believes that mobile homes are the best use of the property."

Maggie let out an exasperated sigh. "What makes Conso think that they can come into a place like this and chop it up into little pieces with no thought to what those of us who have been here for generation after generation think about it?"

"Maggie, the county council, whose members represent the people, voted for the zoning."

"The council doesn't represent me.".

"This region has had a tough time economically in the past several years. Building mobile home sites will mean work for construction companies and their workers. Managing the park and taking care of the grounds will employ a lot of people. The homes will be owned by vacationers who will pump money into the economy. There will be five hundred home sites—"

"Five hundred!" She recoiled in horror, picturing row upon row of little boxes. "What can they be thinking of?"

"Making money," Tate said.

Maggie folded her arms across her chest and squinted into the sun. "How can you work for them? How can you be a part of it?" Her tone was accusatory.

Tate clenched his jaw, and the muscles worked. She saw a vein throbbing at his temple.

"Well?" she said.

"Look, I didn't come over here to get involved in an argument about Conso. I came to return the clothes and to ask if you'd mind if I fished in that little pond above the bend in the river. It's on your property, I believe, and there used to be a sign that said No Fishing."

"You mean the sign is gone?"

"I didn't see it, so I thought maybe you had changed your mind and let people fish there now."

She shook her head. "My father put up the sign years ago after the summer people who rent the A-frames near the highway began to consider it their own private pond. They'd throw their hamburger wrappers and foam cups around, and he and my mother and I had to clean up the mess."

"I'll understand if you don't want me fishing there," Tate said.

"I don't mind if you do," she said, which wasn't at all what she'd intended to say. She'd thought that she didn't want anyone intruding on her privacy, and now she was giving Tate Jennings carte blanche to come on her land.

Then she surprised herself by asking, "Want to walk down to the pond with me? I need to see if that sign's still around. I don't want tourists taking the place over again."

He seemed as surprised as she was at the invitation. "Sure," he said.

"Wait a minute," she said. "I'll bring along a snack." She went back in the cabin and took two shiny red McIntosh apples from the fruit bowl on the dining room table and slid them into a tote bag.

Today the air was rife with the green scent of growing things. Long skirts of wisteria trailed from a vine at the edge of the clearing, delicate lavender petals piling up on the ground below as the breeze tumbled them down. Above them the sky shone clear and bright, dotted with a few scattered clouds. They set off on the path toward the pond, the tote bag swinging against Maggie's legs.

Maggie didn't look at Tate as she walked, but she was aware of him slightly behind her. She felt glad for his company now, which puzzled her. She had come to the cabin to be alone. Now she wasn't, at least for the moment.

The path to the pond was a shadowy tunnel beneath trees leafed out in their first flush of delicate green. Where the trees thinned out, tall grass had overgrown the path, and Maggie moved ahead of Tate to wade into it. Its sharp blades pulled at her socks, stabbed into her knees.

The path culminated in a rocky tree-shaded clearing centered around a round pond, which had been formed long ago by damming up a creek branching off from the river. Once there had been a fence blocking access to it. Now the fence was gone, but there was still a sense of quiet and privacy here.

"I'd forgotten how pretty this place is," Maggie said.

Tate bent and scooped up a tattered paper cup. He stuffed it in his pocket. "In the spirit of keeping it that way, I'll pick up the garbage when I come fishing," he said.

"That's a fair trade," Maggie said. She set down the tote bag and walked around the pond, scuffing at patches of weeds and turning up nothing but shiny foil gum wrappers and a few discarded plastic diapers. In some places, the ubiquitous kudzu had almost taken over, swallowing up whole trees and turning them into unrecognizable shapes.

"I don't see the No Fishing sign anywhere," Maggie said.

"Someone probably stole it," Tate said. He went over to the edge of the water where he stood on a rock and leaned over to peer into the shallows. "The big daddy of all catfish is sitting on the bottom, waiting for a worm on a hook," he reported. "He'd make a decent dinner."

"With hush puppies," Maggie said.

"And corn on the cob. And iced tea. I wish I'd brought along a fishing pole."

"Didn't the Cherokee charm fish out of the water?"

He laughed. "Not quite. They threw pounded walnut bark into small streams to stupefy the fish. Then the fish floated to the surface of the water and were dipped out with a net. Apparently it was an effective way to catch fish, except when a pregnant woman waded into the stream. She was supposed to tie a strip of the walnut bark around her toe so she wouldn't nullify the effect."

"Then I—" Maggie began, stopping just in time. She had almost said that she certainly couldn't step into the stream when such an operation was underway since she herself was pregnant. She had almost spilled the beans about her Awful Predicament.

Tate's smile was warm. "Then you what?"

"Then I suppose we'd better get busy and pound some walnut bark so you can catch old Big Daddy down there," she amended, turning her head away so Tate couldn't see her face.

"No need for that. An ordinary fishing pole will do just fine," he said.

Maggie sat down on a stump and shook the apples out of their bag, handing one to Tate. He telescoped his tall frame until he sat on the ground, resting his back against the stump's weathered bark. Maggie studied him surreptitiously as he took a bite of his apple.

The sun washed his skin with a glaze of gold and blazed a shimmering path across his hair. She, who had only a few weeks ago considered herself madly in love with Kip Baker and in fact might still love him, felt a definite sexual attraction to the man who sat beside her now. The way his jeans clung to his thighs, the broad sweep of his shoulders, even the way he chewed his apple, seemed extraordinarily appealing. Although when he wore street clothes the veneer of civilization rested easily upon him, he carried an air of wildness about him. She looked away, a picture of him in his loincloth flashing through her mind.

"You're not eating your apple," he said.

"Do you want it?" she asked, offering it.

He shook his head and was quiet. "Your parents—do they come here often?" he asked after a while.

"My mother died a few years ago, and she and my father had been divorced since I was ten. My father has a new family in Arizona. I never see him."

He swiveled his head to look at her. "Do you mind?"

"I used to. Now it makes no difference. The only time I even think about him is when I'm at the cabin, which was part of the divorce settlement with the understanding that

it would eventually be mine. It is, and I'm glad. My own-
ership of this property may be the best thing to come out of
the divorce.''

''Do you think you'll ever see him again? Your father, I
mean?''

''I doubt it. I had hard feelings over his leaving my
mother. And he never called me or wanted to see me, not
even on my birthdays. By the time I was a teenager, I'd given
up thinking that he would.'' She could be philosophical
about it by now.

''At least your dad was around during your most forma-
tive years,'' Tate said ruminatively.

Something in his tone made her focus quickly on his face,
but his expression offered no clue as to what he might be
thinking. He seemed aloof and detached, and she remembered what Jacob Pinter had said, that everyone had been
surprised to learn that Phil Jennings had a son. She waited
for Tate to mention something about his father, but he
didn't. He only stared into the distance, his expression unreadable.

Maggie would have liked him to volunteer information
about himself, but apparently he wasn't in the mood. Perhaps she'd rather not hear it anyway, she decided. Better to
keep the conversation light and not too revealing. That way
she wouldn't be tempted to talk too much about her own
situation.

Besides, Maggie thought as she savored her first bite of
the apple, this had turned into a good day for being lazy. For
the first time in years, she had no appointments to keep and
no place to go. Her life in Atlanta was hectic in the extreme, with frequent twelve-hour work days and after-hours
appointments with clients. Sitting here and staring out at the
tranquil surface of the pond with Tate quiet beside her, she
dredged up an infinitesimal amount of guilt about not hav-

ing anything that absolutely needed doing. Her thoughts drifted free, floating effortlessly across her consciousness. *With any luck,* Maggie thought as she allowed herself the luxury of sinking even further into this quiescent state, *I could get used to this pace.*

Time stood still, became irrelevant. She didn't talk, and neither did Tate. The only sounds were those of the forest, the only discernible movement that of dragonflies flitting across the calm surface of the pond. The deep, peaceful silence seemed to penetrate her entire being, suffusing her with pleasure. She sighed with something akin to happiness and wiggled her toes in her boots.

"Ready to go?" Tate said.

"No, I feel as if I could stay here all day," she replied. An inquisitive wasp hovered over the apple and she brushed it away with a lazy hand.

"It's peaceful here on the mountain," Tate said. "I had a hard time getting used to it at first, too."

She turned her head so that the sun fell across her face and closed her eyes to bask in its rays. "Tell me why you made the big decision to take a leave of absence and live in the woods."

Beside her, Tate shifted position, rustling the grass. She waited.

He took his time answering. "I found myself in the middle of a spiritual crisis. My instincts told me that I was about to undergo a vast change in my soul, but when I looked for my soul, I felt only an emptiness. How could my soul change if it wasn't even there? I called my boss at Conso and told him I wanted to take a leave of absence."

Maggie began to chuckle. "Spiritual crisis. Vast change in your soul. Are you for real?"

"As real as I know how to be as one of the Real People," he said soberly. "That's what the Cherokee call themselves. Ourselves, I mean."

She opened her eyes and searched for at least a trace of levity in his expression. She didn't find it. "You're really into this Cherokee stuff, aren't you?"

He smiled. "I was a buttoned-down, white-shirt-and-tie type at Conso. Then my father died, and I met his cousin. Charlie Bearkiller is his name. He took me under his wing, answered questions about my father, told me how to register as a tribal member, and made me start to feel comfortable with the idea that I'm part Indian. For the first time in my life, I began to understand where I came from and where I'm going."

"And where are you going, Tate Jennings?" Maggie asked softly.

"Forward. Charlie showed me that it's more natural for Cherokees to move on to new things rather than live in the past. Looking back was a habit of mine. My mind-set was that if only things had been different in my life, I wouldn't have had to struggle so hard. Now I think that because I struggled, I'm strong enough to face anything. Does this make any sense to you?" His eyes searched her face.

"I'm still at the struggling stage myself," she admitted.

"If I were you, I'd take advantage of this time to reconnect."

"Reconnect with what?"

"Yourself. Nature. The things that nourish your soul."

"You're lucky. You had Charlie to point you in the right direction."

"True, but I've mostly figured things out on my own within the loose framework that Charlie gave me. When I came into the woods and built my *asi*—"

"*Asi?*"

"My sleeping lodge. It's a small hut, not big enough for me to stand up in, and I only sleep in it when the weather is bad. Anyway, at that time, I thought that moving to the woods wasn't a big deal. I'd never felt that I belonged anywhere, so this was just another place where I wouldn't fit. Then, when I was sitting by my campfire that first night, I felt completely and utterly alone. I remember thinking, 'How in the world am I going to manage living here for six months?'"

"What was the general reaction of people when you told them you were going to live in the woods?"

"My colleagues at Conso thought I'd flipped my lid, and my friends expressed grave doubts. I gave away a lot of possessions that I wouldn't need, closed up my apartment in Scot's Cove and ignored my critics. When I established my camp, I threw only a few of the basic necessities on the back of my motorcycle and didn't look back in case something was chasing me." He laughed lightly.

"You ride a motorcycle?"

"Sure. A Harley-Davidson."

"That doesn't sound much like something a Conso executive would do."

"It isn't. But then neither is taking six months off to go live in the woods."

"What do you do when you're in your camp? How do you spend your time?"

"I think a lot. I get in touch with nature. I'm also studying the Cherokee language."

Maggie took another bite of apple. "Did you bring a supply of food up here with you?"

He shook his head. "No, but I haven't gone hungry yet. I fish, set snare lines for small game, harvest edible roots, and support myself quite well."

Maggie shuddered. "It sounds pretty awful," she said. "I can't imagine not being able to go to the freezer and take out a frozen dinner. I expect wine and cheese and banana cream pie to be readily available. I want hot showers and soft towels, preferably warmed on a heated rod. I like a warm bed and a warm body next to mine." Juice from the apple ran down her chin, and she wiped it away carelessly with the back of her hand.

She was unaware that Tate was watching her until she happened to look down at him.

"I like a lot of the same things," he said softly. "Especially that part about the warm body."

She had always talked too much. Maggie knew that. In this case, she had let down her guard and completely forgotten to whom she was talking. Tate wasn't Bronwyn, her trusted confidante, and he wasn't Kip, with whom she was accustomed to sharing all her thoughts. Annoyed with herself and with the way Tate was looking at her, she jumped to her feet and marched to the edge of the pond, where she threw her apple core into the middle of it. Circles spread out from the point of impact; circles begetting circles begetting more circles.

"Maggie?" Tate said. He was close behind her.

She didn't have anyone, that was the problem, and everyone needed someone. *She* needed someone, especially now. Unexpected tears pricked the back of Maggie's eyelids, and the circles in the water blurred into an impressionistic wash of blue and silver. She dug the heels of her hands into her eyes, wishing that her emotions wouldn't hover so close to the surface.

"It's not you that's making me uncomfortable," she admitted in a rush of words. "It's just that I feel so...so alone."

"You wouldn't have to be," he said.

"Yes, well, I thought I had a future with the man I loved, and now look at me."

"I'm looking," Tate said, "and I like what I see."

"You can't mean that," she said, sniffling.

His harsh tone surprised her. "You're beautiful and witty and capable and desirable. Know it and act like it."

Her chin flew up. "I would if I wasn't an emotional basket case," she retorted. It took some nerve to admit her state of mind, especially to him. And, she reminded herself, he didn't know the half of her situation.

There was still a grim set to Tate's lips as his strong arms encircled her and pulled her close. "You'll be okay," he said. "I'm counting on it."

"I wouldn't count on anything if I were you. Nothing is reliable, nothing makes sense," she said, trying to twist away. His lips brushed her temple lightly; they might have been mistaken for dragonfly wings. His arms around her were iron bands, holding her fast.

"Stop wriggling," he said. "I want to kiss you."

"Are you sure? I might be in love with another man."

His arms slowly released her. He backed away. "You think you still love that guy?" he said with a heavy dose of skepticism.

"Well, maybe," she said.

He seemed taken aback. "Maggie, you're too smart for that."

"The situation is complicated. There are a lot of things I need to consider. I don't think that the reconnecting you were talking about a while ago was supposed to be taken literally. Starting a physical relationship isn't going to nourish my soul."

"Why not?" Tate said in all seriousness. She stared at him, at the dark eyes that seemed to know all her secrets, at the determined set of his chin.

She had always been a strong woman, and she didn't want Tate Jennings to perceive her any other way. If she let him kiss her now, he would know that she was giving in. And that would make her look weak.

"Loosen up, Maggie," he said, but this only irritated her. Despite his moments of insight, he didn't know what she was going through, would never be able to understand. She backed off. The clearing was silent, the pond shimmering in the sunlight. She felt the beginnings of a headache behind her eyes.

"Please don't go," he said, but she shook her head violently, denying the open declaration of desire in Tate Jennings' eyes, and then she brushed past him, heading blindly for the path. She halfway expected him to follow her, but when she looked back, she saw only the greenery that had closed around the path, and she heard only the jeering of a lone blue jay hidden among the trees.

Chapter Four

After Maggie fled the pond, Tate, lost in thought and heading back toward his property, saw a great crane rising from the trees. The crane, he knew, was considered a good omen by the Cherokee, and he had adopted it as his own personal good-luck symbol.

That night as he sat beside his campfire growing mesmerized by the flames, he again saw the crane. This time it spread its wings in the blue depths of the fire, finally flying away in a spiral of golden sparks.

As if his spirit were one with the crane in flight, he glided over the cabin where Maggie lived, and the spirits of the ancestors filled his body, telling him to chant in the time-honored Cherokee way. At one time he might have felt self-conscious about chanting alone in his camp, but not any more. It was late when, exhausted, he wrapped himself in his blanket, filled with a sense of joy at the new directions his life was taking and at his newfound oneness with nature.

He didn't know how long he lay there before the doe stepped out of the forest. As she stared at the fire's embers, he marveled at how beautiful she was. He thought she might come closer, and he waited for her to make the move. And when she did, he saw that she was limping.

He sat up as quietly as he could, but she saw the motion and pricked up her ears. He remained as motionless as she was until she turned tail and staggered into the woods.

He felt compelled to help her. It was the time of year when female deer who were about to give birth sought a safe place away from the rest of the herd, and he knew there might be a fawn nearby. The doe, limping as she was, might well need his help.

Tate soundlessly stalked the deer through the night forest, his vision keen, his ears alert for any sound. He saw her ahead on the trail, took a shortcut, and, as she was about to stumble into a thicket, he caught her in his arms.

A sense of urgency overcame him as he bound the doe's leg injury and saw her safely to where her fawn waited. But the doe didn't stay with her fawn; instead she glanced at him over her shoulder and leaped away.

Why, there was nothing wrong with her leg, Tate thought with amazement as he watched her white tail bobbing through the underbrush. She disappeared into the night as the laughter of the Yunwi Tsundsi rang in his ears, and then he realized that he had been tricked by them, fooled into entering the forest.

And then he was running recklessly, crazily, running as if for his life, his heart pounding mightily as he pushed aside tree limbs and leaped over boulders. Dogs were chasing him, howling as they grew near.

At last, as he knew he would, he reached the misty promontory above the river's rapids. There he immediately spotted Maggie waiting anxiously in her canoe below—not an aluminum canoe like the one that had been lost but an old-fashioned dugout. The Little Deer River was muddy and swollen with recent rains; it was so high, the creek where one could normally turn the canoe to head back upstream was flooded over its banks. Maggie cried out, but he couldn't understand what she said. He strained his ears, and he heard her shout something like, "Sunny!" This made no sense, because the fog hung like a shroud over the scene so that the sun was totally obliterated.

He almost stopped breathing when he realized that Maggie was losing control of the canoe.

When he saw her terrified face turned upward, her eyes searching for him against the backdrop of the forest, he knew what he must do. He stepped to the edge of the cliff and jumped.

This time, he missed the canoe. This time, he landed in the water. As he sank beneath the surface, he felt the grasping hands of the Little People who lived in the river clawing at him and dragging him under. He struggled to break free.

"Sunny!" he heard as he came up and gasped for air.

By this time, Maggie had succeeded in turning the canoe and was clinging to the overhanging limb of a tree that had been felled by a recent storm. Through the swirling veil of white mist he saw with relief that the tree's arms had reached out to enclose Maggie and keep her from harm.

Struggle as he might, he could not fight the force of the water carrying him along toward the treacherous falls. He managed one last look at her, at her face contorted with fear and longing as she watched his struggle. He thought he heard her whisper "I love you" as he was swept over the rim of rock, but perhaps it was only the voice of the water.

Tate sat bolt upright, sweat pouring from his body. The dream had frightened him. The sense of falling, of losing Maggie, had been so strong that he could taste it even now that he knew he was safe.

Losing Maggie. Now that was ridiculous, Tate thought as he got up and dipped a gourdful of drinking water from the bucket inside the *asi*. Maggie wasn't his to lose.

He thought of her sleeping snugly inside her cabin, her hair spilling across the pillow in shimmery golden strands, her skin alabaster in the moonlight filtering through the draperies at the window. Not that he had been in her bedroom to see the draperies or the window; he only knew that was how Maggie would look as she slept.

Tate tossed a log on the coals of the fire and closed his eyes, trying to become one with Maggie's thoughts. He centered in on her, made himself see what she saw behind her closed eyelids. Yes, although he didn't understand the way it worked, he could sense her, feel her, could almost be her. Her breath rose and fell in his chest, her thoughts played through his receptive mind. His eyes flew open when he saw, through her, the exact same scene he had seen in his dream—the raging river, the sight of her hanging on to the tree for dear life, the whisper of the words "I love you."

He knew without a doubt that she was dreaming his dream. Shaken, he released Maggie's thoughts. But when he reclaimed his own, they skittered around in his mind like squirrels in a cage, and he was unable to concentrate on any one thing. He knew that he'd been picking up on her thoughts that day that he'd jumped into her canoe, and he'd been startled by his own ability. But this—this was more than that. Wanting nothing so much as to put distance between himself and his conflicting emotions, he got up and ran to the dark river, plunging into the current and swimming against it under the starlit sky until he was exhausted.

After that, he couldn't go back to sleep. Instead he sat staring into the fire all night, imagining that Maggie was saying—really saying—the words *I love you* and that they were meant for him.

Now that was a dream in itself. In his whole life, Tate was sure that no one had loved him, truly loved him.

IN THE MORNING after her upsetting dream, the one where she had watched helplessly from her shelter beneath a tree as Tate was swept over the edge of Maidenhair Falls, Maggie dragged an old patio lounge into the middle of the cabin's clearing and spread a beach towel over it. She lay down in the sun, hoping that its warm rays would dispel the lingering coldness around her heart.

The dream had frightened her. She almost never had nightmares, and this one had been the worst she'd ever had. Even now she could feel her panic when she was struggling to control the canoe, her anguish as she saw Tate swept away over the rapids, and her helplessness when she realized that she could do nothing to save him.

Last night she had awakened desolate after Tate had disappeared over the falls; she'd felt irretrievably broken and as if her sole reason for living had been taken from her. She tried to tell herself that the disturbing dream had been merely a replay of the day when Tate had jumped into her canoe, but the explanation didn't satisfy her. She had the vague unsettling sense that this dream about Tate meant something, although she could not have said what.

She slathered herself with suntan lotion and lifted her chin to the sun so that the pale skin of her neck would tan. She closed her eyes.

A few minutes later, a shadow fell across her face. "You could get skin cancer. Lying in the sun like that is unhealthful." When she opened her eyes, Tate Jennings was looming over her, his long hair fluttering in the breeze like a banner. She felt ridiculously happy to see him, and she realized suddenly that the dream had left her wondering about his safety.

"I'm not the one who goes running around in a loincloth, which as far as I know has no skin protection factor whatsoever," she said. She rose to a half-sitting position, propping herself on her elbows.

"Most of the time I wear clothes. Do I meet with your approval today?"

"Your clothes do," she said. "I'm not sure if you do or not." On second thought, he did. He was wearing thigh-hugging jeans, a T-shirt, and a colorful woven band around his forehead to hold back his luxuriously thick and unfashionably long hair. He looked undeniably virile, a man in his prime. For a moment she imagined what it would be like to lie in bed beside him—but only for a moment.

Uninvited, he sat down on the ground beside her.

"Make yourself comfortable," she said pointedly.

"I didn't think you'd mind company," he said.

"You could've asked."

"Sometimes . . ." he said, but he didn't finish.

"Sometimes what?"

"Sometimes it isn't necessary to ask certain people."

She lay back, wishing that she hadn't worn her oldest bikini, the one with the mustard stain. She also wished that her breasts, already showing signs of her impending motherhood, didn't push the limits of decency by swelling out of the top of her bra.

"What do you mean?" she asked, although she knew perfectly well what Tate meant. It was clear that he occasionally perceived what she was thinking even before she did.

"I think you know," he said. Sunlight warmed his eyes into a quizzical smile, which she did not return.

She flipped over on her stomach. "I know that we're talking in circles," she said. The memory of his lips on her skin yesterday at the pond made her turn her head away and pillow it on her arms. In that position, she couldn't see him, but she was fully aware of him only a foot or so away from her. For a moment, she wanted to tug her swimsuit bottom down to cover more of her derriere but decided against it.

"Right now you're wishing that you had more clothes on," he said only inches from her ear, his voice light and teasing.

She felt herself start to blush and kept her face turned away.

"Don't you have something to do? When are you going to buy me that new canoe?" she said crossly.

"Soon," he said.

"Fine. Now will you please leave me in peace?"

"No. I want to ask you about something."

"Who says I want to answer?"

"Don't get your back up until you know what it's about. Maggie, about the dream that you had last night, the one about Lover's Leap."

Maggie's mouth fell open. She lifted herself on her elbows, the insufficient bikini top forgotten. "How—how did you know?"

He looked steadily into her eyes. "I had the same dream."

"You?" she said, unbelieving.

He nodded. "Me," he said.

"How did you know that I—"

"Call it whatever you like, but I sensed that you were anxious about the dream, and so am I."

"Tell me what you dreamed," she said in a small voice.

He told her, his voice dispassionate and his eyes anything but, and his dream was the same as hers in every detail except that he didn't mention how she had called out that she loved him before she lost sight of him as he was swept over the falls.

"That's the same dream," she said in astonishment. "Exactly the same, Tate. What do you think it means?"

"I don't know. It certainly seemed very real."

Maggie agreed. "Did you feel a kind of déjà vu? As if you'd been there, done that?"

"Yes, and it was similar to the way I felt the day I jumped into your canoe. As if it were meant to happen, as if I'd known all my life that I would meet you in that way, as if I were driven to do it." His brow was furrowed in thought.

She ignored what he said about being driven to meet her, which was, in her opinion, only nonsense. Anyway, she was in the process of making certain connections. "It's the legend," she said softly. "The legend of Peg Macintyre."

"That old Lover's Leap story? I've heard about it, but I thought it was some chamber of commerce publicity hype for the tourists," Tate said. He sounded cynical.

Maggie sat up, eager to enlighten him. "No, Tate, the legend is based in truth. It really happened. Peg Macintyre was my great-grandmother several times over, and the story has been passed down in my family for ages. I've heard it since I was a little girl, how Peg lost her Indian brave lover in an accident at Lover's Leap. I bought a pamphlet that tells the story. Would you like to read it?"

He shrugged. "Sure. I just don't know how much stock I'd put in it, that's all," he said, clearly skeptical.

"Wait," Maggie said. She got up and fairly flew inside the house, returning with the booklet that she'd bought from Jacob Pinter. In her haste she forgot about the skimpiness of her bikini, and as she walked back across the clearing from the cabin, she was aware of the appreciation in Tate's eyes, an appreciation of her form and figure which only minutes ago would have made her unbearably self-conscious. At the moment, it didn't seem to matter. Her body would soon change, and men probably wouldn't look at her with interest again until after the baby was born. She might as well, she thought recklessly, enjoy the attention.

"Look, the story of Peg and her Cherokee lover is in chapter three," she said, sitting down on the lounge and leafing through the pages to the right place. "Read this."

Tate bent his head close to hers, his hair as black and shiny as a raven's wing. It fell loosely across his shoulders, and Maggie fought the childish urge to touch it to find out if it felt as sleek as it looked. She had never seen hair so black; it was as black as ebony, as black as a starless night, as black as—

"Tsani," Tate said suddenly, and she yanked herself back from her dangerous thoughts.

"What?"

"Peg's lover's name was Tsani. I thought you were saying 'Sunny,' but the words sound alike."

"I? I wasn't there. It was Peg Macintyre," Maggie said.

"Yes, of course. In my dream she looked like you."

Gathering her thoughts, she stared off into the distance at Breadloaf Mountain. "I still can't believe that we had the same dream at the same time," she said to Tate. He was paging through the booklet.

He looked up, marking his place with a forefinger. "Neither can I." He was thoughtful and contemplative. After a moment, he continued to read, and she waited for him to finish.

"Peg was going to have a baby," Maggie said when Tate looked up from the printed pages.

"I know. Tsani's baby. The book says that she married someone else shortly after Tsani was swept over the falls to his death."

"According to family legend, she married an older man who had asked for her hand in marriage before she became pregnant with Tsani's child. Peg had refused him and planned to run away with Tsani, whom her parents had forbidden her to marry. She hated the older man, so it must have been awful for her to have to marry him just to have a father for her child." Her eyes welled with tears on behalf of the hapless Peg.

As they threatened to spill down her cheeks, she hated herself for being so emotional. She wasn't normally that way. Usually she could make jokes or toss off quips that got her off any emotional hooks, but since she'd become pregnant, she'd turned into a one-woman waterworks.

Tate saw the tears and reached toward her. "Maggie," he said, but before he could finish, she was up and away, rushing toward the cabin and the blessed privacy it provided.

He caught her just inside the door. "You don't need to hide your emotions from me," he said roughly, reaching for her and pulling her toward him.

"I'm acting ridiculous," she said through a blur of tears. "I don't know why I should care about a woman who lived so long ago."

Tate held her by her upper arms. "You care because you have a kind heart," he said.

Maggie blinked away her tears as she felt him ease his hold on her arms. She didn't want him to release her. She hungered for the touch of another human, and even though she knew that she was inviting a continuation of the scene that had begun yesterday at the pond, she couldn't make herself pull away. She needed his strength and solidity. She took a deep breath; the scent of him was wonderfully redolent of pine and cedar with a slight undertone of wood smoke.

"I thought—I thought for a moment that I felt Peg's anguish as she must have felt it," Maggie whispered. She had also heard the faint strain of dulcimer music that had become so familiar, a sad, poignant tune.

"Oh, Maggie," Tate said, wrapping his arms around her.

She stood motionless. Somewhere a faucet dripped, but it seemed far away. Outside, she heard the trill of a mockingbird. She felt insulated from the world in Tate's embrace, separated from reality by a lovely warm luminescence that enveloped both of them. At the moment, the urge to cry was gone. Taking its place was the urge to do something entirely different.

Tate's hands inscribed slow circles on her bare back. It felt so good to be held and touched and pressed against the long length of him. The hard metal of his belt buckle cut into her stomach, and the firm muscles of his chest flattened her sensitive breasts.

His hands moved upward, still circling, until his fingers threaded through the hair on the nape of her neck. They massaged gently, and she let her eyes drift shut as she gave in to his ministrations. His fingers were cool against her sun-warmed scalp and she leaned toward him, thinking that Kip had never been so thoughtful or so nurturing.

Tate moved one hand slowly to her waist, skimming his hand over the fastening of her bra, but she didn't react. Instead she thought about how easy it would be to guide his cool hands to the scraps of fabric that clothed her; the fabric could be easily pushed aside. His hands, those hands that understood how to soothe her so well, would know exactly how to hold her breasts, the thumbs brushing her aching nipples until she arched backward and invited more intimate caresses. Thinking of it, her skin tingled in anticipation and desire. She drew a long shuddering breath, desperately wanting to let instinct take over, to stop thinking about what she should or shouldn't do and let it happen.

Let it happen, urged her inner voice. *Just let it.* Or *was* it her inner voice? She angled her head to look up at Tate, wondering if it was he who had said those words. But no, he was only looking at her with compassion, a look that melted her resistance. She felt drenched in a sudden, inexplicable eroticism; it made her tremble within his embrace.

She lifted her head only a fraction more, and the light of understanding leaped in his eyes.

For a moment his pupils darkened, and he slid both of his hands through her hair until it spilled from his fingers. "Yes," he whispered, and he dipped his head and kissed her.

The kiss was very tender and very brief, and it engendered a dizzying wave of emotion. It also brought her immediately to her senses.

"Tate, no," she said. With those words, whatever spell had held her in its grip was broken. The magic was gone.

He immediately dropped his arms, those strong arms that could enfold her completely if he chose to do so and if she chose to let them. But their eyes held fast until Maggie made herself look away.

Her swimsuit had never seemed so brief; she felt as if she were all bare skin and raw emotions. She made tracks across the room, putting distance between them as quickly as possible, and tried to make light of what had just happened.

"I mean, I know you must think I'm teasing you, acting the way I do, but the truth is I'm confused and upset, and now this dream, and—oh, I don't know what I think," she said. She knew that she was babbling as was her habit when nervous, and she hated herself for it.

"That's obvious, since you keep sending mixed signals," Tate agreed equably. When she risked a look at him, she saw that he had folded his arms across his chest and stood regarding her with an upraised eyebrow.

"I hate sending conflicting messages. I never say one thing and mean another, and now I do it all the time. I wish I could stop."

"I don't. I like you exactly the way you are."

"You don't know me. You don't know how I am or about my life or—listen, Tate, what you like isn't reliable or real, it isn't even me." She covered her face with her hands, then realized that there were other places that she should be covering first. She went into the bedroom and slipped on a robe.

When she returned, Tate was standing in front of the living room window and looking out. He turned when he heard her approach. His gaze traveled beyond her to the bedroom, and for a split second she knew that he was looking at the picture of Kip on the dresser. His eyes quickly focused on her face, his expression unreadable.

"Look, Tate," she began.

"I've looked at you. That was part of the problem."

She ran trembling fingers through her hair, then realized from the way he was studying her that it had been an unconsciously provocative gesture.

"This is getting out of hand," she muttered, turning away.

"I'm not going to take advantage of you. That's a promise," he said, and there was something so fierce in his voice that she whirled to look at him.

"What I mean is that someone has already hurt you. I'm not going to pursue you if that's not what you want. I don't want to add to your pain in any way." His nostrils flared, and she sensed a passion that, once unleashed, would be impossible to restrain. She knew that she had caught a glimpse of Tate's nature that was usually well hidden. It piqued her curiosity, but only for a moment.

"And if I were to encourage you?" She was immediately sorry after these words escaped her lips. She had never been coy.

He looked down at her from his considerable height. "Believe me, Maggie Macintyre, if that was the case, I'd take you up on it. So don't start any fires that you intend to put out. There will be no quenching mine once it is lit.''

If this was a comic strip, Maggie thought, *this is the time when my character would say Gulp.* But there was nothing remotely funny about this. Tate was dead serious.

Walk over to him and put your arms around him, urged the voice.

''No,'' said Maggie, clearly and distinctly.

Tate stared at her for one long moment, his eyes burning into her like black coals. It struck her that he thought she had spoken to him; how could she explain otherwise? How could she tell him she'd lately heard a female voice that instructed her about how to act, what to do? If she so much as mentioned it, Tate Jennings would be sure that her head wasn't screwed on right.

Tate shook his head as if to clear it. ''I don't know how you do it, but whenever I'm around you I want to touch you and kiss you and—my God, woman, I think you bewitch me!'' With a muttered oath he wheeled and stalked out of the cabin, slamming the door behind him.

Me and the Tsagoomahs, she almost said, but he was gone too fast. In the echoing aftermath of his dramatic exit, while she stood both shocked and titillated by his display of temper, Maggie thought she heard the echo of distant laughter. Voices, laughter, music—what did they mean? Did Tate hear them, too?

She turned to the window to watch him go. He was striding toward the forest as if—well, as if some of his annoying Little People were chasing him. This brought a smile to her lips, but it faded when she saw that the bird's nest with the robin's egg, which she had left on the sill since the day she'd found it, was gone.

Tate must have taken it. Did that also mean that he had left it in the first place?

And exactly what kind of kicks did Tate Jennings get out of depositing a bird's nest on her windowsill and then taking it away again?

THE NEXT DAY Tate felt a need for a break from Maggie. He wasn't comfortable with what had happened yesterday at the cabin; they'd both acted strangely. He'd heard dulcimer music, and he was willing to bet that Maggie had heard it, too. He hadn't mentioned it because they'd had other things to say to each other that were more important. Still, he kept playing the plaintive tune over and over in his mind, and he kept thinking about the dream that he and Maggie had shared.

Tate decided that it was high time to buy the canoe and that he would go into Scot's Cove to do it. At the last minute, he decided to stop by his apartment and put on a suit, a rare occurrence these days, and on the way into town, he dropped in to see his boss at Conso. He'd been back only a few times since beginning his leave of absence, and a visit was way overdue.

The development company had built a large ultramodern office building on the highway, and Tate parked his motorcycle in the reserved parking space that bore his name. When he went inside and asked to see his boss, he was amused at first that he was announced like a visitor rather than an employee and less amused when he was made to cool his heels for an aggravating period of time in the anteroom to the corporate executives' offices.

As he was becoming even more impatient, his colleague, Don Chalmers, who was manager of the marketing department, saw him waiting and strolled out of his office to chat. Tate had the feeling that Don was using this opportunity to size him up, although they were equals in the corporate structure and had always been friendly. Now he thought he sensed a cautious reserve in Don's manner. It puzzled him.

When at last Tate was ushered into the inner sanctum, Karl Shaeffer, who was not only his boss and Don's but also vice president of Marketing and Public Relations, walked around his big carved desk and clapped Tate on the back. "Good to see you!" he said heartily, pumping Tate's hand.

Karl invited Tate to sit down and returned to the big leather chair behind his desk. "So," he said. "I suppose you're ready to get back to work soon." He thumbed through a stack of file folders, trying to find something. "I'm glad you showed up, since there are some points that we should discuss. Lots of things will be going on when you return," he said.

"You'd better clue me in," Tate said.

Karl ran a stubby forefinger down a list. "As soon as you come back, you'll be making the rounds of all the local civic clubs for lunch. We've booked you with Kiwanis, Civitan, Rotary and so on. We want you to make similar speeches to all of them to quiet their fears about the Balsam Heights mobile home park on Breadloaf Mountain, which, as you know, is slated to begin construction this summer. You'll say something positive about how construction will bring jobs and dollars into town, keep the young people at home doing healthful outdoors work instead of wandering off to the cities to get jobs flipping burgers, that kind of thing. You know the drill."

Tate did. He had helped carve out the original strategy to create a positive corporate image in Scot's Cove. He felt a sick lump growing in the pit of his stomach now when he thought about how easy it had been to insinuate himself into the locals' good graces. In their innocence, they had wanted to believe that Conso would end economic deprivation here; they'd been delighted with the sprucing up of their deteriorating downtown area, and they hadn't thought about the larger consequences of development.

"Another thing," Karl was saying. "We'll want you to attend all county council meetings and report back to us everything that's said about Conso. We think somebody's doctoring the minutes of the meetings, and we can't depend on Albie Fentress at the newspaper for the real story—he's hand in glove with the council."

Albie Fentress, the editor and publisher of the *Scot's Cove Messenger,* was Tate's good friend, and he regarded Albie as a fine newspaperman. But Tate held his tongue, waiting to see what else Karl had to say.

Karl shoved the folder to one side. "I'm sure you know that the company is pleased with your work. The PR department doesn't function as well these days without you. The company has big things in mind for you, Tate."

Tate's collar was too tight, and he resisted the urge to tug at his tie. He shifted in his chair. "Well, Karl, you'd better tell me what you're talking about," he said. He happened to know that Karl was a gossip who could never keep anything under his hat. This particular quality of his boss's had often caused trouble that Tate had found himself mopping up in the past. Now, he thought, he might be able to play Karl's shortcoming to his advantage.

Karl leaned across the desk. "They're talking about a vice presidency for you next year," he whispered with a watchful eye toward the door beyond which his assistant sat. "Don't tell a soul."

"A vice presidency?" Tate said. True, he had risen through the ranks quickly. But a vice presidency at his age of thirty-two, thirty-three in a few months, was almost unheard of within the company.

"If you can handle the brewing crisis, that is, and of course, if you're top management, you'll have to get a haircut. That mop of yours," Karl said with obvious distaste, "looks rebellious."

Tate, although outraged, forced himself to ignore the comment about his hair. "I've been out of touch," he said warily and through gritted teeth. "I'm not sure what crisis you're talking about."

Karl leaned close again. "When Conso came here to develop the town into a resort area with ski slopes and condominiums and housing developments, they had to fight for zoning variances from the county council, especially for the Balsam Heights mobile home development on Breadloaf. One of the conditions that the council insisted upon when they approved the variance was that the company must deed a huge chunk of land to the county and develop it as a park."

"I remember," Tate said. "The park will be a perpetual wilderness area and ensure that the local people will always have access to Breadloaf Mountain."

"That was the plan. At the time, land values were high and the company felt that the park was feasible considering how much money they'd make selling lots in the various subdivisions. And we had to agree to it in order to get what we wanted. Now land values have tumbled so that we're not getting as much money as we'd planned for those big homes over in Cherokee Acres. The company needs to make up the money somewhere else, and guess where?"

"The wilderness park?" Tate said unbelievingly.

"The park," verified Karl. "The company's going to renege on the deal. There's a legal loophole, and the wilderness park acreage is going to be used to develop five hundred more mobile home sites in addition to the ones planned. It will double the size of Balsam Heights."

"I don't believe it," Tate said. "I was on the committee that convinced the county council members to give the variance based on our promise of the wilderness park. Those people trusted us."

Karl shrugged. "It's all going to hit the fan shortly after you come back to work, so be prepared. You'll have to mount a campaign to whitewash the whole ploy, make the locals think that we're doing it to provide even more jobs, point out to the merchants how twice as many mobile homes means more people to shop here, that kind of thing. I don't need to tell you how to go about it, man. You know what to do."

Tate stared at the outline of Breadloaf Mountain in the distance. The local mountaineers, who were for the most part descended from hardy Scotch-Irish stock, were fiercely independent and until a decade or so ago had managed to eke out an existence on their hardscrabble farms. Conso was changing that; now the local people were becoming a servant class for the wealthy newcomers to Scot's Cove. Many old-time landowners couldn't afford taxes that had tripled in the past few years, and some had been forced to sell their ancestral lands to Conso. This state of affairs was difficult for these proud people to swallow.

But it was Tate's job to soothe the locals and help them to accept the inevitable.

"Yes," Tate said heavily. "I know what to do."

A sudden thought struck him. He said, "What if I don't want to?" His eyes swung back to Karl, who looked unbelieving at first and then flushed with anger.

"What do you mean?" Karl said in a dangerously level tone.

"What if I refuse to whitewash the company? Scuttling the wilderness park is a rotten thing to do to these good-hearted people, Karl. The county council never planned on one thousand mobile home sites with their corresponding one thousand septic tanks on Breadloaf Mountain. Even five hundred was pushing it.'' He stared at Karl, but the older man refused to look away.

"It's your job to do and say exactly what the Consolidated Development Corporation tells you. That's what a public relations flack does.'' Karl's voice was cold, and his eyes had turned to agate.

"I don't consider myself a flack,'' Tate said forcefully. "I'm a public relations professional.''

"Then *be* professional. You're no babe in the woods, Tate. You know the score. I don't need to tell you that there will be no vice presidency if you foul this up.''

"Of course,'' Tate said, keeping his voice as neutral as possible.

Karl skewered him with a look of pure vitriol, and Tate thought with sudden and unnerving insight, *It's not just the fact that I've objected to the company line. Something else is bugging Karl.*

Tate cast around for some explanation of Karl's animosity and came up with Don Chalmers. Karl had always felt threatened by Don, since both of them had risen through the marketing department and had carried on a personal feud for years. If Don was to become the next vice president, he could eventually jockey himself into position to get rid of Karl, and since Karl was known to have many enemies within the company, he was always watching his flanks. On the other hand, if Tate was promoted to the next vice presidency, Karl probably thought he wouldn't have to worry. In the past, Tate had always aligned himself solidly and unquestioningly behind his boss.

Karl thinks his survival at Conso is riding on my success, Tate thought. *But can I continue to support Karl if I disagree with what he and the company are asking of me?*

Karl relaxed slightly and adopted a cordial tone of voice. "Enough about all that. It'll be good to have you back,

Tate. How about lunch today? I'll be free—oh, in half an hour or so."

So Karl was going to act as if nothing were going on. At one time, Tate would have followed his lead, but not any more.

"Sorry," Tate said, getting to his feet. "I've got an appointment."

"Too bad," Karl said. "We'll have to make it when you come back to work."

"Right," Tate said. "When I come back."

He stopped briefly to collect his mail and threw most of it into the circular file. Then he hurried through the hallways at breakneck speed and burst out into the cool, sweet-smelling air. He inhaled a long, deep breath in hopes of clearing the stuffiness of Conso from his head.

As he wheeled out of the parking lot on his bike, Tate knew what he had to do. He had to go see Charlie Bear-killer and get his head straight. As a first step in that direction, he ripped off his tie and let it fly away into the dusty weeds on the side of the road.

Chapter Five

After Tate left Karl Shaeffer's office at Conso, he rode to his apartment in town, ditched the suit for shorts and a shirt, and locked the place up again before going to see Charlie Bearkiller.

Tate parked his motorcycle behind Charlie's scarred red pickup truck outside the neat frame house where his mentor lived and rang the doorbell. As Tate expected, his friend appeared at the screen door and ushered him into the amiable clutter of the living room. Tate took in the television set blaring in the corner, the potato chips in the dish by the recliner, and the marmalade tomcat named Oscar reclining on the couch.

"*A'siyu,*" said Charlie, his face all smiles. "Welcome."

"*Wadan,* thank you," Tate replied automatically. Even though he was new to Cherokee ways, certain things, such as the Cherokee language greeting and response, came easily to him now.

"I knew you'd come today," Charlie said gleefully as Tate settled on the couch beside the cat. "I knew it." Small-boned and wiry, Charlie looked like the personification of one of the fabled Little People, one who perhaps had been created to star in Disney's *Snow White* cartoon feature.

"How'd you know I was coming?"

Charlie tapped his head. "I get messages," he said. "Like you do."

Tate was stunned. "How did you know?" he said.

"I recognized the gift in you from the first time I met you," Charlie said. "Some of our people have always had it."

"I wasn't aware of it until—well, until recently," Tate said, not wanting to bring Maggie into this conversation if it wasn't necessary.

"Didn't I tell you that your new way of life would open new windows and let fresh air into the old, stale places?"

"Sure. You never mentioned how I'm supposed to deal with it, though, and I don't only mean reading other peoples' minds. For instance, right now I'm having a hard time reconciling the Cherokee belief that the land, the air, the trees, the water should belong to all of us."

"Humph." Charlie slid him a sly look out of the corners of his eyes. "That's certainly not what Conso thinks, is it?"

"I worry about that, Charlie. I see everything in a new way now that I'm living more simply. I find that different things are important to me." He helped himself to the potato chips.

"Like what?" Charlie leaned forward in the recliner, all ears.

"I want peace in my heart. I'm still searching for a sense of who I am and where I'm going, but I know now that I want to be comfortable with who I am and what I do."

Charlie waited, but Tate said no more.

"Well?" Charlie said. "That's not all, is it, Tate?"

Tate flushed. "I should have known that you'd realize I'm holding out on you. Yes, Charlie, there's one more thing. I've met someone." Oscar the cat stood up, circled around, and curled up with his chin on Tate's knee.

Charlie cackled. "I knew it. You've got the look."

"The look of what?" This unsettled Tate; he didn't like to think that his demeanor or appearance would give a clue to what was going on in the most private sections of his heart.

"The look of a man who wants," Charlie said.

Tate cleared his throat. "It's not only sex," he said earnestly. "There's certainly more to my relationship with Maggie than that."

"Oh, I don't doubt that. You're one of those deep ones, Tate, You don't love easily, but when you do, look out."

"I never said anything about love. And my interest in Maggie did happen easily, which makes me wonder what it's all about." Tate related how he had dreamed of a woman, then recognized Maggie as that woman as she was swept past him at Lover's Leap. He told how he had jumped into her canoe, and Charlie regarded him soberly, remaining quiet for so long that Tate grew impatient.

Finally Charlie spoke. "Maggie needs to know why you feel as you do for the relationship between you to develop to its greatest potential," he said. He looked Tate full in the face, his expression keen. "Can you talk to her?"

Tate shifted his position so that Oscar reproached him through narrowed eyes. He scratched the cat's ear in apology. "Talk to Maggie about my life?" He didn't like the idea much. He had learned never to get involved, never to get too close, and never, never to trust anyone, man or woman, with his innermost thoughts. Opening up to his friends was new to him; it hadn't come easily, even with Charlie.

Charlie's voice was gentle. "You must tell Maggie about your past. It is the only way you can make her part of your future."

"I can't imagine that she'd want to listen to my version of a hard-luck story." Oscar was purring now in the rhythm that Cherokee children would say sounded like counting; in the Cherokee language, purring sounded as if the cat were saying "sixteen four, sixteen four."

After a moment's quiet, during which Tate wasn't sure if the older man was communing with his own spirit or something outside of himself, Charlie said, "Maggie needs you. She doesn't know how desperately she needs you yet, and neither do you. And soon you will find an opportunity to talk to her in a natural way, and it will make a big difference."

"Maggie seems pretty self-sufficient."

"You can't always trust appearances, Tate."

"Don't you think I know that after working for Conso?" Tate said.

"I think you know more than you think you know."

"Now that," Tate said, "is what is known as a cryptic comment."

"Yeah. That's what I'm best at," Charlie said with a grin.

Tate moved the cat aside and stood up. "I'd better get going. I've made up my mind to buy a canoe today. Thanks, Charlie. You always manage to make me feel as if I'm on the right track."

"That's because you usually are," Charlie said. He walked Tate outside, one hand on his shoulder.

Tate had already swung onto his bike when Charlie said, "One more thing. You aren't going back to your job after your leave of absence."

Tate stared for a moment, and then he broke into laughter. "Well, Grandfather," he said, using the word as a term of respect for one's elders in the tribe. "I don't think I have much choice."

Charlie was still standing in the driveway as Tate kick-started the motorcycle, and Tate waved as he drove away. He hoped that Charlie was right about his not going back to Conso; the whole idea of it left a bad taste in his mouth. But if he didn't go back, how was he going to support himself? Did Charlie know that, too?

He chalked Charlie's prediction up to another cryptic comment and wished for a moment that he could read the old fellow's mind as well as he could read Maggie's.

"KEEP YOUR BABY!" exclaimed Bronwyn at the top of her lungs.

Maggie cringed. "Must you inform everyone in the offices of MMB&O of my decision? Couldn't you let me do that in my own way?"

"I didn't think that you'd decide to keep it, that's all."

"I want to. I love this baby already, Bronwyn. I can't explain it. I know the baby is still a tiny embryo, a mere dot of protoplasm, but to me it's real and wonderful and all I can think about right now. I couldn't possibly give up my child." She knew she wasn't explaining this well, but then Bronwyn wasn't receiving it well, either.

"Your apartment in Atlanta only has one bedroom, not to mention that your neighbors will complain if the baby cries in the middle of the night. You know how those people bang on the wall with their fists when you play music too loudly."

"I'll move," said Maggie. "The place is too small anyway. The landlord won't let me have a pet."

"You never wanted a pet," said Bronwyn. "You've always said they were too much trouble."

"The baby will need a pet. A nice little dog, maybe. A Yorkie. A cockapoo. A cat."

"You don't even like cats."

"It's a sacrifice I'm willing to make for my child," Maggie said, hoping that she sounded noble, but Bronwyn guffawed.

"I have never known anyone less altruistic in my life," Bronwyn said. "What's come over you? Awful Predicaments don't normally affect one's sanity."

"I'm going to change, Bronwyn. This baby is the most important thing in the world to me. It's going to make a difference in my whole life-style." How could she tell Bronwyn that she had come to picture herself as a benevolent mother surrounded by animals and children? She would speak to them in gentle tones like Marmee in *Little Women*, and she would wear smocks and sensible shoes. A halo would also be a nice touch.

"Why don't we talk about this when you come back to the office after your vacation? We'll take a long lunch hour, treat ourselves to a feast at the Ritz."

Maggie drew a deep breath. "I'm thinking I might take a leave of absence from MMB&O," she said.

"Leave of absence?" Bronwyn said. "No one at MMB&O takes leaves of absence!"

"Well, what if someone wanted to? In order to get her life together?"

"Are we talking about a *paid* leave of absence?"

"I hope so," Maggie said blithely, but she was worried. Bronwyn wasn't exactly lapping up this idea.

"Would you go for an unpaid leave?"

Maggie calculated rapidly in her head. She had a small inheritance from her mother, but not much in the way of savings. She would have doctor bills, things to buy for the baby and miscellaneous expenses that she hadn't even begun to anticipate.

"I think it would have to be a paid leave," she said not so blithely.

"You're asking a lot, Maggie." This delivered in a doubtful voice.

"Will you see if it flies with our superiors?"

A long silence, and then Bronwyn said carefully, "How long would this leave need to be?"

"Oh, I was thinking of six months."

"Maggie! Our work load is heavier than it's ever been. Have you flipped out?"

"No, but let's face it—having this baby means making major changes. I'd want my present job to be waiting for me when I came back from a leave of absence, of course. I'll need to support the baby."

"Do you know how hard it is to be your boss as well as your best friend? You are really putting me in a difficult position, Maggie."

At that moment, a bouquet of wildflowers flew in the open kitchen window. Not knowing at first what this flying projectile was, Maggie dodged it, dropping the phone in the process. She was glad for the interruption, since she didn't like the way the conversation was going anyway.

"Maggie? Maggie? What's wrong? Maggie?" Bronwyn was saying when Maggie managed to convey the phone back up to her ear.

"Some flowers have just been delivered," Maggie said, eyeing the spray of cerise azaleas surrounded by lavender trillium and pale pink lady's slipper. When she picked up the bunch of flowers, a note fell out.

"Meet me at the river. I can—canoe?" It was signed Tate.

"Who sent them?" Bronwyn wanted to know.

"Remember the man I met the other day?" Maggie said cautiously. She didn't want to sound enthusiastic and thereby give away her ridiculous happiness at this sign that Tate wasn't angry with her.

"The naked Cherokee man?"

"Half-naked."

"I remember," Bronwyn said, sounding resigned.

"He's ready to smoke a peace pipe."

"You shouldn't smoke, Maggie. It wouldn't be good for the baby." This caution was delivered with the fervor of a reformed chain smoker, which Bronwyn was.

Maggie stuck her head out the kitchen window in an effort to find out if Tate had left the clearing. "Must you take everything literally? I'm not going to smoke anything. I hate tobacco smoke, you know that."

"You've said you were going to change."

"I'm not going to go off the deep end. I think I'd better hang up." She didn't see Tate anywhere.

"Call me back," said Bronwyn, but Maggie hung up without promising and, having learned her lesson on the day that she'd had to swim for her life, grabbed a life jacket off a hook in the utility room before hurrying outside and toward the path to the river.

WHEN MAGGIE REACHED the river, she found Tate standing on the bank with his hands on his hips looking at the shiny new aluminum canoe.

"Hi," she said. It wasn't the most original greeting she could have thought of, but it certainly sufficed. She took in the bare muscular torso, the clean but tattered jeans cut off at the knees. He had plaited his hair in a single queue at the nape of his neck and fastened it with a leather thong. She'd almost forgotten the long clean line of his throat; she was newly conscious of the high cheekbones sloping into the straight planes of his cheeks.

"Hi," he said, his eyes lighting up when he saw her.

"Thanks for the flowers."

"I figured I needed to make something up to you," he said.

"You didn't," she said. "Except for the canoe, of course."

He grinned at her in benign munificence and thunked the side of the canoe with a moccasined foot. "What do you think of her?"

"She's bigger and better than the one I bought. You wouldn't have had to go, well, overboard," she said, and he laughed.

"I did that once," he said, and she laughed, too. But she felt suddenly shy with him looking at her with such intensity.

"Let's take her out," she said, and he moved closer and took the life jacket from her. He held it up so that she could slip her arms through the armholes, and she stood very still as he straightened it across her shoulders. His hands lingered for a moment beneath her hair before he pulled it free of the jacket; she held her breath. She thought, in that heart-stopping moment, that he was going to kiss her. Instead he turned suddenly and said, "Let's go."

In a few minutes she was in the bow and he was in the stern and they were paddling upstream. She wished that she had the ability to read Tate's thoughts as he seemed able to read hers; she would have loved to know what was running through his mind at the moment.

The canoe handled beautifully, and for the first time, Maggie considered that Tate Jennings should not have gone to the extra expense. The canoe that she'd bought had been of the plain-vanilla variety. She certainly would never have bought this spiffed-up, top-of-the-line, and obviously expensive canoe for herself.

When she looked back at Tate, she flashed him a smile. "I like the canoe," she said. "You, ah...really outdid yourself." She aimed for a tone between friendly and casual, wanting him to know that she approved of his choice without seeming to lead him on in a romantic or sexual way.

"Good," he chuckled. "We're fair and square now, aren't we?" He was paddling with bold, rhythmic strokes, the muscles in his arms rippling with the effort. She felt a catch in her throat and thought about the day before when those arms had held her so securely; she had almost lost control, and he knew it.

She turned back around. "Yes. Fair and square," she replied. She felt awkward about saying anything more.

Paddling against the current provided enough exercise so that Tate apparently felt no need to break the silence either, but eventually he spoke.

"I went to the office to see my boss today," he said.

"Oh? And are you eager to go back to work?"

"It will be a major change, that's for sure."

"You don't sound happy about it."

"I didn't feel comfortable at the office. Either the corporation has changed or I have. And somehow, I don't think it's Conso."

"No," Maggie said. "Conso seems to expect everyone else to do the changing."

"They're the ones with the money. That gives them the power to dictate, or so they think. It's not only the locals who are under Conso's thumb—it's everyone who has anything to do with them, including the employees."

A butterfly landed on Maggie's arm and rested there for a moment before flitting away. "Even you?" she said.

"Even me. For instance, Karl told me today that I may get a hefty promotion. If I don't screw up on the job, that is. Oh, and if I get a haircut."

The words hung heavy with irony, a fact that was not lost on Maggie.

She stopped paddling and looked around. "How do you feel about that?"

"I'm still trying to deal with it," he said, but he didn't look pleased.

"It must be nice to know that they're considering you for a promotion. Usually when you're not around, it's out of sight, out of mind." She thought of telling him how his venture had given her the nerve to request her own leave of absence, but she didn't want to talk about it until she heard a yes or a no from Bronwyn.

"I'm glad to know that the company thinks highly enough of me to push a promotion, but..."

"But?"

"But I'm not comfortable with the company politics involved. Also, I find myself wondering if I'll be able to toe the company line now that I've experienced freedom of thought. I'm more independent out here in the woods, and I'm comfortable with who I am for the first time in my life. Going back to my full-time position will mean giving up a part of myself." He saw her start to dip her paddle in the water again and said, "No, Maggie, let me paddle. I don't want you to get too tired."

She rested, glad that he was taking over.

"Something you said a few minutes ago sticks in my mind," she said over her shoulder. "What do you mean about being comfortable with who you are now that you've lived in the woods?"

She listened to the dip and swing of Tate's paddle. It was a while before he answered. "I'm only half Cherokee," he said. "I wasn't ready to accept that part of my heritage until recently. I hardly knew anything about it, in fact. For most of my life, it seemed like something of which I was supposed to be ashamed, like a lot of other things about my past."

"Like what?" Maggie blurted the words. Once she'd asked, she almost wished she hadn't. Tate didn't speak, and she turned to look at him. "If you don't want to talk about it . . ." she began, but Tate interrupted her.

"I could tell you," he said, "if you're in the mood to listen to a long story. Want to take a break? We could pull over here under the willow trees. I know of a quiet place on the bank where we can rest."

Maggie assured Tate that she was eager to hear what he had to say, and after a searching look, he glided the canoe up onto the grassy bank. He helped her out, and they climbed to a level spot above the river where the sun peeped through a dark canopy of leaves. It was calm there, and the only sound was the music of the water purling over the stones below.

Tate threw himself down upon a bed of moss, and, uncertain where she should sit at first, Maggie finally lowered herself to a soft mat of fallen leaves opposite him so she could watch the dappled sunlight play across his features.

She had always found the way he looked fascinating, but today he seemed even more exotic. His eyes were slightly slanted with an almost oriental cast to them; they were so black that it was almost impossible to distinguish iris from pupil, especially in this shady glen where his pupils expanded to let in more light. She had never before noticed how precisely arched his eyebrows were, and her gaze lingered on them, avoiding his mouth. She waited for him to speak.

He threw his head back and stared at the specks of sky beyond the leaves above. "I don't talk about this much," he said finally, lowering his head to look at her. He sounded faintly apologetic.

"Why do you want to now?" she asked.

"It's easy to talk to you," he said, sounding halfway surprised. "You probably don't realize it, but for me you opened the door for confidences when you shared the news of your breakup with Kip.''

''Did I?'' she said, surprised.

''Yes, and I'm glad. I think we both need a friend right now, Maggie.''

Suddenly she couldn't look at him anymore. Yes, she needed a friend; Tate couldn't know how much. *Tell him,* said the soft and insistent voice in her head, disconcerting her. It was the first time she'd heard it away from the cabin. But she couldn't tell Tate that she was pregnant, not now when he was primed to talk about himself. Any misguided revelation would immediately and inappropriately train the spotlight on her. Mentally, she told the voice to mind its own business.

Tate, for once, seemed oblivious to her thoughts. He picked up a leaf and began to shred it methodically. ''All right. The early history of Tate Jennings. Well, here goes.'' He shot her a quick look but apparently saw nothing amiss in her expression. With a look of determination, he went on.

''My mother was a singer at the Golden Fleece Tavern in Nashville and my father was in town peddling songs to record companies. He and his pals persuaded my mother to party with them, and she and Phil Jennings ended up at a no-tell motel on the outskirts of town. She had the presence of mind to check his driver's license before she crept away at dawn, and that's how she learned his address. If she hadn't done that, I might never have known who my father was.'' He spoke quickly at first, then more calmly, but Maggie sensed that his words hid a carefully concealed pain.

''My mother had been trying to make it big in Nashville's country music scene for four long years by the time I made my appearance in the world. There was no doubt that I looked like an Indian when I was born. The nurses in the hospital nursery, I was told, exclaimed over my black hair and my dark eyes.

"'He's a cute kid,'" people would tell my mother, 'but he doesn't look like you had anything to do with him.'

"'Looks like his daddy,'" Ma would say. My mother was a blue-eyed blonde. Nothing about me resembled her, and I think that bothered her. Maybe that's one reason that the motherhood bit got to be too much for her and why she finally contacted Phil Jennings to ask for help. My father's letter of reply was swift and to the point. 'I'm not ready for a family. Please don't contact me again,' it said. In the morning Ma strapped me in my stroller, wheeled it to the landlady's door, popped my pacifier in my mouth, and left me there. She didn't come back for three years." He stopped speaking suddenly and stared into the distance as if at an invisible wall.

"I can't imagine it," Maggie said, shaken by Tate's story. "I can't imagine walking off and leaving a baby with anyone." She placed a comforting hand on Tate's arm, and he rested his on it. "What happened after that?"

"I was shuffled from one foster home to another. The first real memory I have of my mother is of her sudden appearance on a frosty December morning when I was four. She showed up at the foster home where I lived, handed me a present wrapped in gilt paper, fussed over me, and told me that she loved me more than anything. I asked my mother if she would take me home with her.

"'Oh, I don't think that would be such a good idea,' she said. 'Mother thinks it's best for you to live with these nice people. Mother has to leave you here because she loves you so much.'"

"You must have been so unhappy," Maggie said softly, her eyes searching Tate's face. He still held her hand, and she didn't try to pull it away.

"I was bewildered. If she loved me, wouldn't she want me with her? If she loved me, why did she pry my fingers loose from her coat and thrust me away when I begged to leave with her? Why didn't she wave to me after she got in the car?"

Maggie sat very still, letting Tate talk. She sensed that this was a catharsis for him, and she wondered how many other people he had ever told about his childhood. *Not many,* said the voice. Maggie wished for a dial with which she could turn off this pesky and insistent nuisance, and as she wished it, she heard a peal of laughter. With a tremendous effort of will, she pushed the voice out of her mind and concentrated on Tate.

He paused for a moment before continuing. "After I left that foster home, I spent a brief time in a group home. The house parents were cruel to all of us kids." He gazed at the river for a moment before continuing.

"I finally ran away. Police caught up with me two days later in the bus station, a bedraggled seven-year-old begging strangers for the fare to go to New Orleans, where I thought my mother was."

"Did you find her?" Maggie asked.

He shook his head. "I was sent to another foster home."

A chipmunk poked its head out of its burrow, spotted them, and quickly disappeared. The leaves above rustled and shifted, the scudding clouds overhead dimming the light in the clearing.

"You've had a hard life," she said.

"Harder than most," he agreed. "In a way, it's why I've never wanted to marry and have a family. The idea is foreign to me, since I don't know the meaning of a happy home life. I put all my effort into building a career, trying to overcome my background."

"Would you say your values have changed while you've lived on the mountain?"

"I've been forced to examine my life honestly, and I've discovered that all those supposedly worthwhile reasons for working at a job in which I exchange my personal values for a certain amount of economic power have more or less faded away. Gone. Kaput. *Finito.*" He gave a little half laugh.

"Would you ever quit your job at Conso, Tate? Just not go back?"

He seemed to consider this carefully. "I've thought about it," he confessed. "I haven't figured out a way to do it, that's all."

Maggie thought about Bronwyn's reaction to the very mention of a leave of absence. She could only imagine what Bronwyn would say if Maggie decided not to return to MMB&O. Not that this was in the cards; Maggie liked the creative aspects of her job, although she was increasingly aware that she disliked the hustle and bustle of the busy office. Also, with a baby on the way, she couldn't afford to quit.

"You know, Tate," she said, "it seems as if there are all kinds of supports built into working at jobs we don't enjoy. Our bosses set examples that we're supposed to live up to, even if we don't believe in the corporate ethic. We're ostracized if we don't fall into place and spout the company line. And there are hardly any precedents for doing what you did, for taking time out to consider what we're really doing with our lives. It's sad, I think."

"I'm through with sadness," Tate said with conviction. "I've made up my mind to be happy. If that requires that I return to Conso, then that's what I'll do. If not, well, I'll have to figure out something else, won't I?"

"Mmm," said Maggie. She leaned back against a boulder and gazed up at the sky. "I thought I had a hard life when I was growing up, but it wasn't nearly as awful as yours.''

"You said you had a hard time with your parents' divorce.''

"Don't most children?''

"Probably. That's why if I marry, I hope to get it right the first time.''

"That's important to me, too,'' she said. "Like a lot of people in my generation, my parents' divorce made it that much more important for me to find the right person. I can't imagine putting kids through that kind of turmoil. Growing up is hard enough as it is.'' It seemed so natural to be having this conversation with Tate; they were relating as friends, all pretense gone.

"Growing up is a difficult time, isn't it?. Yet so many babies come into the world without the benefit of a real family,'' Tate said.

Maggie froze. It was almost as if Tate knew her secret. Was he reading her mind?

Or—giving him the benefit of a doubt—maybe he was really talking about his own situation. She didn't know him well enough to know what he was getting at, but she certainly had no intention of giving herself away, especially now that she knew his feelings about single mothers keeping their babies. She adopted what she hoped was a nonchalant expression.

"After my father left, you couldn't say that my mother and I were what the rest of the world considers a real family, yet Mom did a great job bringing me up, and I admire her for it,'' she said.

"That's different. When you were born, your mother had every reason to expect her marriage to last. I'm sure she never expected to be a single mother, but she coped. I worry about single mothers who have babies and keep them when there's no father around to support them, either financially or emotionally. I know it works out well a lot of the time, but I don't think it's right."

Tell him about the baby, said the voice inside Maggie's head.

But this wasn't the time. Maybe she'd tell him later. Or maybe she never would. And where was this voice coming from? Chalking it up to her condition no longer seemed a viable answer.

A distant rumble of thunder rolled down the mountain, and Maggie, who would have grasped at any interruption at that moment, said too brightly, "It sounds as if our afternoon thunderboomer is arriving early today. We'd better head back to my place before it starts to rain."

"I'm game. Anything to get out of telling you the rest of my story," he said.

"We got off the track, didn't we? I still want to know how you ended up here, in Scot's Cove. Don't think you're going to get out of telling me, Tate Jennings. I'll remind you sometime that you left me dangling." She grinned at him.

They got up and brushed the leaves and bits of forest debris from their clothes. Tate cast a worried eye at the dark clouds gathering above the trees.

"That looks like a big storm. We'd better hurry. We don't want to be out on the river if there's lightning," he said. He slid his arm around Maggie's shoulders and hurried her toward the canoe; her arm went naturally around his waist.

"You'd better ask those Little People of yours to send the lightning in a different direction," she said, striving for a cheerful tone.

"I don't think you can tell the Yunwi Tsundsi anything. They have minds of their own. Besides, the Cherokee say that when there's lightning, you should sit under a basswood tree because of all the trees in the forest, they're never struck. But personally, I don't want to take any chances.''

"Seems to me everything is full of chances," she said. "Like jumping into my canoe.''

He smiled down at her. "Are you still angry at me?''

"Don't you think I should be?''

"If you were, we wouldn't be friends," he said soberly.

"No," she agreed. "We probably wouldn't.''

You're much more than friends, you know, said the voice, and for the first time, Maggie had no desire to tell it to shut up.

Chapter Six

Maggie and Tate were running up the path from the river, borne along on a cool rush of air sweeping ahead of the storm, as the first drops of rain spattered on their faces.

"We made it just in time," Tate said as an out-of-breath Maggie pushed open the front door and drew him inside with her.

Gazing out the window at the wind-tossed trees, she said, "I guess you'll have to stay awhile," and secretly she was glad.

Looking for something to do, Maggie picked up the wildflower bouquet that Tate had tossed through the window earlier and made a show of arranging it in a cut-glass vase. Tate busied himself by taking one of the books down from the bookcase and thumbing through it, then replacing it in its slot and studying one of the prints on the wall. "It looks like you've been keeping busy," he said when he saw the quilt squares that she had arranged on the coffee table.

"This quilt as my mother planned it was a work of art. The first couple of squares show Peg Macintyre's early childhood," she said.

She spread the finished squares out so that he could see them. "Here's the square that shows her living here in this cabin with her parents, all of them occupied by daily tasks. This one shows the family farm, and you can see the approach of a dark-haired boy through the cornfield. According to family history, Tsani was employed by Angus Macintyre, Peg's father, to help out with the work.''

"So Tsani moved freely about the white man's world," Tate mused. "Or was he in it but not of it, like I always thought I was?"

"I wonder," Maggie said quietly, and she and Tate shared a rueful smile.

Maggie rummaged in a work bag and withdrew the square she had finished yesterday. "Look, Tate. Here's Tsani sitting in the cabin—this cabin. See how Peg is looking shyly at him out of the corners of her eyes and how the mother is hovering protectively over her daughter? My mother had already appliquéd the figures. All I had to do to finish this square was to whipstitch the loose edges."

"I didn't know you had any interest in this sort of thing," said Tate as he picked up one of the squares and inspected it.

"I didn't until now, but this was my mother's last craft project. When I finish it, I'll donate it to the local history museum as she planned to do. It will be a memorial to Mom. She loved these mountains." Maggie, who had so eagerly gravitated toward the excitement and glamour of the big city after college, had never been able to understand her mother's attraction to this place, but the longer she lived here it became more clear.

Outside, a flash of lightning forked through the dark clouds, and rain began to pour down in sheets. Thunder shook the cabin as Maggie ran to close the open living room window.

The robin's egg reposed in its nest on the sill, quivering slightly from the reverberations of the thunder.

Maggie closed the window and picked up the egg, turning to confront Tate with what seemed like an inexplicable foible of his.

"Tate, why do you keep putting this robin's egg on my windowsill? Is it supposed to be a joke? If so, I have to admit that I don't get it."

Tate put down the quilt square and regarded the egg cupped in her two hands with puzzlement that appeared to be genuine. "I don't know what you're talking about," he said, moving toward her.

"This egg in its nest appears and disappears from one day to the next on the sill of the open window. I know you're the one who is responsible."

"Not me," he said evenly, and she somehow knew that he was speaking the truth.

"No one else has been to the cabin since I arrived a little over a week ago. Who else could be doing it?"

He reached out toward the egg in her hands, whether to touch it or to take it from her she didn't know. As his finger barely contacted the egg's smooth surface, lightning struck so close in the clearing that Maggie felt a zing of electricity from her head to her toes. In sudden shock, she dropped the egg, and Tate's outstretched hand caught it in midair.

Tate, his face limned in the blue-white light as thunder shook the cabin, looked as startled as anyone would be when lightning had struck so close. And then something shifted subtly in his expression; the air around them sharpened and grew heavy with a blue-green glow, and a huge buzzing arose in Maggie's ears. When she lifted her eyes to Tate's, she saw that he was looking down at her with an intensity that bespoke a deep emotion, and Maggie found that she could not look away.

The buzzing stopped suddenly. Maggie shook her head to clear it. And when Tate spoke, the timbre of his voice was familiar, although the accent was not. She stood transfixed, held captive by his gaze and by the impassioned delivery of his words.

"Dearest, I found this nest under the tree where we first kissed, and I thought it would be a fine memento of that moment. Now when you're free to see me at night, all you'll have to do is set the nest in the window as a signal, and when I walk by on my way to your father's fields, I will know," he said. His eyes burned into her, and she could look nowhere else.

Maggie hesitated. She felt light-headed under the intensity of his gaze, and her knees were weak. "What if my father finds out?" she heard herself saying, but the voice was not her voice. It originated in her head and emitted from her mouth, but the words were not those that she, Maggie Macintyre, would say.

Tate carefully set the robin's egg in the nest on the windowsill and took her in his arms. "Your father will come to see it our way. He cannot hold out against our love forever."

"I hope not," she said, her heart beating rapidly. Her palms were damp, and she felt very nervous. "I—I have something to tell you."

"Tell me you love me. That's all I need to hear." He smoothed her hair back and looked deep into her eyes.

"I do love you, my darling, so much. That's why I'm completely happy about what has happened." She stared resolutely at his chin.

"And what is that, my Margaret?" He smiled at her, all warmth and invitation. She knew that he had no idea about the gravity of the circumstance that she was about to reveal.

"I am with child," she whispered softly, her eyes searching his face. His expression changed to utter shock.

He gripped her arms so hard that she rocked against him. "Are you sure?" he said.

"I am sure," she said, keeping her voice steady although she thought she might faint.

"How many moons?"

"Almost four."

To her relief, he swept her against him and murmured into her hair. "Why did you not tell me sooner?"

"I didn't know what we would do. Father wishes me to marry Old Garvey—"

"You can't marry him, that should be clear," he said biting off the words fiercely. "You will marry no one but me. It is what we have always wanted."

"Yes, oh yes," she said.

"Do your parents suspect your condition?"

"Father knows nothing. Nor does Mother. They will never let me marry you, Tsani. We both know that."

"We will run away together, it's the only way. Before the next full moon, I will make the arrangements. No more sneaking and hiding, Margaret. From now on we will live openly together far away from here where no one knows us."

It suddenly came to Maggie in that moment. She and Tate were playing out a scene that had happened between Peg Macintyre and Tsani many generations ago. How or why this could happen, she did not know. And then she didn't care, because Tate—Tsani—was threading his fingers through her hair and lowering his lips to hers. He kissed her with great tenderness, which slowly grew into passion. His hands traced the curves of her cheeks, slid down to cup her shoulders for a moment, and then he wrapped his arms around her slender body until the contours of her shape

were fitted to his. Her own arms slid upward until they
looped around his neck and loosened the leather thong that
bound his hair, which slid forward and brushed against the
sides of her face. She thought, *Tsani, Tsani,* and felt a sharp
pang of love.

This scene might not be real, but the taste of the man who
held her in his arms was certainly no illusion, and neither
was the sweet seeking of his lips. Her mouth parted beneath his, and he kissed her deeply and surely as if he had
done so many times before. She heard him moan deep in his
throat, and she wondered fleetingly if it was Tate or Tsani
whose tongue traced the outlines of her lips, and she wondered if it was Maggie or Peg who responded so eagerly.
And then it didn't matter; all that mattered was their
tongues tangling in haste.

This man wanted her; she knew it, had known it and denied it. Now she felt as if she had been admitted somehow
to the silent part of his soul where his deepest secrets lay, and
opening to him, she tentatively let him know that she wanted
him as well.

His lips feathered downward, his breath rippling against
the soft skin of her throat. "Margaret," he said. "Margaret, the mother of my child."

Whoever she was, whoever he was, she was Margaret, his
Margaret.

Now and forever, said the voice.

A quicksilver shiver coursed through her, and she
clutched him tightly, feeling his muscles tense beneath her
fingertips. It seemed so natural to slide her hands down his
arms and interweave her fingers with his, to touch her
tongue to his earlobe, to flutter her hands upward to tangle
in his hair. Every cell of her body seemed electric, alive,
joyous with the thrill of the moment, and when he slid his
hands under her clothes and cupped the lush contours of her

breasts, her senses swam with the knowledge that their lovemaking was absolutely right in whatever time and place they happened to be.

If he undid buttons, she didn't know; if he grappled with sleeves or armholes, she didn't notice. It seemed to her that her clothes drifted away, wafted elsewhere by a magic wind, and the first she knew of being naked from the waist up was when he held her breasts in his hands, his mouth abandoning her lips to touch his seeking lips first to one rosy tip, then the other. His tongue was damp upon her skin, and his breath was hot upon her nipples. And she floated along with him downward to the rug beside the fireplace, whispering urgently, "Quickly, we must hurry, someone may walk in." As she gazed up at him in wonder, he slid his body over hers.

His eyes were darkly luminous in the glow of the fire in the grate, and his lips were eager upon her mouth, his hands gentle upon her breasts. The fire warmed her body and his kisses warmed her soul; she heard nothing but the sound of their quickened breathing and the beat of her own pulse in her ears. Her fingers knotted in his hair, urging him closer.

She wanted more than anything to feel him tight inside her, and her eyes closed as she reveled in the liquid fire rippling though her veins, the same as the fire that crackled and sparked beside them in the fireplace. She was lost in the sensation of his mouth upon her, of her body rising to meet his, of two spirits blending in sublime pleasure, of longing beyond longing to know him in the most intimate way.

Twin forks of lightning rent the sky, and the ensuing thunder rattled the window panes, startling her. She said, "Tsani?"

When she spoke the name, Tate recoiled in consternation, the light of reason flaring in his eyes as he stared down at her, his body poised above.

"What? What did you call me?" The words uttered on a gasp, sharp and incredulous.

In that moment, Maggie knew she could not let this go on. *You can, you can, you can,* chanted the familiar insistent voice, but she pushed Tate aside and rolled away, distracted by the rain clattering against the window and the bewildered look in Tate's eyes.

They stared at each other for a time, and they might have been miles away from each other, not inches apart on the hearth rug. The dulcimer music that Maggie had not even realized she heard until now terminated suddenly on one discordant note.

For a long time, neither of them spoke. Finally Maggie stirred, pushing her tumbled hair away from her face.

"Tsani," she said dully. "I thought you were Tsani. And you thought I was Peg." She reached for the afghan spread across the seat of the couch and pulled it across her, not daring to look at Tate. There was no fire in the fireplace; there weren't even any logs, and the cold ashes from last year's fires had been swept away long ago.

Tate sat up and adjusted his clothes, staring at her. "I don't understand what happened," he said.

Maggie closed her eyes, hoping that this was all a bad dream but certain that it wasn't. She took her time answering, waiting until she was sure that her voice would hold steady.

"Somehow we became them."

Tate digested this, his features dimly lit in the pearly gray light from the rain-washed window. "We must have been replaying something that happened between them long ago," he said.

Maggie, drained by the experience, shivered. "I knew something was happening, but I was powerless to stop it," she said.

"I knew it, too," Tate admitted. "It was as though I could think and feel but another person was inside me."

"We were two other people," Maggie said in a small voice. "We weren't us." She was lying on the hearth rug, her hair spread out around her, the afghan pulled across her bare breasts. She knew she had behaved wantonly, and she was embarrassed at her lack of control. She had, during those moments, felt love for him, and she was totally bewildered by the feelings.

"Tsani was only doing what I've been wanting to do since I met you," Tate said slowly, touching a finger to her cheek.

"And I—" she began, but she couldn't possibly tell him how deeply his kisses had affected her.

"You liked it," he said. "You might as well admit it. I sensed your thoughts, knew that you were willing."

"It wasn't me," she said resolutely. "It was Peg."

"It wasn't Peg's hand that touched me like this," he said, drawing her hand toward him and placing it on his nipple. It was hard and tight beneath her fingers, and she felt a thrill of misplaced anticipation.

"And it wasn't Tsani's mouth that kissed you like this," he whispered, his lips seeking hers.

His kiss was warm and thorough and completely absorbing, and yes, she liked it better when she, Maggie, was experiencing Tate's kisses and not Tsani's. He infused the kiss with a tantalizing blend of longing and barely suppressed excitement so that she felt an answering tremor spiraling up from somewhere deep inside her. He ended the kiss prematurely, leaving her with an unsatisfying sense of disappointment.

Tell him about the baby, said the voice, Peg's voice, and this time Maggie heeded it. They couldn't go on, not like this, becoming increasingly intimate when she was in an Awful Predicament.

She took a deep breath. "Tate," she said, "I have to tell you something."

His eyebrows shot up, but not as if he didn't want to hear what she had to say. Gently he caressed her lips with a fingertip. "What could you possibly have to tell me at a moment like this?" he said.

She stared at him, at his eyes black as ebony, at his lips curved upward in an indulgent smile.

"I'm pregnant," she said.

He recoiled, an expression of disbelief washing over his features. "You...*what?*"

"I'm going to have a baby. Kip's baby."

He shook his head in denial. "You're joking. Right?" he said, even as the recognition dawned that she was entirely serious.

She swallowed and shook her head.

"Are you sure?"

"Of course I'm sure. I came here to think it over. To decide what to do."

Tate jumped to his feet and gazed at her from above, still shocked, still stunned. "And?" was all he said.

"And I'm going to keep the baby," she said.

He turned away as if he couldn't bear to look at her, then wheeled around and stared again. "My God," he said.

"I wasn't going to tell you. But now—" she said, and she lifted her shoulders and let them fall.

He paced from one end of the cabin to the other as if physical activity would dispel his anger. "You should have mentioned it earlier," he said.

"I didn't know how you'd react."

"So you waited until *now?* When we're—" He left the sentence unfinished and stared at the ceiling for a moment. When he looked back at her, the pain in his eyes went straight to her heart.

"Why'd you tell me?" he said.

"I—I thought it would be unfair not to let you know. Peg told Tsani, and I told you."

"What did you think I'd say? My reaction couldn't be the same as Tsani's. Did you'd think I'd be happy for you? Telling me you're going to have another man's baby is hardly the same as telling me you won the lottery, you know."

"I didn't think ahead," she said miserably.

He let out a long deep breath. "Look, I don't know what to think," he said. When she was silent, he shook his head. "I'd better go. The rain has let up." Tate strode to the door and after one last baffled glance at her, he let himself out. The door slammed behind him, perhaps driven by the wind, perhaps not.

Maggie's first impulse was to run after him, to beg for reassurance that he didn't think less of her. But she knew that if she got up, she'd be dizzy, and already she felt nauseated. Why, oh why, had she told him?

Between her and the window, a slight shadow passed, a mere blip. No, not a blip. *Someone.* Maggie blinked, but she knew who it was.

You had to tell him, said the voice. *Just like I had to tell Tsani.*

Maggie knew now whose voice she had been hearing, and in her despair over Tate's reaction to her news, oddly enough she was comforted. Peg Macintyre had been a fragile presence in this cabin ever since Maggie had arrived, and now she knew why. Something at this juncture in her life had drawn Peg to her, had made her communicate with Maggie. Maybe it was Maggie's pregnancy and the problem with Kip that made Peg sympathetic, or maybe it was some reason that Maggie couldn't fathom.

One thing she knew was that she wasn't the least bit afraid of Peg. She could never be afraid of this woman whose aura conveyed only a lingering, loving presence with which, Maggie now realized, she had become increasingly familiar over the past week and a half.

And Peg was her only comfort now, when she felt more desolate than ever. Tate had gone, maybe for good. Why would he come back after the strange interlude with Tsani and Peg? And what must he think after finding out that he had almost made love to a pregnant woman?

After an hour or more of huddling under the afghan and holding back the nausea with some success and the tears with far less, Maggie thought to look at the windowsill. The nest with the robin's egg had again disappeared. This time, she thought as she pulled herself together and retrieved her clothes, she knew Tate wasn't the one who was playing mind games with her, but at last she knew who was.

PREGNANT! Tate thought as he made his way through the wet woods toward his camp.

Maggie was pregnant, and by a man who didn't love her, couldn't love her if he could leave her at a time like this. And she was going to keep her baby. If Tate had known about the baby, things would have been different from the very beginning. He wouldn't have become so deeply involved.

But he was involved, and that had dire ramifications. He was still too stunned to know what effects this new knowledge would have on his life; how could he know when he was still reeling from the shock?

Grimly he decided, as he pressed through tangles of rain-drenched laurel, to embark upon a vision quest. The goal of such spiritual seeking was to produce a vision that would offer insight into the problems being faced. There was no doubt in Tate's mind that his problems at the moment were mind-boggling. He didn't know what to do about his job. He didn't know what to do about Maggie and her astonishing news. And how did Peg and Tsani enter into any of it?

When he reached his camp, Tate silently went about preparing for his vision quest. His sweat lodge, which was about ten yards from the *asi,* consisted of a dome frame of peeled willow saplings covered with canvas. In the ground in the center of this structure he had dug a hole approximately twelve inches deep and twenty-four inches wide; it was lined with large rocks.

He stripped off his wet clothes. Then he lit a fire in the sweat lodge and waited outside until the fire grew hot. He searched for a crane in the trees, but all he saw was one reticent owl that landed at the top of a huge oak tree and studied him with thickly hooded golden eyes. Tate didn't know how to interpret this as an omen; he still had so much to learn about native ways.

When the owl flapped away into the night, Tate said, "Go, little brother, and bring me the crane." The owl answered with a muffled cry, which Tate interpreted as a positive sign. Then he went into the sweat lodge and tossed water on the hot stones. He sat naked amid the rising steam and concentrated on finding solutions to his problems as the sweat poured from his body.

Tate delved deep into his emotions, tried to figure out what they were, tried to feel them in his heart. For so long he had made himself feel nothing; the circumstances of his life were such that it was better not to feel. Now he was feeling something for Maggie, and it frightened him.

Once the vision presented itself, he would know what to do. Until then, he would not see her. Until then, he would not go back to Maggie's cabin.

He threw more water on the stones and gazed into the fire, knowing that he might have a long wait before he found the answers he so desperately sought.

ONE DAY. Two days. Three days. Tate didn't come to the cabin, and Maggie didn't know where to find him. At times she was sure she'd never see him again; other times, she knew she would. Occasionally she broke down in despair over his reaction to her pregnancy. She had, she realized, counted on him to be a friend. Now she couldn't count on him for anything.

Maggie ticked the time off on her Filofax calendar, which was seeing a lot less action than it had when she was in Atlanta. She spent her days working on her mother's quilt, which was coming along faster than she had expected. Her fingers fairly flew when she was sewing, guiding the needle in and out, in and out, with a skill she had never known she possessed.

The appliquéd squares were pure artistry. Most of them were almost finished; others had been pinned and were ready to be whipstitched onto the background fabric. Maggie found herself empathizing with the Peg and Tsani she grew to know through the quilt. The squares showed them kissing beside the waterfall, picnicking in the woods, riding on horseback along a winding mountain trail—all things that Peg and Tsani probably did in real life. The last piece that Maggie's mother had completed, however, was the scene of Tsani being swept over the waterfall as Peg looked on, horrified. There was room for two more squares that were needed to complete the quilt, and Maggie knew that it was up to her to create them.

The trouble was that she had no idea what her mother had in mind. What scenes had she planned to depict? Peg married to the old man who had become her husband? Peg with her baby, Tsani's child? Peg living out her life in this cabin, an unhappy woman? Maggie had no idea.

At least working on the quilt kept her mind off Tate Jennings. Then again, it didn't always. Sometimes she could almost forget how he had stormed out of the cabin, and at those times she caught herself smiling a slow secret smile whenever she thought about the way he had kissed her. She fantasized about making love with him, thinking about his long limbs entwined with hers, about his dark skin sliding against her body, hot with passion and urgent with need. She remembered all too well how eagerly her body had responded to his touch.

She thought about him so much that she stopped sewing one day when the shock of it hit her: she was mooning over Tate Jennings as if she were in love with him.

Nonsense, she told herself. She sternly made herself think about the baby instead. Her dear little Awful Predicament. Except that she hardly ever thought about the baby as her Awful Predicament anymore.

She would have told Bronwyn this, except that Bronwyn wasn't on her wavelength these days. She was being helpful, though, for which Maggie was extremely grateful. Bronwyn had talked their boss into letting Maggie work at the cabin. She even interrupted her lunch hour one day to call and relay the good news to Maggie.

"A lot of companies are encouraging employees to work at home these days, since it saves on office space and expenses. How would you feel about that?" Bronwyn asked.

"Hey, I might like it," Maggie said in surprise. She hadn't considered this solution before, but it would be ideal. She could write creative ad copy anyplace, not just at a confining desk in a claustrophobic office.

"I thought you'd go for it. Do you think you could get a fax machine up there, Maggie?"

"Oh, yes."

"So, you do want me to pursue the matter?"

"Bronwyn, it's a great idea and a good solution for all of us. I've been trying to figure out a budget since I last talked with you, and I've realized that I can't afford to take any unpaid leave."

"Why don't you go ahead and line up the fax machine, and I'll check into sending your computer up there to that miserable place. What's the name of it?"

"The town is called Scot's Cove. You know that."

"I know that. You're right. I just refuse to admit that such a backwater town exists in your consciousness," Bronwyn said.

Maggie thought it prudent not to mention what else existed in her consciousness, like people who had been dead for over a hundred years but tried to impose their will on the living in a most remarkable way. She held her tongue, but it wasn't easy.

Not wanting to discuss the deficiencies of Scot's Cove again, Maggie changed the subject. "I'm going to have to start wearing maternity clothes soon," she said.

"Is this news? Should I be surprised?"

Maggie sighed impatiently. "Somehow, I didn't expect to gain so much weight in the early months."

"Here's a helpful hint. My sister-in-law wore stretchy leggings during the first several months of her pregnancy," Bronwyn said.

Maggie wrote Stretchy Leggings on a pad of paper beside the phone. "Good idea. I'll try it."

"How are you feeling? Any more stomach upsets?" Bronwyn asked.

"I feel super fantastic, but strong odors bother me sometimes. I tried to sauté onions yesterday but had to quit because my stomach rebelled."

"I can't believe *you're* not rebelling against this mother-hood bit," Bronwyn said with a sigh.

"I'm happy about it. The baby is going to be cute."

"Cute. Well, I can't argue with that. All right, Mags, you line up the fax machine, and I'll talk to you soon," promised Bronwyn, and she hastily hung up.

The baby was becoming more and more of a reality to Maggie, especially since it was clearly rounding out the bottom part of her abdomen. This interested her. Somehow she had believed that it wouldn't be until the very end of her pregnancy that she'd have to wear maternity clothes, and now almost none of her clothes fit.

Then came the day when she could no longer force her jeans to button at the waist one morning. One broken thumbnail later, she gave up and slipped on a pair of Kip's old shorts. The seat bagged, but she could fasten them. Unfortunately, when she looked in the mirror and saw how frumpy she looked, she dissolved into tears.

Also on that day, Maggie started asking herself agonizing questions. Had becoming intimate with a pregnant woman turned Tate off? Did he find her breasts with their darkening areolas unattractive? Had his hands detected the firm little lump in her abdomen that was the baby?

She reminded herself that Tate hadn't been making love to her; Tsani had been making love to Peg. This hardly consoled her. It was Tate's kisses that had made her feel wonderful. And, heaven help her, she wanted to feel that way again.

Heaven did not help her. Tate did not appear, and if Peg was around, she wasn't talking. Even the bird's nest seemed gone from the windowsill for good. Maggie faced facts: maybe Tate and Maggie's love scene the other day had broken whatever spell existed here in this cabin. Maybe Tsani and Peg had received the solace they had needed and had finally gone the way of all good spirits, leaving her with sensuous memories of Tate and a yearning that was destined to remain forever unfulfilled.

Chapter Seven

By the third day in the sweat lodge, Tate had almost given up on his vision quest. He became frustrated waiting for an elusive experience that he wasn't even sure would take place. He had meditated, he had sweated so many buckets that he was sure he must be the most purified person alive, and he was growing weak from fasting. He had sprinkled river water over the hot stones to make steam, and still all he saw through his light-headed haze were the canvas walls of the sweat lodge and swirling billows of smoke.

Finally, late on the third night when Tate had despaired of ever having a vision, the white crane appeared as a tiny white speck in the darkness, growing until it had distinguishable features, growing again until it towered over him.

"Hello, my brother," it said.

"Who are you?" Tate demanded.

In the blink of an eye, the crane's head transformed into a ceremonial mask which he lowered to reveal a face that Tate instinctively recognized as Tsani's. Tate was stunned; Tsani's face was the twin of his own. He blinked, scarcely able to comprehend it.

"You see now that I am really Tsani. For good luck, I showed myself to you in the guise of a crane."

"*You* are my good-luck crane?"

"Yes. You must come with me."

Tate started to say that he could not leave the sweat lodge, but Tsani's eyes mesmerized him so that the words would not come. Suddenly, as if he had been cut loose from the bonds of earth, Tate was borne up and away, weightless and free. In the blink of an eye, Tate was standing before a cabin similar to Maggie's but not as attractive. Crows hunched silently in a leafless dead tree, staring at him with unblinking eyes. Not far away a stooped and bent man stumped past a tumbledown chicken coop on a wooden leg, the expression on his leathery face as bleak as the surroundings.

"That is Old Garvey," said Tsani, and Tate realized with surprise that although they could see the old man, he couldn't see them. "This is the man that Margaret's parents wanted her to marry."

"We must have gone back in time," Tate said. He darted a look at Tsani for confirmation.

"Yes, but do not worry. We'll not stay."

Tate stared at the old man. He could not imagine a young and beautiful woman married to this dirty old codger.

At that moment, two ugly heavyset men appeared at the edge of the forest. They were shouting and raining blows on each others' heads. Tsani leaned close and spoke.

"I received a message from Old Garvey the night before I was to run away with Margaret. The acquaintance who had helped me plan our escape had become drunk in a tavern in town, and when he talked too much, Harry Garvey's sons learned that we were planning to leave. When I was summoned to the Garvey farm, I was stupid enough to think that I could explain how much I loved Margaret. I believed that when he knew of my sincerity and good intentions, Old Garvey would accept my love for her, especially if he loved her himself. Wouldn't he want her to be happy? I thought so until I learned that he only wanted her as his prize, a bit of information that I found out too late. When I came here on that night, I was ambushed by Garvey's two loutish sons, who tied me up and locked me in the shed over there. They left me there and went away to debate what to do with me. I heard them arguing with their father over my fate."

"Is that why you were late for your meeting with Peg?" Tate asked.

Tsani nodded. "In order to get away from here, I had to break the rawhide thongs with which they had bound my wrists, and then I tore away the boards of the shed with my bare hands to make an opening through which I escaped. The dogs heard the noise and began to bark, and they chased me, and—you know the rest. You saw it in your dream. So did your woman."

"Are you saying that the nightmare that Maggie and I shared really happened?"

"Yes. I sent it to both of you so you would understand our desperation. Tate, the woman you know as Peg—my Margaret—and I need your help."

"But I can't—"

"Oh, but you can, Tsani."

"I am Tate," he said in a mystified voice.

"What has gone before will come around again. Tsani and Tate are the same. Peg and Maggie are the same. Our destinies are intertwined. Didn't you guess that?"

Of course he had. He hadn't wanted to admit it, that's all.

Tsani leaned close and said, "Listen well, my brother. Know this—I will live unhappily forever with the Little People beneath the waterfall and my Margaret will wander the earth searching for me for all time if you and your woman do not find a way to be together. You have one chance in this lifetime, and one chance only. You must correct times past."

"Correct times past? I don't even know how to manage the present," Tate said with more than a hint of ruefulness.

"Don't you understand? The ghosts of my Margaret and I will not be released to travel to the Nightland together until our spirits are joined in you two."

"Joined?"

"Not only in sex. In the mind and soul as well. The souls of you and Maggie must come into each other as my Margaret's and mine have done. And then we will go to the Nightland and be together for all eternity. It is our only chance to know peace and your only chance to know true love. You must do this, not only for us, Tate, but for yourself! You must!" Tsani's eyes burned into him like two black coals.

This all sounded like some kind of weird riddle. Tate was sure that he didn't know how to make his soul come into another's, and he certainly didn't know how to join the spirits of Tsani and his Margaret. As for true love, well, did it really exist? Tate had his doubts.

"I wish I was back in my sweat lodge. I wish I had never sought a vision," Tate said.

"Wait," Tsani said, and before Tate knew what was happening, he was lying on the floor of the sweat lodge, his face pressed into the dirt. Tate struggled to rise to his feet, but three days of fasting had left him as weak as a baby, and he wove back and forth on his knees as the steam curled past his head. He wanted to be free of the heat and the steam and the sweat lodge; he wanted to be free of Tsani or the crane or whoever or whatever he was.

"I can't help you," he told Tsani. "I can't even help myself."

Tsani shoved him so that he fell back on the earth. "You reclaimed your heritage as one of the Real People. Also, in your present life you have recently asked that your name be added to the tribal rolls, as is your right. You want the privileges of the Cherokee. How can you not accept the responsibilities as well? You are the one who sought this vision, my brother."

Tate considered this. He had desperately wanted to have an instructive vision, and now he was refusing to listen to the advice and insight he was given. Tsani was telling him that he must not only live like a Cherokee, he must also be a Cherokee inside where it counted. This indeed was the revelation he had sought, and now he felt humble in the face of such wisdom.

Tate pushed himself to a sitting position. "I will accept the vision and learn from it," he said. "I will try to do as you ask."

"That is good." Tsani knelt at his side and leaned close. "I ruined everything," he said. "I lost my woman through my own stupidity. I was too late for our meeting. This caused both of us much misery. Do it right this time, my brother. Do not let yourself be confused by unimportant consequences."

Before Tate could answer, Tsani rose, wrapped the feathers of the crane around him and, with a rapid flutter of wings, disappeared.

"Wait," Tate cried, but it was too late. No one was there to hear his plea.

"What about Maggie's baby?" he cried into the darkness. Was her pregnancy what Tsani had meant by an "unimportant consequence?" It certainly didn't seem so to him. But there was no answer to his question.

"Tsani?" he called into the blackness. "Tsani?"

In answer he heard nothing but the raucous laughter of the Little People who lived beneath the waterfall.

When Tate woke up, he was still in his sweat lodge, his head pillowed on his arms. The fire had gone out, which

explained the blackness surrounding him. He sat up, thinking of what had happened to him. Or had it happened at all?
Perhaps he had never left the sweat lodge. Perhaps there had
been no Tsani, no visit to the past and no white crane.

But what then, he asked himself, would explain the lone
white feather floating slowly, slowly to the floor?

A SPATE OF TREACHEROUS spring weather rocked the entire
country that week. A storm front spawned deadly torna-
does in Texas, unleashed extensive flooding in New Orleans, and was responsible for widespread power failures in
Atlanta. The tail end of the storm wreaked one final insult
by dipping into Scot's Cove and its environs long enough to
cause damage to several storefronts and to uproot a giant
oak tree on Maggie's property during the night.

After surveying the storm's damage, Maggie decided to
drive into town. She had reached the craving stage of her
pregnancy and had developed an uncommon longing for dill
pickles and pistachio ice cream. Also, she needed to ar-
range for the services of Jacob Pinter's grandson, who
owned a chain saw and had cut firewood for her in the past.

In the aftermath of such a devastating storm, his grandson had several weeks of work waiting for him all over the
county, Jacob told her, but the boy would see to her downed
tree eventually. Maggie, feigning nonchalance, took the
opportunity to ask Jacob if he knew how Tate had fared.

"Tate Jennings? No, I ain't heard tell of how the storm
affected Stoker's Knob," said Jacob Pinter as he loaded a
large box of groceries into Maggie's car.

"I thought maybe someone might have mentioned it,"
Maggie said carefully.

"I heard that Flat Top Mountain got tore up pretty bad
up near the tree line."

"Is that where Tate's camp is?" For the first time, Maggie wished she had thought to ask Tate to take her there.

"It's not that high up. If you want to get to the old Jennings home site, you go up past the road to your place, see, and then you veer off to the right near that tumbledown fence afore you get to the bridge. Then you walk due south. Can't help but run into it. You'll know you're almost there when you pass a stone marker. It used to have a mailbox on it, but they don't deliver mail up there anymore, so alls that might be there is a heap of stones."

Maggie got in the car. "Thanks, Jacob. Tell your grandson to come any time."

"Will do, Maggie," said Jacob. He hesitated as she started the motor. "Say, Maggie, have you found any tenants for the summer?"

"Not yet. Do you know of anyone who is looking for a cabin?"

"Nope, sure don't. I got nothing against your place, Maggie, but I have to tell you that some of your renters haven't been too happy there." He seemed reluctant to say more.

Maggie's hand stopped halfway to the ignition. "They never mentioned any problems to me," she said.

"Maybe they're too polite. The folks last summer complained to my wife about not being able to sleep because of strange noises. They seemed kinda worried about it."

"Strange voices?" she said, deliberately misunderstanding.

"No, just noises."

So Peg hadn't talked to them, or if she had, Jacob didn't know about it. Her former tenants must have heard the faint dulcimer music that drifted in and out of Maggie's consciousness day and night. By this time she was sure that the music had something to do with Peg Macintyre, but she didn't want to mention this to Jacob Pinter for fear that word would get around that the old Macintyre place was haunted. She'd probably find it impossible to get tenants if Peg's presence became common knowledge.

"Thanks for telling me, Jacob," was all she said before starting the car. She fluttered a hand out the car window as she drove away.

Maggie was thoughtful as she headed out the highway away from town. Jacob's information convinced her that she wasn't the only one who was aware of Peg's presence in the cabin. This was reassuring in a way, but in another way, it was not. If she wanted to rent the cabin for the summer, an ancestral ghost didn't bode well.

She passed her own driveway and accelerated along the bumpy road leading farther uphill. Maybe she'd run into Tate on his way down the mountain, which would reassure her that he was all right.

When she reached the old weathered rail fence, she slowed the BMW to a crawl. The fence was covered with delicate yellow rambling rosebuds not yet in full bloom. On impulse, she pulled the car onto the shoulder and got out. She saw no sign of Tate.

She scuffed at a few leaves and waited, hoping against hope that Tate would choose that moment to appear. She felt ridiculously eager to see him. She leaned against the fence and closed her eyes, willing him to be there when she opened them. But when she opened her eyes, she saw nothing but the old fence, the roses, and a squirrel that ran down the trunk of a tree and scolded her.

Why? Why do I want to see him, need to see him, think I won't live if I don't see him? If she had expected an answer, she was disappointed.

Well, Maggie told herself with a mixture of longing and hopefulness, *there's nothing like a brisk walk in the after-*

noon, and she hitched up Kip's shorts and climbed over the fence, taking care not to let the thorns on the roses scratch her legs.

At the stone marker near Tate's camp, Maggie stopped to catch her breath. The way to the camp had been an uphill struggle, and she doubted that she would have started out if she'd known how far she'd have had to walk.

A bright red cardinal fluttered in front of her as if showing the way. She followed its lead until she saw a plume of smoke rising over the treetops, and she knew she was almost there.

"Tate?" she called through the thicket of hardwoods that blocked her vision. "Tate, are you there? It's Maggie."

She heard no answering call, so she kept going. Soon she broke through a clutch of rhododendrons and found herself in a clearing with a small log hut adjoined by a cramped lean-to which sheltered Tate's motorcycle. A rudimentary garden sprouted nearby. In the middle of the clearing burned a campfire, and she smelled the succulent odor of a savory stew. To one side stood a peculiar domed structure covered with canvas. A thin wisp of smoke issued from a small hole in the middle.

After a moment's hesitation, she walked to the dome and lifted the canvas. The smoke within made her sneeze. Backing away, she wondered whether she should go looking for Tate. She sneezed again, and when she opened her eyes, she saw him.

He was walking up the slope from the river wearing only his loincloth. She hadn't seen him like this since the day they had met, and she stood as if rooted to the spot, bowled over by the beauty of him.

For if any man could be said to be beautiful, then Tate Jennings was. His body was smooth and slick with water that ran off in glistening rivulets, making the ripple and flow of his muscles even more pronounced. He saw her in that instant, and his eyes widened. He halted, standing like stone so that his bronzed skin blended with the moving shadows of the forest beyond.

"*A'siyu*," he said. "Greetings."

The Cherokee language surprised her and she said nothing, but her heart was beating a tattoo against her ribs. For two cents, she would have turned and run like a startled deer. If she could have, she would have transformed herself into a tree trunk so that she would not be noticed. But not having the magical capabilities necessary for such transmogrifications, she merely stood. And looked. And waited.

"Maggie," he said. "I can't believe you're really here."

"Are you glad?" she managed to say.

He smiled at that. "Glad doesn't even begin to describe it."

She felt childishly pleased. "I wondered if you were okay after the storm," she confessed.

"I hardly even noticed the weather." He indicated the domed canvas. "I was in there."

Maggie cast a bemused look at the sweat lodge. "Why?" she asked.

"I was on a spiritual quest. Won't you join me for dinner? I've been fasting for three days."

Maggie was incredulous. "This is the first time you've eaten in three whole days?" she repeated.

"I drank some broth earlier."

"I came up here to see how you had fared during the big storm, and I find out that the storm wasn't the problem. You've nearly starved."

"I had reasons," he replied patiently. "Sit down. The stew is almost ready."

Maggie peered into the pot over the fire and saw that there was plenty of fish stew, but any man who hadn't eaten for three days would have a powerful appetite. "Are you sure that's enough to eat? I left my car loaded with groceries on the road," she said.

"In my present state of hunger, it's too far away," he said. He went into the *asi* and brought out bowls and spoons. He handed one of each to Maggie, who sat down cross-legged and watched Tate as he ladled generous helpings into each bowl.

She watched him surreptitiously from under her lashes as he ate. His attention seemed to be focused on slaking his hunger, not on her presence or what might happen later or any of the other things that kept tumbling over and over in her mind. She tried to make small talk, but Tate seemed uninterested; she could understand why. Dropping the bombshell of her pregnancy had created a barrier between them. Was that what had caused Tate to embark on a spiritual quest? Should she ask him about it, or would that be a bad idea?

She realized that she might have made a mistake coming here, and she thought that perhaps he didn't want her around. On the other hand, he kept looking over at her with an unfathomable expression on his face. She had no idea what it meant.

The more she thought about it, the more she wondered what she was doing here. And the worst of it was that Tate didn't seem to know, either.

AFTER HIS VISION, Tate could hardly believe that Maggie was real. He kept expecting her to lower her mask and become someone else, or to disappear in a puff of smoke. But she *was* real. She was eating and talking and, well, being Maggie. His heart warmed toward her.

Looking at her, watching her as she conveyed delectable morsels of fish to her even more delectable mouth, he felt a stirring in his groin, and he couldn't for the life of him figure out why he found a pregnant woman so sexy. Maybe he had been without a woman for too long, but he didn't think that was it. He certainly hadn't wanted to bed any of the other women he'd encountered in the past five months.

He cleared his throat. "Maggie—" he began.

"Yes?" she said too quickly.

"About your pregnancy—do you want to talk about it?"

"I think we should," she replied. She set down her bowl and spoon and stared at him through the thickening twilight. "Tate, if you were offended by—by my body, it's okay. If touching me and kissing me was a turnoff for you, I understand, and—"

"A turnoff? Is that what you think?" He was incredulous.

"Well," she said in a low tone, "yes."

"Maggie," he said with the utmost patience, "I find you beautiful beyond compare, sexy beyond belief, and touching and kissing you was one of the most—perhaps *the* most—erotic experience imaginable. I didn't know you were pregnant. I was stunned to learn that you were. But when I walked away from your cabin, in my heart I still wished we had made love."

She stared at him blankly, saw the fervor in his eyes, blushed and looked away. "Oh," she said.

"Have I convinced you?"

"Kind of."

He wondered what would make her truly believe, but short of making a move on her, he couldn't think of a way. They sat in silence, listening to the flutter of birds overhead. The fragrance of cedar wafted over them, perfuming the air with its pungent scent.

"Tate," Maggie said after a while, "how do you think Peg and Tsani were able to actually become us during the storm?"

"I've always sensed something special about your cabin," he said.

"Oh, so have I," Maggie agreed. "It's almost as if the cabin is surrounded by a special enchantment. I thought it was because I feel close to my mother in the place where we had so many good times, but now I realize that there's more. Peg is there. I feel her. And I hear her laughing sometimes, and dulcimer music, although I don't know why."

"I've heard the music, too," he said. "Also, I felt a peculiar sensation the first night I visited your cabin, almost as if someone were looking over my shoulder."

"I had a peculiar sensation, too, as I recall. It started in the pit of my stomach." This she said with a wry twist to her lips.

Recalling how she had run out of the room and been sick, Tate smiled. "Maybe we should blame that on Peg," he said.

"I can't blame Peg for anything," she said seriously. "I feel so close to her. Not only because I'm going to have a baby and so was she, but her thoughts were running through my head when you and I were—well, at the time, I was actually feeling the emotions she felt. I don't know how I could, but it was so real, Tate. I knew her fear that her parents would find out that she was going to bear Tsani's baby, and—" Maggie cast her eyes down "—her deep love for him as he began to make love to her."

"Ah," Tate said. "That." He understood perfectly because he, when he had been Tsani, had felt love for Maggie as well. Or at least it was love as he had always dreamed it should be. He, who had conditioned himself not to feel emotion, had loved her in those moments with every fiber of his being, and she had returned his ardor as passionately as any woman ever could. After such a breathtaking experience, he now knew what love and sex intermingled could be, and he was certain that he could never settle for anything less. He wanted to feel the emotion of love again, over and over. In this lifetime. And for keeps.

Maggie lifted her shoulders and let them fall. "Have you ever loved anyone, Tate?" she asked with a certain prescience.

"I've wanted to," he said slowly, "but I never quite understood what I was supposed to feel. Because of the way my mother used the word *love* to manipulate me and excuse herself from her obligations, I thought that love was a bad thing. It's hard for me to hear the word even now without conjuring up a negative connotation."

Maggie was silent for a long time. "I thought I loved Kip," she said. "Maybe I never really did, since it didn't last the way love should. Sometime I'd like to feel so much in love that I don't know where I leave off and the other person begins. I'd like a really deep soul connection that lasts forever. Do you believe that's possible?" she asked wistfully, gazing into the fire.

"I've heard the love songs and read the books. I hope that the people who write those terrific things know what they're talking about." Tate thought about Tsani and Peg and how they wanted to be together in the Nightland for all eternity. He had the idea that they would both do whatever it took to achieve that goal. And having felt what Tsani felt when he was with Peg, he understood.

"Certain kinds of love are forever. They defy all boundaries and evade all reason," he said.

Maggie smiled waveringly at him. "I hope so," was all she said, but she reached over and took his hand. "I seem to recall that you were going to finish telling me about yourself."

He turned her hand over. It was small and smooth, and he traced the lines on her palm with his forefinger. "Too boring," he said, pulling himself back from his agreeable fantasies.

"When we got chased home by the thunderstorm, we were at the point where the police had picked you up begging for bus fare to go visit your mother in New Orleans," she prompted.

"Are you sure you want to hear this? Couldn't we talk about you instead?"

"Later. I have news, but I want to know what happened to you before we get into that." She smiled her encouragement, and Tate thought with surprise, *She really cares*.

As he had done before, he kept emotion out of it, relating his own story as he would if he was reporting it for a newspaper. Not that this was so difficult; right after college, he had held a reporter's job on the staff of the *Raleigh Express* for three interesting years.

As Maggie listened, Tate told her how, as the years of his childhood passed, he often asked his mother Chantelle if he could live with her, but because she loved him so much, she thought he'd better stay where he was. Once he wrote to her and asked if he couldn't live with her, could he please go to North Carolina to live with his father? Chantelle wrote back that his father was a no-good bum who hated them both. Tate believed it. What other choice did he have?

His ninth set of foster parents wanted to adopt Tate, but Chantelle refused to sign a release. When she got her life together, when she finally signed a recording contract, she wanted Tate to come to live with her. She loved him too much to let him go, she said.

"At least you had a family who wanted to adopt you," Maggie said.

"They were nice," Tate said reflectively. "The father spent hours playing basketball with me in the driveway, and the mother taught me to make toasted cheese sandwiches, but after the adoption fell through, I was sent to another foster family. I was heartbroken and withdrew into an angry, impenetrable shell where no one and nothing could reach me. By the time I was twelve, I was a chronic runaway. I had hardened my heart to the world. I didn't fit in anywhere. I had no identity, no family, no friends. No one could reach me—not my teachers, not my caseworker, not anyone. And then my middle school physical education teacher discovered that I could play basketball."

Finally, he told her, he had found a place where he felt comfortable. To his amazement, he became the star forward on his team, and when he got to high school, he was the star on that team, too.

When he finally realized that others respected him, he began to respect himself. His grades improved dramatically, and he won a full scholarship to the University of North Carolina, where he played championship ball for four years. In college, he was stunned to realize that he was popular; people liked him. Before long he had melded into the multicultural student population and was dating, joining a fraternity, planning a career. He thought he'd never look back.

And then his father died, which changed everything. Suddenly he'd been brought face-to-face with the part of him that he had so long denied—his Cherokee heritage.

"What happened to your mother?" Maggie asked.

"I sent her an invitation to my college graduation, and it came back stamped Addressee Unknown.

"And that's the last you've heard of her?"

Tate shook his head. "I was often interviewed on television as a spokesman for Conso, and once Ma's friend Agnes, who was vacationing here, recognized me from a picture that my mother had sent her. She called me at work. She said that my mother had died alone in a hotel in Dallas a few years ago."

He glanced at Maggie to see how she was taking all this, and her expression was pained and more serious than he had ever seen it. He hadn't told her his story so that she'd pity him, and he hoped she didn't. Maybe it was time to let her know that he didn't hold any grudges.

"The thing to remember, Maggie, is that I made it. I became a success in spite of everything that happened to me."

"I'm sure you wish your father could have known how well you've done," she said.

"He knew where I was when I was a college basketball star because my name was all over the papers in those days, and by that time I was using his last name, Jennings. He never tried to contact me."

"Why not?"

"I don't know. He moved away from Scot's Cove about the time that I graduated from UNC, so he must have lost track of me. After college, I worked for a newspaper and later got a job in a public relations department for a big company near the coast. That led to my job with Conso, and eventually they transferred me to the office here. My dad never knew that I'd landed right here where he'd grown up. When he died in New York City, I read the obituary in the local paper and called Charlie Bearkiller, who was listed as one of the survivors. Through him I found out that my father had left me everything he owned, including this piece of land."

"And now you and Charlie are good friends," Maggie finished softly.

"That's about it."

It had grown dark, and in the brush, fireflies winked and blinked. Overhead a sickle moon was suspended in a velvety sky; he could not have been more content. Maggie slid her hand out of his and brushed back a strand of blond hair, hooking it behind her ear. He swallowed, wanting nothing so much as to kiss that pale expanse of skin along her exposed neck.

If she knew that his thoughts had swerved toward the pleasures of the flesh, she gave no sign. Maggie seemed comfortable, both with the place and with him. She grinned at him and linked her arms loosely around her legs. He liked the way she lit up the clearing with her bright face and luminous eyes. He had no need of firelight or moonlight when Maggie was near.

"You won't believe what I did about my job," she said.

Tate lay back and propped himself on one arm. "Try me," he said, making himself match her casual manner.

"I called my boss at MMB&O and asked her for six months' leave like you did with Conso," Maggie told him, looking pleased with herself. "I think Bronwyn was fit to be tied. Which is about what I would expect from her since she's been working on that Irwin Twine campaign."

Tate laughed at that. "Do you think the company will go for it?" he asked.

"Bronwyn called back today and offered to let me work at home. At the cabin, I mean. Today I bought a fax machine, and as soon as my computer arrives from the office, I'll be in business. I can't afford to quit, since I'll certainly need the job to support my baby once he or she is born."

"What about whatsisname?" he asked as though her answer wouldn't interest him much. "Will he contribute to the baby's support?"

Maggie's face became somber. "I don't know. I hope so. On the other hand, I would dearly love to tell Kip Baker to take a long walk off a short pier so I won't have to accept money from him ever."

"I don't think you still love this guy," Tate said, testing the waters.

"I never said I did. I said I wasn't sure. And the longer I stay here on Flat Top Mountain, the less relevant to the situation he seems."

"Any second thoughts you're having about Kip Baker are good news to me," he said mildly.

She studied him for a moment, and he took that opportunity to reassure her. "I care about you, Maggie," he said quietly with all the force of the conviction that he felt in his heart. He waited to see how she would respond.

"I care about you, too," she said in a troubled voice.

"I won't pressure you for more than you're willing to give. I promised," he said, wondering if this was realistic even as he said the words. They had already seen and touched each other intimately, and telling himself that it had been Peg and Tsani might well be a cop-out and a refusal to face reality.

"You won't?" she said hesitantly.

"I promised," he repeated.

He knew she was thinking this over, and he realized suddenly that what she was worried about was not how to fend him off if he became amorous but how to convince him to continue the other day's proceedings if she decided that she wanted to. He turned away to smother a chuckle, camouflaging it as a cough.

"Then," Maggie said in a very small voice, "I guess you wouldn't be interested in making love to me tonight, would you?"

Chapter Eight

The cough almost choked him.

"What did you say?"

Maggie sighed. "All right, maybe it was a bad idea," she conceded.

He studied her eyes, so deep and mysterious, and her lips, so full and inviting. Impulsively he reached over and covered her hand with his. "It was a very good idea. But I'm not sure it's what you really want."

"It was when I said it," she told him.

"I hope it was you talking and not Peg," he suggested with a glint of humor.

"It was me. I had this kind of spur-of-the-moment feeling that if we don't make love now, we never will. And that would be sad, I think." He didn't doubt her earnestness at all, and he certainly agreed with her that it would be a tragedy if they never made love. He was taken by surprise by her unexpected suggestion, that's all.

He touched her hair, which was bound up in a braid. It was the softest hair he had ever felt, so different from his own. "And why, if we don't make love now, do you think we never will?"

She gazed at him mutely, and he thought she might not answer. "Because I'm pregnant," she said finally. "Because soon you'll leave your camp to go back to work. You'll move back to your apartment in town, you won't live on the mountain any more. We might not even be friends.''

"We'll be friends no matter where I live," he said with great conviction.

"That's good," she said. "My pregnancy—" she began, but she stopped when she saw his expression.

"What about it?"

"I know that I'll become less desirable as I get bigger," she continued in a resolute tone. "I won't be attractive when I'm huge with child."

She sounded so woebegone that Tate leaned over and kissed her on the cheek. "You will be beautiful no matter how big you get. I know you will."

"To whom? The only thing I'll be able to have a relationship with is the Goodyear blimp, and I'm not sure what gender it is. Come to think of it, maybe that's the point." Tate was not surprised to see tears welling in Maggie's eyes, and he reached out and tipped one with his finger. It quivered there, a prism in the firelight, before it fell to the dust.

"Are you sure you're not just feeling sorry for yourself? What's this about, anyway?" he said.

"I can't get my jeans on anymore," she said. "My stomach is too big."

He looked at Maggie's stomach and saw nothing different about it other than she was wearing what appeared to be a man's shorts. "You look fine to me," he said.

She took his hand and moved it to the triangle where her belly curved so gently. "There," she said, pressing his hand into her. "Feel it?"

He did feel something under the fabric and zipper, a kind of a round hard mound above Maggie's pelvic bone. He didn't move his hand; he didn't know what to do. He felt himself beginning to get aroused, but if Maggie realized it, she gave no sign.

"I just—just—" and Maggie began to sob.

Tate removed his hand from her abdomen and took her in his arms. "Shh," he said as she wept, "it's going to be okay. It's going to be all right." Reluctantly he reminded himself to take it easy.

Finally when her sobbing quieted and all they could hear was the crackling of the fire and the dulcet calls of night birds in the darkness surrounding them, he moved slightly apart from Maggie.

"I would love to make love to you if I thought it was what you really want. What you want—what you need—is someone to care about you. When and if we make love, Maggie, it will be for a better reason than loneliness."

She sighed deeply and stirred in his arms. "Tate," she said. "I'd better go." He saw the beginnings of an even greater distress building in her, and he felt her unhappiness like a stab in his own heart. He couldn't let her leave now.

"Go? And be even more lonely when you're back at your cabin and start replaying this conversation in your mind? I don't want you to regret any of this, Maggie. Dear Maggie, I want to comfort you, but not in a way that you might regret later."

He drew her down on the bed of fresh juniper boughs where he laid his blanket at night. He slid his arm under her head, and she stared at him in the darkness. Neither of them spoke for a long time. He caressed her face with his eyes, lost himself in the symmetry of her features, inhaled her sweet natural fragrance.

She lifted a hand and touched her fingertips to his face. The whites of her eyes glistened in the firelight, and her lips were slightly parted. She was more beautiful than ever in that moment, and he knew that he wanted her to fall in love with him as deeply as he was falling in love with her. He wanted it more desperately than he had wanted anything in his whole life, and not just to save Tsani and Peg from wandering in search of each other. This had to do with him and with Maggie and the way they had met when each was at a major turning point in life, when they both needed solace and comfort.

She smiled at him. "You seem so different here in your camp," she said softly.

"How different?"

"More free."

"I hope so. You know, Maggie, I've learned a lot by taking this six-month leave. Now the hard part is going to be to translate what I've learned as one of the Real People to my ordinary life."

He smoothed her hair, and her braid came undone. He unraveled it by threading his fingers through the pale strands again and again until her hair framed her face in soft waves. He took in her lovely gray eyes, the small nose, the pale freckle at the right corner of her mouth. He wanted more than anything in the world to kiss that freckle.

Maggie pulled his head down and kissed him on the lips, slowly and gently. She gazed at him, her eyes wide and serious. She hesitated, perhaps gauging his mood. "I want to stay here tonight," she said.

He certainly didn't want her to go. "In that case, I think you're entirely too far away from me," he said. He took her in his arms. She sighed, or maybe it was a low moan, and nestled closer to him. He felt protective of her, as if she had been entrusted to him—as perhaps she had. His conversations with Maggie had made him feel closer to her than he had felt to anyone in his life.

While he pondered this, a whippoorwill cried overhead. When he next looked down at Maggie, her long tangled lashes were curled against her cheek, and she slept peacefully. He found that he couldn't look at her without desiring her, and so he stared into the fire for a long time until he finally slept.

He was awakened once during the night when Maggie said clearly and distinctly against his shoulder, "Pickles. Ice cream."

He was sure that she was awake, but the light of Grandfather Moon showed her eyes to be closed; her eyelids twitched as if she were deep in sleep. He listened to her soft regular breathing for a time before getting up and tossing more wood on the fire. Then he went into the *asi* and brought out a blanket, which he tucked carefully around both of them.

If she had truly awakened and asked for pickles and ice cream, he would have done anything in his power to get them for her. But she didn't. Finally, smiling to himself, he fell soundly asleep.

MAGGIE WOKE AT DAWN, and for a moment she couldn't figure out where she was. Then she remembered. The warm musky smell of him reminded her that it was Tate who slept beside her. The hand on the back of her thigh was his. Memory flooded into her consciousness: his camp. Asking him if he wanted to make love to her. Her cheeks grew hot with the memory. Apparently pickles and ice cream weren't the only things she craved at this stage.

She couldn't imagine what Tate must have thought last night when she'd so awkwardly come on to him. Thank goodness he had cautioned against making love; otherwise, she'd feel like a first-class fool this morning.

She turned her head to look at him and saw that he was lying on his back, his chest rising and falling gently. His free hand rested on his diaphragm, and it too rose and fell to the rhythm of his breathing. He looked like the little boy he must have been, a little boy who had suffered in so many ways. No wonder he didn't like the idea of single mothers raising their children alone; his mother had really botched the job.

But her own mother hadn't, and Maggie was sure she couldn't fail as a parent with such a good role model. Eventually Tate might understand why Maggie felt equal to bringing up a child on her own. He understood so many other things about her; certainly last night as they poured their hearts out to each other, they had bonded.

Yet she wasn't at all sure how much feeling Tate had for her over and above kindness and compassion. And lust, of course. She could hardly ignore that, even after the sweetness of last night.

Thinking about it, about how much she had wanted him to make love to her, she was embarrassed. Now maybe he wouldn't ever want to make love, and it was all her fault. Suddenly she wanted to be up and gone, saving both of them from the inevitable embarrassment of the morning after a night when nothing had happened.

Or had it?

Carefully she eased away from Tate, lifting his hand and setting it down beside him. He sighed and rolled onto his side so that his face was toward her. She wouldn't disturb him.

In the fresh morning air, the lingering aroma of smoke blended with the scent of juniper. The fire had gone out, and birds were beginning to try to drown out each others' songs in the branches overhead. Once she'd washed her face, she would head back to her car.

Maggie followed what she surmised was the path to the river. Preoccupied with her thoughts, she suddenly heard a freshet of birdsong rippling from a nearby glade and for some reason, it was so prepossessing that she automatically turned and headed down the narrow trail leading in that direction. She stopped in her tracks when she saw what lay within the circle of trees ahead, greeting its jewel-like beauty with a sharp intake of breath.

It was a small limestone pool secluded in an out-of-the-way place. In the rays of the early morning sun slanting through the forest, the surface of the still water gleamed like golden glass. Delicate spiderwebs, jeweled with tiny drops of dew, trembled in the light breeze, and flowers swayed on the opposite shore. As if spellbound, Maggie knelt on the sloping bank and brought handfuls of the fresh, sweet water to her face.

The water clung to her eyelashes in crystal droplets so that she saw the scene before her through a misty veil. When she looked down, it was to see her image in the water rippling and wavering as the pool grew still again. As she stared into her image, she thought she heard familiar silvery laughter, and she quickly glanced up. Beneath a rainbow's arch, a cardinal rose with a scarlet flash of wings from a dog hobble bush, setting its dangling white blossoms aquiver, and she thought she must have been mistaken. She hadn't heard laughter after all; it was only a bird.

But when she again looked down at her image in the mirrored surface of the pond, she saw that her hair was piled on top of her head in braids. She was wearing a dress with a lace collar. And then she realized that she wasn't looking at her own reflection at all—she was looking at Peg Macintyre.

Maggie blinked, and the image in the pond was again her own, her eyes swollen with sleep, her hair tumbling over her shoulders in an unruly mass.

She did not want to become Peg Macintyre again, and certainly she didn't want Peg to take over her thoughts, her emotions or her body. And if she and Tate made love, she wanted it to be the two of them, not people from a long time ago.

But since it had happened before, what was to keep it from happening again? With a fierce surge of longing, she wanted to keep her emotions for herself. She wanted her body to be her own when and if she and Tate ever made love because she knew that the act was going to be so special that she would want to remember it as long as she lived.

Make love this morning, Peg told her. *He's ready. You're ready. Why wait?*

Maggie's breath caught in her throat. Why indeed? She knew in that moment that she couldn't leave Tate Jennings this morning without making sure that he knew how much she loved him. It might be crazy, but she did love him, liked him, was attuned to him in an uncanny way.

As if in a dream, Maggie stood up and unbuttoned her shirt. She slipped off the shorts, unfastened her bra and laid it neatly on top of the other clothes. Then she slid the panties down her legs and stood naked, her hands crossed over her breasts.

She stepped into the pool and waded into the shallows. The water was warmer than she had expected; perhaps it was fed by a hot spring. She leaned back and let the water support her weight, dipping her head back to let the current flow through the strands of her hair. She half floated, her breasts buoyant and as white as two pale moons; the rounded shell of her abdomen made another moon farther down. Below that the soft springy hair between her legs drifted on the current like seaweed.

Slowly she submerged and opened her eyes underwater. She surfaced quickly, listening for the Little People that Tate so often mentioned. She didn't hear them and she didn't see them, but she had an idea that they were around. If they were, she hoped that they would not confuse or confound either Tate or her this morning.

They won't, I promise. Don't you know it was only their job to bring you to this magic place? said Peg's voice in her ear.

"Go away," Maggie said out loud, her words echoing from the banks, the trees, the mist-shrouded forest beyond. "We don't need you." She didn't feel the least bit constrained about talking to someone who wasn't there; she suspected that Peg was with her more often than not.

I'll go, agreed Peg, and her voice slid down the scale into a chord of faint dulcimer music.

Maggie smoothed her wet hair back from her face and was wading toward shore when Tate appeared soundlessly in the shadows, brushing his way past the rainbow and setting the blossoms of the dog hobble to trembling.

Maggie understood as soon as she saw the expression in Tate's eyes that speech was unnecessary. He knew what she had in mind, had known before he even started out from the camp. Had Tsani sent him here? Or had he come of his own accord?

And then there was no doubt. She knew as well as she knew her own name that Tate had come because he had wanted her, that his sixth sense had told him exactly where to look. He never had needed words to understand what she was thinking.

Without taking his eyes off her, he slipped out of his loincloth with a minimum of motion. He stepped into the pond and came to her slowly, his body parting the water so that it curved out in a wide wake toward the shore. He held out his hands, and when she extended hers, he gripped them tightly, warm current flowing from his body to hers. Did he love her? Did she love him? Oh, yes.

Water streamed down her body, dripped from her nipples, lapped between her legs. He crushed her to him and kissed her deeply, his tongue invading her mouth, his hands pressing her buttocks so that the tiny round form of the baby was drawn against him. She, who was always aware of the child, wondered if he could feel it between them or if he even thought about it. She doubted it; now he was gripping her head tightly between his hands, angling it so that his seeking mouth had better access to hers; he was sliding his fingers down her slippery neck to count the bones in her spine; he was cupping her breasts in his wet hands and rubbing his chest back and forth against them until her nipples were hard, tight, water-glazed berries.

"Oh," she said, clinging to him tightly. "Oh, Tate."

"Yes, and you are Maggie and no one else," he said, and then he pulled her up against him so that her feet no longer touched the bottom of the pool, and he gripped her tightly so that her legs went around him, holding him fast. She felt the heat of his erection against her belly; she moaned low in her throat as he captured her lips.

And then she ceased to think and was lost to the passion that had been so long building. He waded with her up the sandy bank and laid her reverently upon a cushion of soft green ferns; he lay beside her and pressed his hand with its bronze skin upon her pale breast, his fingers splayed. "How lovely you are," he murmured, almost to himself. She looked at the contrast of their skins. "How lovely *we* are," she said.

He bent to kiss the taut skin below her breasts, skimmed lower and dipped his tongue into her navel. His hair slid silkily against her skin, and she sighed deeply. He cupped both hands over the small convexity of the baby and lifted his head in concern. "Will I hurt you, Maggie, if I touch you here?"

She put her hands over his. "No," she said.

Slowly he lowered his lips to touch the place where the baby was sheltered. "How amazing it is that your body can produce a child. How miraculous," he said.

"I know."

His lips feathered up until they reached the sensitive lower contours of her breast. He nibbled there, sucked at the translucent skin with its blue veins so close beneath the surface, then eased his mouth over her ripe nipple. His lips were hard and then soft by turns, evoking sensation from deep within the most secret recesses of her body.

Slowly he eased over onto her, watching her for any sign of discomfort. Her hipbones bit into his stomach, and her rib cage rose to meet his. She felt as if the breath were crushing out of her and being replaced by some new essence, and she smiled against the smooth dark skin of his neck. Her tongue licked droplets of water from its crease, and he lifted himself on his elbows to place his hands on either side of her face. His hair curtained them off from the sky, now a brilliant shade of blue sifted through a leafy net of green, creating a shifting mosaic on their naked bodies. The ferns beneath her were hopelessly crushed. She felt the gentle impressions of their curled fronds biting into her skin.

"Kiss me," she said, and Tate kissed her, slowly and with great feeling. "Again," she murmured against his lips, and when he did, she wondered how she could have lived this long without feeling this way about a man before. He knew exactly how to touch her in order to elicit the maximum feeling; he knew when to increase pressure and when to lessen it; he fit himself to her as if he had known the shape of her body all his life.

There was no hurry. Here in this quiet place with birdsong cascading overhead, with the wind rustling the ferns beside them and with the sweet scent of wildflowers drifting over and about them, they could pursue this happiness unfettered by the concerns of everyday life. They had nothing to do and nowhere to go; all they had to do was to concentrate on giving each other pleasure.

He kissed her until he said he knew every inch of her body, and she touched him, exploring all the curves and crevices. She pressed her ear against his heartbeat; he traced her eyebrows with his tongue. She discovered a birthmark behind his ear, and he found that she was ticklish in the crease between buttocks and thigh. She laughed with him, let her tongue linger on the most tasty parts of him, learned the different fragrances of him. Finally, after what seemed like forever or only a moment, Maggie wasn't sure which, he said, "Are you ready for me, love?" and she nodded as he wrapped his arms completely around her and drew her hips upward to meet him.

Maggie closed her eyes, expecting a hard, ramming jolt; instead there was only a delicious pressure that kept on and on and on until she was warm and full with him. She rose against him, crying out, wanting more, and when she shuddered beneath him, whispering his name, he drove into her again and again until she thought she had never known such joy. It burst within her with the force of a thousand pinwheels, a million shooting stars, a hundred suns exploding behind her eyes. At last he collapsed above her, damp and sated, and she buried her face in his shoulder and let the tears come.

He kissed them away. "You are mine now," he said, brushing her tangled hair from her face.

"I think I always was," Maggie said unsteadily, and then she pulled him down to her for another kiss.

MAGGIE WAS SOPPING UP the melted ice cream from the trunk of her car shortly after noon that day when the familiar gray compact car wheeled into the clearing of her cabin and pulled around to the side where Maggie was parked. Bronwyn jumped out of her car and said, "Where in the world have you been?"

Maggie straightened and took in the gold buttons marching in lines down the front of Bronwyn's double-breasted red blazer. A Hermès scarf adorned the neckline, and Bronwyn wore neat navy pumps that had cost three hundred dollars. Maggie had been with her when she bought them.

"How nice to see you, Bronwyn," Maggie said with exaggerated politeness. "Couldn't you at least say something pleasant before confronting me with what I suspect is a belligerent question?" She went back to mopping up the ice cream, which unfortunately was pistachio. The whole trunk compartment was crisscrossed with dried puddles of pale green goo.

"Sorry. I *am* glad to see you, Maggie. Especially since I left Atlanta at the crack of dawn this morning to bring your computer to you, not daring to trust it to the packers and shippers, and I arrived here over an hour ago. I waited around wondering where in the world you could be before riding back into town to ask if I was in the right place. Mr. Pincher at the general store said—"

"Mr. Pinter," Maggie said. "His name is Jacob Pinter."

"Well, all right, but anyway, he said that indeed this was the right cabin seeing as there aren't too many others on this road, and he wanted to know if I was interested in renting. I said no, and he said that maybe you'd gone away on a trip, and I said that you wouldn't do that without telling me, though I'm not at all sure that you *would* tell me, and— where *were* you, Maggie?"

"Away on a trip," Maggie said. She crumpled up the rag and reached for a clean one.

Bronwyn narrowed her eyes. "Away on a trip from which you return with a gallon of pistachio ice cream melted all over the trunk of your car? And what is this in your hair?" She plucked a green thing from the top of Maggie's head.

Maggie inspected it. "It looks like fiddlehead fern," she said equably.

"Indeed it does," Bronwyn said, flicking it away.

"I bought the fax machine," Maggie said for the sake of distraction.

"Good. Will you be able to set it up?"

"It will be operational by this time tomorrow, I promise."

Hands on her hips, Bronwyn took in the fallen tree at the other end of the clearing, and she spared a cursory glance for the cabin. "I thought I'd spend the weekend here. We can yak and giggle and talk over things like we usually do."

Maggie's heart fell to her toes. Tate had claimed errands in town today, and she had invited him to come over afterward. She had not planned on having company.

"So, where would you like me to put my suitcase?" Maggie's guest looked at her expectantly, overnight bag in hand, and bared her teeth in what she probably hoped would pass for a cheerful grin in an obvious attempt at trying to be a good sport.

"In the bedroom will be fine," Maggie said weakly, and Bronwyn disappeared into the cabin, leaving Maggie in blessed quiet.

Maggie finished mopping the rubber liner of the trunk with a wet sponge and, girding herself for conflict, went in to see how Bronwyn was managing.

Bronwyn was managing to be a nuisance. By the time Maggie reached her, she had changed into a pair of silk slacks as well as a matching top and had found out that the obscure long-distance telephone company that held the local franchise would not accept her credit card.

"You have to get used to things being, well, a little bit slower here," Maggie cautioned, but she was secretly amused.

"It's not going to be easy being incommunicado until I get back to Atlanta," Bronwyn said.

"Which will be when?" Maggie asked hopefully.

"Monday," Bronwyn said with heartfelt longing.

"Slow down. Take it easy. That's what this place is for."

Bronwyn spared a glance at Maggie's attire. "I don't know, Maggie. You seem to have slowed down so much that we might have to jump-start you to get you going again."

"Living here isn't half-bad," Maggie said. "You might like it. I do."

Bronwyn muttered something that sounded a lot like "Hmphf." As Maggie washed her hands, Bronwyn added, "I brought you some of my sister-in-law's maternity clothes. Not that I think your wardrobe needs sprucing up or anything," she said pointedly.

Maggie looked at the clothes, which Bronwyn had hung from a hook on the back of the bedroom door. "Thanks," she said with a marked lack of enthusiasm. Wearing such garments was the furthest thing from her mind. This morning she had felt womanly and sexy and beautiful again. Remembering Tate's lovemaking, she felt a thrill of happiness. The intensity of it was still with her; the glow had not faded.

"Maggie? I asked you how you've been feeling," Bronwyn said, looking at her strangely.

"Absolutely wonderful," Maggie said in a dreamy voice. Realizing that this sounded oddly suspect, she added hastily, "Most of the time, anyway."

"You're looking fantastic," Bronwyn said with her usual critical frown.

"Thank you." Maggie dried her hands on a paper towel and tried to mind her manners. "Have you eaten lunch?"

"Have you?"

Neither she nor Tate had been hungry—at least for food—after their tumultuous session of lovemaking in Tate's secluded sylvan hideaway. Maggie smiled now, treasuring those moments. No matter that neither of them had actually spoken those special words *I love you*. They each knew what the other felt.

"Maggie, I asked you if you had eaten lunch."

"No. No, I haven't. How about a barbecue sandwich?"

"Whatever. Is that what you eat here?" In Atlanta, they both enjoyed eating out at fashionable lunch spots. They usually ordered delectable fresh seafood salads, or homemade potato chips served with bleu cheese at the Buckhead Diner, or tomato Montrachet at their favorite little café.

"I eat whatever is easy," Maggie said. She took a hunk of barbecue out of the freezer along with two frozen buns. She popped the barbecue in the microwave oven first.

"I heard from Kip the other day," Bronwyn said. She had perched on a bar stool and was dangling one expensive shoe. "He called the office."

Maggie turned and leaned with her back against the counter, her arms folded across her chest. "And what did that no-good bum have to say for himself?" She didn't feel one iota of interest in Kip Baker, which surprised her. She'd have thought that she'd be eager to know how he was, or if the battle of the South American beauty queens was wearing on his nerves, or if he missed her. She only felt a kind of detachment, as if he were the friend of a friend of a friend whose name had come up in desultory conversation.

"He wondered how you were. He wondered *where* you were. It seems that he's tried to phone you at your apartment several times, but you were never there."

"I don't suppose he mentioned the baby," Maggie said.

Bronwyn studied her cuticles. "Actually, he didn't. I kept waiting, but..." and here Bronwyn spread her hands in a gesture of resignation, "nothing. He didn't even say any other words that start with *B*—no *begrudge, boondoggle* or *Biafra.*"

"No *begrudge, boondoggle,* or *Biafra,* maybe, but I bet Kip Baker can still throw around a lot of bull," muttered Maggie.

"If you have a message for him, I'd be happy to relay it if he calls again," Bronwyn said.

"Just one," Maggie said, taking the barbecue out of the microwave and replacing it with the buns. "Drop dead."

"That's a bit extreme. Are you sure you want me to tell him that?"

"I don't care what you tell him as long as you keep in mind that my life is in turmoil because of him. We were together for over two years, Bronwyn. I thought we were happy together."

"Obviously he wasn't too happy about the idea that baby makes three."

"Until I showed him the results of the pregnancy test, Kip had never mentioned one thing about going anywhere. Then he acted like he had been planning on going to South America all his life and as if photographing a bunch of beauty contestants was his big chance for lasting fame. I'm glad he's gone. I've been doing a lot of thinking, Bronwyn, and I don't need Kip Baker. This baby and I are going to manage without him, thank you very much, and we won't need his help." She pushed a sandwich across the counter to Bronwyn and appropriated the other bar stool for herself.

"Seriously, Maggie, I think you'd better consider coming back to Atlanta soon. I know you want to give yourself a chance to work here, and that's fine with the boss and with me, but you still have your apartment there."

"I can wiggle out of my apartment lease. I'll move my things up here, raise the child here."

Bronwyn very carefully set her sandwich down. "You can't mean that you're thinking of moving to Flat Top Mountain permanently?" she said incredulously.

"Why not? I don't have one single tenant for this place lined up for the summer season. I wouldn't have to pay rent here like I do in Atlanta, and if our arrangement works out, I'll be able to keep my job. Scot's Cove is a good environment for children, very outdoorsy and healthful." Maggie didn't say so, but she felt a million miles removed from the city instead of only a few hours away.

"There are a few things you need to consider about the mountains—for instance, the winters. They're cold and damp, and you could be snowed in for days. And no restaurants around here serve quiche—now Maggie, don't try to tell me anything different. I know. I went looking for such a restaurant when I was in town today scouting out news of you. No one ever even heard of quiche in Scot's Cove. And they put cole slaw and chili on their hamburgers here, for goodness' sake."

"If you were hungry for something that tastes familiar, there's a Taco Bell on the corner in town where the stoplight is," Maggie pointed out.

"Well, believe me, I didn't hear Taco Bell ringing. Anyway, I wasn't in the mood for Mexican food. And what about the overly bucolic atmosphere here, which will surely drive you bonkers if you stay in Scot's Cove? I passed two trucks hauling hogs down Main Street, Maggie. They blocked traffic." Bronwyn adopted a glum expression.

Maggie was mustering her forces to counter all these truths, but at that moment, Tate chose to walk past the kitchen window. Maggie thought he was probably headed to look at the oak tree that had been toppled by the storm.

Bronwyn did a fast double take and said, "Who's that?"

Maggie cursed Tate's timing. She would have preferred that Bronwyn know as little as possible about Tate Jennings.

"That's the man I told you about," she said reluctantly. "The one who jumped into my canoe at Lover's Leap."

Bronwyn stood up and went to the window. She stared out at Tate, who was walking around the fallen oak and studying it gravely. Finally he stopped and balanced his hands on his hips. He was wearing a pair of shorts and nothing else; his hair fell loosely to his shoulders, gleaming with the brilliance of jet.

Bronwyn let out a low and decidedly unladylike whistle. She seemingly couldn't take her eyes off him.

"Well, Mags," she said finally. "Now I understand everything." And she turned and stared at Maggie with an expression that could only be described as flabbergasted.

Chapter Nine

The next day, Saturday, Maggie and Bronwyn treated themselves to the local sights. They picnicked below Maidenhair Falls and they mined for gems at the local Ruby Ranch Gem Mine where neither of them found anything of value. Maggie had a good time, but she missed Tate. She wondered if he missed her even half as much.

He was around, she knew that. On Sunday morning, he left a bouquet of tiny wild violets on the doorstep so that she saw them when she opened the door to greet the morning. She and Bronwyn spent the day sitting in the sun outside, and she halfway hoped that Tate would appear, but he didn't.

Tate had met Bronwyn briefly after lunch on the first day of her visit. The two of them had looked each other over warily, finally warming to each other after Tate had won Bronwyn's admiration by successfully hooking up the new fax machine. But Tate, saying that she and Bronwyn needed time together, had stayed away since.

Maggie wondered how she would explain the sound of dulcimer music if Bronwyn heard it, but fortunately, Peg had apparently decided to stay away, too. Finally, on Monday morning, Bronwyn left in a flurry of activity, declaring that she was expecting a visit from Maggie in Atlanta soon.

"I'll have to come back and clean out the apartment, put my furniture in storage, and all that fun stuff," Maggie said.

"Bring Tate with you. We'll show him a good time," Bronwyn said.

"Yes," Maggie said as she lugged Bronwyn's overnight case to the car. "And you be sure to come back here to see us soon, too."

"Not a chance," Bronwyn said cheerfully, and then she was driving away in a cloud of yellow dust.

Maggie watched her go with mixed feelings. Once Bronwyn, who had seemed savvy and smart to Maggie when she'd first arrived in Atlanta, had embodied everything that Maggie wanted to be, but now—well, the baby had changed things. Or maybe it wasn't only the baby; maybe it was her new attitude. Maggie no longer wanted to make the most money or be seen with the best people; she no longer cared about fancy clothes and traveling to exotic places. Funny, but for the first time in her life, she was actually feeling content with the way things were.

After she saw Bronwyn off and went back inside the cabin, Maggie was startled to see that the robin's egg with its nest had mysteriously reappeared on the window sill. She almost laughed with glee. This meant that Peg was back. She had capriciously placed this sign in the window so that Tate and Maggie would get together.

Time to get down to business and start talking commitment, said Peg's familiar voice.

"What if I'm not ready?" Maggie said aloud. For an answer, she only heard a bit of incredulous laughter.

"Well, why *should* I be ready?" Maggie said with more than a little irritation.

Because you love him, was the answer.

"Yes, but—"

No buts, Maggie, and you need to stop blocking his thoughts so he can't get closer to you. That's not a nice thing to do, Peg said.

"It feels too intimate when he knows what I'm thinking even before I do," Maggie said.

There is no such thing as too intimate if you really love each other, Peg replied.

"I never *said* I loved him."

That's another part of the problem. What's stopping you?

"Look what happened to me when I loved Kip."

Tate needs to know that you love him and you need to know that he loves you.

"We know. We can't bring ourselves to say the words, that's all. Saying 'I love you' makes everything so... so serious."

It's supposed to be serious, you ninny.

"Can't we just enjoy each other?" Maggie said on a pleaful note.

She heard another peal of laughter laced with dulcimer music. It faded toward the bedroom, and Maggie followed it.

The curtains had been pulled wide so that the sun shone brightly into the room, and for a moment, Maggie's eyes were blinded by it. She closed her eyes, opened them, and then she saw her.

She was no more than a shadowy outline in front of the window, but there was no doubt in Maggie's mind that the image she saw was of Peg Macintyre—and a very pregnant Peg Macintyre at that.

Peg gave her a reproachful look and faded into a sunbeam.

Maggie blinked. "We haven't even touched on the issue of trust. How can I ever trust a man again?" she asked plaintively.

Peg, if she had an answer to this question, wasn't talking.

That night, Maggie waited eagerly to see if Tate had noticed the bird's nest in the window, and he showed up at her door precisely at nine o'clock.

She went into his arms eagerly, naturally.

"Ah, this feels so good," he said, holding her close.

"I've missed you, Tate," she said.

"And I've missed you. I spent the whole time we were apart wanting to be with you, even though I went into town and hung out with Albie, my buddy from the newspaper, and Charlie. Did you and Bronwyn have a good time together?"

Maggie led him to the couch and pulled him down beside her. "We had fun, but I missed you, too. What did you think of Bronwyn?"

Tate kept hold of her hand. "I like her, but I don't believe she thinks much of our mountain ways," he said.

"She's a city person, like—" Maggie had been going to say that Bronwyn was a city person like her, but she decided to amend this observation. "Corrected version— Bronwyn is a city person like I used to be."

"Are you sure that's past tense?" Tate was running a finger up and down the inside of her forearm, which made it hard to concentrate on what she was saying.

"Almost. Stop it, Tate. I can't think when you do that." She brushed his finger away.

"That's the general idea," he said, not stopping anything.

"I can't imagine ever going back to the city," she said.

"That's even better. What did Bronwyn say about me?"

"She said that you aren't as wild as you look," Maggie said, and giggled.

Tate laughed. "Does she know that you're even wilder than you look? Does she know that you're a tiger when you make love? Tell me, are you like her when you're in Atlanta?"

"What do you mean, like her?"

"You know. Sophisticated."

"Maybe. Probably," Maggie admitted. "You might not like me there."

"Be assured, Ms. Macintyre, that I like you everywhere," he said. "All of you. Your eyes, because they look silver in the starlight. Your hair, because it's the most beautiful color I've ever seen. Your ears, because I have never seen more beautiful earlobes in my life. Your—"

Maggie dissolved in laughter. "My earlobes? Is there a standard of beauty for earlobes?"

"I'm not sure, but there should be. Yours are beyond compare. Slightly fleshy, but not to the point of droopiness. Elegantly rounded, and a delightful pale pink. I'd describe them as delectable. What else do I like? Oh, yes. These," and he touched her breasts, caressing them softly through her clothes.

Maggie looked down. "They're only this large because I'm going to have a baby."

"It's not the size that I admire so much as the shape. They're almost perfectly rounded. And the peaks are perfection." He slid his hands downward to cup them over her abdomen. "How's the baby?"

"Not complaining," Maggie said.

"Are you sure you're feeling all right?" He looked at her anxiously, lovingly.

"Oh, yes. Very," she whispered, wishing he would look at her like that forever.

"I love making love with you," he said quietly. "Have I mentioned that?"

"Only five or six times. Not nearly enough."

"I'll tell you many more times. Many, many more times. Take this off," he said, untying the knot of the blouse that she had carelessly knotted at her midriff.

Her heart melted, and she knew that she wanted him as much as he wanted her. To tell the truth, maybe even more.

"Wait," she said. She stood and led him into the bedroom, where she had lit several candles earlier. The candlelight cast a golden glow over the bird's-eye maple of the furniture; it reflected in the old beveled mirror over the bed and made dancing shadows on the ceiling. Tate and Maggie became two of those shadows moving toward the bed.

Maggie kicked off her shoes, and Tate wrapped his arms around her from behind and kissed the top of her head. As she leaned blissfully backward, his hands found her breasts, circled slowly, enticingly. One hand dropped to her pelvis and tucked her close to him; she felt his arousal growing through her clothes. Gently he stroked her abdomen over the place where the baby grew.

Her need made her swallow and reach around for him, urging his thighs closer.

"I wonder if they're here, Peg and Tsani, watching us," Tate said.

"I hope they have better manners than that," Maggie said, and Tate laughed low in his throat. Maggie couldn't think about Peg and Tsani. It was Tate who filled her consciousness so completely that she thought of nothing and no one else. Tate with his long dark eyes smudged like shadows beneath his prominent brows, Tate whose features were softened by candlelight. Slowly he slid his hands under her shirt and unhooked her bra. He removed his shirt and drew her down onto the bed before lying back on lacy pillowcases to feast eager eyes on her breasts.

"So beautiful," he said as if to himself. The way he was looking at her made her feel voluptuous and desirable. She thought about this; only a few weeks ago she had been so miserable that she had known deep within her soul that she would never feel sexual again.

He was touching her nipples now, rolling them lightly between thumb and forefinger; he watched her face for expressions of desire. She smiled and touched his chest, tracing the contours of the muscles, moving her hand lower to circle his navel. She unbuttoned his jeans and reached for him, touching him as lightly as he touched her.

"Don't stay so far away," he murmured, reaching out and encircling her waist with his arm. Maggie shifted her weight so that she leaned closer, and she closed her eyes for a moment against the flickering candlelight.

He traced her lips with a forefinger. "How I've dreamed of kissing you," he said, and he shaped his palms to her face and brought it in line with his. He kissed her, and she held her breath, wanting it to go on forever yet feeling the most excruciating longing for more.

When he released her lips, he smiled at her. "You are so wonderful, Maggie. I've done a lot of thinking about us. I told you that I care about you. I even think," and he stopped to moisten his lips, never taking his eyes from her face, "I even think I'm falling in love with you."

She stared at him. "Do you mean that, Tate? Because if you don't, it's the cruelest thing you've ever said."

"I mean it," he said evenly.

She digested this. She knew she loved him; how could she help it? In the short time that they had known each other, he had become part of her life. At the same time, the thought of loving him terrified her. She had committed to a man once; she didn't think she could ever do it again.

"I don't trust love, Maggie. Maybe it's not fair even to tell you what I'm thinking. But more and more, I want you to know all my thoughts, as I want to know yours."

She put a finger over his lips. "I don't mind telling you that I'm scared to death," she said solemnly.

He kissed her fingertip and took her hand, moving it away from his mouth. Her fingers interlocked with his.

"Is that why you're blocking me from your mind? You are, you know."

"Not always."

"Sometimes, then. It seems as if you do it at the very times that I want to be inside your head the most."

"It's not fair for you to know what I'm thinking when I don't have the same advantage about you," she said. "How do you do it, anyway?"

"I concentrate on you and suddenly it's there. The messages, I mean. Chalk it up to my Cherokee heritage. Charlie says that there have always been those among us who have the gift."

She smiled at him. "And what a gift! Tell me, Tate Jennings, what's on my mind now?"

He turned solemn. "Maggie, the message I'm getting is too deep for words, and you've admitted that you're scared, which only makes it more complicated. I understand why you'd be afraid of commitment after what Kip did to you, and in many ways I feel the same. Love is scary."

"Tate," she said, drawing him toward her. "I don't know how much of this is real and how much is fantasy. Maybe we can make sense of it together."

"Together," he said, the syllables expelled on a breath that stirred her hair. "A beautiful word."

"It never was before," she said, stroking his cheek.

"I'm finding meanings that never existed for me in all sorts of things," he said. "It started when I came to live on

Flat Top Mountain, but nothing had any significance until I met you. I want to make love to you now, Maggie. I want to show you how much I adore you."

He gathered her to him, and she wondered how this man had come to mean so much to her in so short a time. In that moment, he seemed like all she ever wanted in a man and more. He made it possible to lock everyone and everything else in the world from her consciousness; they were again floating in their own special place, far away from normal cares. There was no reality, there were only the two of them pleasuring each other in their own special way.

The only reality that Maggie knew was Tate kissing her, Tate caressing her, Tate banishing her sense of separateness. His hands shaped her buttocks, urging her against him, communicating exquisite passion. With heightening arousal, he slid his hands inside her shorts, touched the roundness that was the baby, passed over it and found what he was seeking. Maggie gasped, all bodily sensation, all electricity, tiny sparks becoming huge fires that threatened to consume her very soul. Making love together was nirvana and heaven and paradise all rolled into one; it was Tate and it was Maggie and all that they meant to each other.

He helped her out of her clothes, and she helped him out of his, and he covered her body with his, pressing her backward into a nest of soft pillows. In a moment of possessiveness born of desperation, she wanted to feel all of him, wanted to hold him inside her so that he would never get away. She buried her face in his chest and clutched his back, wrapping her legs around him as if to bind him to her forever. The pulse of his heartbeat bore her forward as if on a huge wave, the crush of his body drove her toward a rush and swell that crashed and boomed on a distant shore.

Again and again he rocked against her, gasping with pleasure at each magnificent thrust. She no longer cared about anything but loving him, holding him, pleasing him. Their climaxes broke over a vast landscape of unbounded light, and they were drowning, drowning in each other and the light and the intensity of their lovemaking. For a long time, all they could do was cling to each other, still shimmering in the afterglow of their experience.

"Maggie," Tate said. "Oh, Maggie." He rained gentle grateful kisses on her ear, her nose, her lips. Slowly they drifted down together. She breathed slowly and deeply, her rhythm adjusting to his.

After a time, he slid his sweat-slick body to one side and exhaled, his breath stirring tendrils of her hair. One hand rested possessively on her stomach. She still could not speak; all she could do was relive those glorious moments. But still she could not bring herself to say the words that were engraved upon her heart. She could not say, "I love you." And he didn't, either.

Tate's hand circled the place where the baby grew. "Do you think the little kiddo knows what we're doing out here?" he said, his eyes alight with humor.

"Maybe," she said. She smiled at him and placed her hand over his. In that moment, she felt a deep pang of loss for what could never be. She wished desperately that Tate Jennings was the father of her child. A child conceived in a moment of joyful lovemaking such as they had just shared would be a lucky child indeed.

After a while, a time when Maggie allowed herself to feel the sheer and utter pain of regrets that she had never anticipated, Tate turned on his stomach and rested on his elbows. "You're still planning to keep the baby?"

Slowly she nodded, watching him. He showed no expression of surprise or displeasure; instead he seemed to accept it.

"I thought you would," he said. "I couldn't see you changing your mind."

"Does it make a difference between us?" she asked, holding her breath.

He didn't hesitate. "No. No, Maggie, it doesn't. At least not now."

"How about later?"

"I don't know," he said. "I never have approved of the idea of single mothers keeping their babies, you know that."

"It won't be like it was with your mother, Tate. I have a good job, and I want this baby. It's real to me, an honest-to-goodness little human being."

"You really love this baby, don't you?"

"Yes. Oh, yes," she said.

"I bet your baby is going to look exactly like you. It's going to have blond hair and gray eyes and a freckle right at the corner of its mouth," Tate said. He smoothed her hair back from her face and took her in his arms, cradling her gently.

"You see, Maggie, I'm looking forward to the baby, too. Because it's part of you," he murmured, his mouth close to her ear.

"You don't have to accept—"

"I know, but I want to. Something that means so much to you is bound to be important to me."

She was touched beyond words. "You're very good to me," she whispered, her heart in her throat.

"Good? I'd like to be better. Even best." He was smiling down at her, his eyes bright with happiness. "How can I go about being very, very good to you, Maggie my love?"

What a wonderful man he was, and how proud she was to be the woman with whom she shared his life, if only for a little while. In that moment, she realized that whatever they decided about their future, they shared an incomparable now.

"Try this," she said, guiding his hands. "And this. And this."

And for the rest of the night, he was very good to her indeed.

THE NEXT DAY, Maggie woke and stretched and yawned and nudged the sleeping Tate in the back.

"Lazybones," she said when he opened his eyes.

He reached for her and tickled her, and she started to giggle and tried to roll away, and they both almost fell out of bed. Maggie righted herself, plumped the pillows and fell back with a sigh of sheer happiness. Tate rested his head on her bare stomach, which grumbled noises of protest.

"There's nothing like an organ recital before breakfast," he said, and she picked up a feather pillow and whacked him.

"That may be the person that you so touchingly refer to as 'the kiddo' registering his protest over last night," she told him.

"I don't hear anyone else protesting."

"Not even Peg and Tsani," Maggie said blissfully.

"I think," Tate said carefully, "that they would have approved wholeheartedly."

Maggie sat up and kissed him lightly. "I think," she said, "that you're right. Who showers first—me or you?"

He slanted her a look. "How big is the shower?"

"Oh, it's—" she began unthinkingly, then realized what he was suggesting. "Big enough for two," she finished.

"Three counting the little guy," he amended, and in a matter of seconds they were embracing each other under the warm spray.

"This is nice," he said.

"Until you drop the soap."

"There are shower Tsagasi, you know. They cause people to slip on the wet tile, they make the hot water heater run out of hot water, they cause faucet handles to fall off and disintegrate—"

"You're joking," she said, but she did drop the soap.

He looked down at it. It had landed near his big toe. "Doesn't that prove that there are really shower Tsagasi?" he said, and she giggled and kissed the tip of his nose.

Later, sitting around in big terry cloth robes, they had bananas and orange juice, which Maggie told him were her usual breakfast along with a prenatal vitamin, and he said she should eat more for breakfast now that she was eating for two and that she should eat a better variety of food as well. He offered to cook bacon and eggs, but Maggie shook her head and told him that the odor of bacon frying often made her sick these days and that she'd just have another banana, please and thank you. Tate insisted on peeling the banana for her, which she said made him look like a monkey, and he mugged and scratched and made what he thought passed for monkey noises, which cracked Maggie up. Maggie said that bananas were considered a grain, did he know that? Tate said that he was sure that bananas were a fruit, and they argued about it until they both got tired of arguing, and then Tate cut two bananas up in a bowl, mashed them, added a spoonful of sugar, and poured orange juice over them, saying that this conglomeration was one of his favorite snacks, and Maggie wrinkled her nose but was persuaded to taste a bite, after which she declared that the concoction was pretty good and in fact tasted like Juicy Fruit gum. Tate said that the flavor of Juicy Fruit gum had always turned him on when he was a kid, and Maggie said, "You mean sexually?" and he picked her up right off the breakfast stool and carried her to bed, where he proved that the flavor of Juicy Fruit, or at least bananas and orange juice, *still* turned him on.

They stayed in bed most of the morning, watching the leaf-filtered light play over each others' faces, finding new ways to please each other, laughing over private jokes. The fax machine, now operative in the dining room where Maggie was using the table for a desk, beeped from time to time, but they ignored it. The telephone rang, but Maggie, in a fit of impatience, finally flounced out of bed and yanked its cord out of the wall.

It was almost nightfall before they got up and dressed, and then they wondered why they had bothered since it was so late. Tate said he might as well not even go back to his camp unless she was ready for him to leave, and she gave him an are-you-kidding? look and asked him what he'd like for dinner. She happened to have steaks in the refrigerator, and he cooked them on the charcoal grill he found in the shed behind the cabin.

"What a perfect day," Maggie told him later, and he grinned. "How are you feeling?" he asked her. He was always asking her, worrying about her, concerned that she might feel sick to her stomach or woozy or something, but she assured him that she felt fine.

"I could fix the television set," Tate said after they cleaned up the kitchen.

"I don't even remember what programs are on or when."

Tate studied the back of the TV. "The little doohickey that fits around the screws in the back of the set and connects with the antenna on the roof is broken," he said after his inspection. "I'll have to get a new one, but I can buy it in town."

Maggie sat down in the rocking chair and picked up the quilt. "It'll be nice to be able to watch TV while I'm working on the quilt. Come to think of it, I haven't been working on this as diligently as I could have been," she said.

"You've had other things to do."

"Other much more interesting things," she agreed.

"Go ahead and work on the quilt now," he said. "I know it means a lot to you to finish it."

"Are you sure you wouldn't mind?"

"I like the way your hair falls over your cheeks when you bend your head to sew," he said. "I won't mind at all as long as I can sit here with you and watch."

She smiled at him fondly. Soon the only sound was of the old-fashioned clock ticking on the bookcase. Tate read tattered copies of out-of-date magazines, every now and then stealing looks at Maggie whose head was bowed diligently over an appliquéd square as her fingers plied the needle in and out of the fabric.

"I feel close to Peg when I'm working on the quilt," Maggie said after a while. "Sometimes when I'm here alone, I hear dulcimer music as I'm sewing. I wish I knew why that seems to go along with her. The mountain dulcimer must have been special to her. I'd like to know more about Peg's life. We know from the pamphlet that she married the old man, and I've always thought of her as pining away here in this cabin. That doesn't square with the feeling I get when she's around—a light, happy feeling, and then there's the laughter, which makes me think that Peg must have been a particularly happy person."

"I think she was, too," Tate said.

Maggie went on talking. "You know, Tate, I've always wondered how, if Peg married the old man whose name was Harry Garvey, and if I'm descended from her, why has my family name always been Macintyre? Women in those days didn't keep their birth names."

"Good question," Tate said. He watched the fireflies winking on in the shrubbery outside the window. Beyond the line of trees bordering the clearing, Breadloaf Mountain was silhouetted against the sunset, and he thought distractedly how this view would be so different in a year's time. But then everything would be different in a year's time—Maggie, her baby and even him.

"It would be fun to do some research about my family. It seems like I ought to learn more about my ancestors now that I'm going to have a baby who will presumably want to know someday." She set the sewing aside. "You know, I happened to think of something. There's an old family Bible stored on the top shelf of the wardrobe in the bedroom. Let's take a look."

Maggie led the way into the bedroom and pulled open the wardrobe door. "The cabin was originally built without closets, so this wardrobe has been here since time out of mind. The stuff I'm looking for is on the top shelf. Can you see what's in that bundle on the left side?"

"Sure," Tate said. He reached up, shoved a small box out of the way, and retrieved a bundle of objects wrapped in a faded flour sack. "Is this it?"

"Here, put it on the bed so that we can open it and spread things out." Maggie sat down on one side of the bed, and Tate sat beside her. She tugged at the knot that bound the bundle, her nose twitching as dust fluttered upward.

"No telling what we'll find in here," she said.

It was a motley collection of keepsakes. A child's top, circa the early 1930s. A wedding ring, apparently real gold. A baby's woolen hand-knit bonnet, so old that it was falling apart. And on the bottom, a family Bible.

Maggie touched it with reverence. It was so old that the cover was crumbling into dust; the pages were so brittle that she feared that they would disintegrate beneath her finger-tips. But she found what she wanted.

"Births," she said when she had turned to the right page. The ink was faded to a faint brown.

"Is Peg listed?"

"Margaret Mary Macintyre," Maggie read in triumph. "Born May 31, 1825." When she said the name, she felt a definite breeze swish by.

"Did you feel that?" she asked Tate.

"I felt—something," he said.

"It was like a butterfly's wings brushing my cheek," Maggie said. She looked around the room, which was golden with the afternoon sunlight. The rag rug on the floor glowed with brilliant colors; the handmade sampler on the wall looked as it had ever since Maggie was a child and, probably, as it had looked before that. Yet there was an indefinable change in the room.

"She's here," Maggie said unsteadily. "Peg Macintyre is in this room now, Tate."

"I sense her, too," he said.

Maggie collected herself. "If anyone had told me that I would ever think I was in a room with a—a ghost, I would have laughed myself silly."

"This ghost probably would have laughed right back."

Maggie herself laughed at this.

"See how many children Peg had," Tate urged.

Maggie ran her forefinger down the column of names. "John Garvey, born in 1842. John Garvey?"

"John is the English form of the Cherokee name Tsani. Peg named her son after his natural father," Tate said. He reached across her to turn the tattered page. "Marriages," he read. "Margaret Mary Macintyre to Harry Garvey, June 2, 1842. And then..." He checked the page for Deaths and found Harry Garvey listed. "He died in November of the same year shortly after Peg gave birth to John."

Maggie shifted her position so that she could more easily read the pages. She found what she was looking for on the Marriage page. "Margaret Macintyre Garvey married Laurence Macintyre, her third cousin, two years after Harry Garvey's death!" she read excitedly. "I didn't know this, Tate. Family gossip was that Peg mourned Tsani's death for the rest of her life, that she died miserable and lonely."

"You know how stories get mixed up over the years, and the Lover's Leap legend was certainly more interesting if people could think that Peg pined away here on the mountain," said Tate.

"If she had been sad, I would know it," Maggie said with certainty. "Maybe that's what she's been trying to tell me. That she was happy here in her later years. She knows I've been unhappy over Kip's leaving and not knowing what to do about the baby, and it was as if she were telling me not to worry, that everything would be all right. And it *is* all right, Tate. I'm happy about the baby now, and I know I don't need Kip."

He smiled at her. "I'm glad," he said.

Maggie returned her attention to the Bible. "Peg and Laurence had three children. First, Polly Macintyre, born to Peg and Laurence four years after their marriage. And Carter Macintyre, born two years after that, and David Macintyre nine years later. My father's name is David Laurence Macintyre. Those names have always been traditional in our family. So, I think we can safely assume that I'm descended from the union between Peg and her cousin. I wish I knew more about them."

Tate slid an arm around her shoulders. "Let's go visit the Scot's Cove Historical Society tomorrow. It's located in a little museum in the old railroad station."

"A great idea!"

"And while we're in town, I can pick up the part I need to get the television working again."

"Another great idea."

"In fact, for the rest of the week, let's do exactly what we want to do. No schedule, no work—"

"I might have to check the fax machine once in a while so that Bronwyn doesn't go ballistic," Maggie interjected.

"I can deal with the fax machine. And if you want to sew, that's okay. But we should go fishing for that big catfish in the pond and grill it over charcoal, and we should lie in the sun, and we should—"

"Unplug the phone and make love as often as possible?" Maggie asked innocently.

"I'm not the only one who has great ideas," he said, grinning.

"You're going back to work when?"

"Monday."

"You don't sound too happy about it."

"I'm not. I don't think I fit in at Conso anymore."

"Perhaps you'll readjust quickly," she said comfortingly.

Tate didn't say anything, only stared out the window at Breadloaf Mountain. Maggie's eyes followed the line of his gaze to the site of the future Balsam Heights mobile home park.

"So that's it," she said softly. "A case of the guilts."

"Yeah, I guess so." He knew he sounded discouraged.

"I know you don't want Conso to build that mobile home park on Breadloaf," she said.

"It's worse than you know." He told her how Conso was planning to renege on their agreement to preserve a wilderness park in order to double the size of the Balsam Heights mobile home park and how he was the one who was supposed to win over the townspeople to the company's new plan.

Maggie's eyes reflected her horror. "That's awful," she said flatly.

"I know," he said. "A lot of things that Conso does are awful, but in a job like mine, you learn to live with them."

"It's a good job by anyone's standards," she agreed, her voice thoughtful.

"I worked hard to get where I am," he said. "It wasn't easy. That's why I can't just . . ." He shrugged.

"Why you can't what?" Maggie said.

"Why I can't chuck it all," he said.

"Maybe you won't have to. Maybe you'll find a way to mediate a different solution."

"That's not my job. Karl Shaeffer made it clear to me that if I want to be a vice president, I'd better do exactly what they say."

Neither of them spoke for a long time, and then Maggie said, "How much do you really want to be a VP of Conso, Tate?"

"The job is worth a lot of money," he said.

"Is it also worth your integrity?"

He stared at her. "No," he said unhappily.

She leaned closer for a kiss. He kissed her hungrily, deeply, as if he would never stop. When at last they parted, she rested her head on his shoulder.

"I've planned on your staying here tonight," she said. "Will you?"

"I'd like to," he said.

"And how about every night?" she said in a shaky voice.

"You mean move in here?"

"Would you like to?"

"I want to be with you every moment that I can," he said truthfully.

"You wouldn't have to give up your apartment in town," she said. "I'm not asking for that."

"You're not going back to Atlanta, then?"

"Not for a long time. A long, long time. Maybe never."

Briefly Tate thought about Kip and what that fool had so easily given up. He also thought about Kip's picture, which even in this tender moment was staring at him from atop Maggie's dresser.

He disengaged himself from Maggie, went to the dresser and picked up the picture frame.

"I don't mind a ghost or two, but if I'm going to live here, I won't be able to sleep very well with this staring at me from across the room," he said.

Maggie grinned and held out her hands. He tossed her the frame and she pulled out the photograph.

"I think it's a good night to build a fire in the fireplace, don't you?" she said, tearing Kip's picture into little pieces.

"Exactly," Tate said, returning her grin, and he went out to get the firewood.

Chapter Ten

The director of the Scot's Cove Historical Society Museum, a tiny birdlike woman named Lucille Dunn, was delighted that someone was asking about the real people behind the local Lover's Leap legend and even more pleased when Maggie told her that she was descended from Peg Macintyre.

"The Lover's Leap legend has overshadowed the real people behind the story," Lucille told them. "Actually, there was more to Peg and Tsani than the legend leads us to believe."

Maggie and Tate followed Lucille to a dusty file room where she pulled out a folder and spread the contents on a library table. She invited them to join her in sifting through the contents.

The first thing she pointed out was an obituary clipping, yellow with age, about John Garvey Macintyre, who had been mayor of the town of Scot's Cove for twenty years. Lucille told them that this son of Peg and Tsani had added his stepfather's surname to his birth name when he reached legal age to do so.

"Peg's marriage to Harry Garvey was widely known to be unhappy, even though it lasted less than a year. Everyone knew that her son John was the son of Tsani, not Harry

Garvey," Lucille said. "You can bet it wasn't talked about much in those days, though. John went on to become a hero in the War Between the States, fighting for the South, of course. He almost single-handedly revived the town during the Reconstruction years, and later he was mayor until he died in the early 1900s."

"Why, he's the spit and image of Tsani," Tate said before he thought, quickly adding, "the way Tsani must have looked, I mean." Although Maggie looked at him strangely, she didn't say anything.

"Yes, he most definitely resembled the Cherokee side of the family," Lucille said briskly.

Good thing Ms. Dunn was too preoccupied with the past to notice Tate's uncanny resemblance to Tsani.

"Are there any pictures of Peg?" Maggie asked.

"None have survived, but she was reputed to have been a beauty," Lucille said. "She moved back to the cabin where she grew up with her parents after she was widowed, her parents having both died of a fever by that time. Peg became well-known in these parts as a musician."

Maggie and Tate exchanged glances.

"Do you know what instrument she played?" ventured Maggie.

"She was an expert player of the mountain dulcimer," Lucille said as the telephone rang in another room. She excused herself, and Maggie and Tate stared at each other, their eyes wide.

"Wow," Maggie breathed.

"If there ever was any doubt about what the music and voices mean, this puts it to rest," Tate said.

"This absolutely blows me away," Maggie said. "I mean, I wondered what exactly was going on in the cabin, and now I find out that she played the dulcimer. It must have been the thing that people associated with her most. She must have gained great pleasure from her music."

"I think so, too," Tate said as Lucille hung up the phone.

When Lucille returned, she seemed oblivious to their sense of discovery. "As it happens, Peg Macintyre lived to be more than ninety years old," she said briskly. "In the early nineteen hundreds, when a couple of Princeton University ethnologists passed through here to learn about the customs of the people who lived in these mountains, they recorded Peg playing her dulcimer. Would you like to hear the recording?"

"Yes!" was Maggie's answer, and Lucille went to a closet and removed a primitive phonograph with a big black horn protruding from the top.

"We're so accustomed to all our high-tech stereo equipment that this Graphophone looks funny to us now, but it probably looked even funnier to the mountain folk who lived around here at the turn of the century. I'm sure it appeared very modern to them."

"How does it work?" asked Maggie.

"Wax cylinders were inserted into the machine, and whatever was to be recorded was spoken or played into the horn. A stylus made impressions on the wax. Then it could be played back." She held up a spool. "We have a small collection of these cylinders, willed to one of the local people who befriended the university ethnologists. This is one on which was recorded Peg Macintyre's playing of the mountain dulcimer."

Lucille inserted the cylinder and cranked the machine with a handle. She set an arm with a needle on the cylinder's wax surface. "Listen," she said.

The sound emitting from the phonograph was scratchy in the extreme, but Maggie caught her breath as she recognized the tune. It was the same plaintive, simple melody that she had heard over and over in her cabin.

"What is the name of that song?" she asked.

"It's called 'If I Could Fly,' and it's a ballad of lost love. Peg may have written it herself; it's often been attributed to her." Lucille paused for a moment, picked up the tune at the beginning of a verse, and began to sing.

"I'd be with my love if I could fly,
I'd soar like an eagle up in the sky.
He can't return to the ties that bind,
But if I could fly, my love I would find.
Oh, sweet love, my love I would find."

"I can see why that would be Peg's favorite song," Maggie said softly. "She wanted to be with Tsani."

When the final chords of the music died, Lucille glanced at her watch. "It's time for my lunch hour," she said. "Since you're so interested, why don't you stay and look over the other items in the folder? When you're through, you can leave the folder on my desk."

"I know now what the next square of the quilt will be," Maggie said after Lucille had left. "I'll show Peg playing the dulcimer with all her children gathered around her, looking happy. I think that's what her dulcimer music was supposed to tell me, Tate. She wanted me to know that she was happy in the cabin, finally."

They studied old photos and letters from various Macintyres to other Macintyres, none of them important to Maggie, until Tate finally stretched and pushed his chair back from the table. "Aren't you and the kiddo hungry?" he asked.

Maggie laughed. "The kiddo and I are starving," she said as she began to put the things back into the folder. Her fingers lingered on the picture of John Garvey Macintyre, the son of Peg and Tsani.

"What makes you think that he looks so much like Tsani?" she asked him curiously.

"I saw Tsani in my vision," Tate said.

"You never mentioned that," she said in surprise.

He shrugged.

"Neither Tsani nor Peg has been around lately," Maggie said. "Have you noticed?"

"Perhaps they think that we're getting along well enough without their help."

Maggie laughed. "They've got that right," she said.

THE TINY SANDWICH SHOP down the street from the museum was crowded, and before she placed her order, Maggie checked the menu. As Bronwyn had said, they didn't serve quiche. But they did, Maggie found out after she ordered one, make a fantastic chicken salad sandwich.

Because there was a crowd waiting for seats, Maggie and Tate ate as quickly as possible and vacated their booth as soon as they had finished. When they stepped outside, the reason for the crowd became obvious. People were flocking toward the courthouse in droves.

"What's going on?" Maggie asked.

"I don't know. It looks like some kind of rally," Tate replied as someone almost elbowed him off the narrow sidewalk in haste. He was as surprised by the situation as she was.

Scot's Cove was teeming with people. Tate spied a van with the logo of an Asheville television station emblazoned on its side, and he recognized the station's chief reporter, Casey Nichols. As public relations manager at Conso, Tate had often dealt with Casey but had never liked him much; he had an idea that Casey didn't care for him, either.

Several people ran up the street carrying signs, and one of them almost knocked Maggie over as she ran past.

"Sorry!" the woman called back to them, but by that time Tate had pulled Maggie into a niche between two buildings. He kept his arm around her.

"Did you see what those signs said?" Maggie asked him.

"Something about Conso," Tate told her.

The crowd was growing by the minute. By craning his neck around the corner, Tate could see that a dais had been erected in front of the Confederate monument near the courthouse steps. A few members of the crowd looked angry, others merely excited. Tate knew some of the fellows who looked the angriest; they were the notorious town rowdies and sure to turn up wherever they could find trouble.

Everyone else, however, looked peaceable, including several mild-mannered grandmotherly types with children in tow. He finally decided that he and Maggie might as well attend. First, however, he thought he'd saunter over and say hello to Casey Nichols.

"Wait here," he told Maggie, and he went across the street to confront Casey.

"Well," said Casey, looking Tate up and down and taking in the long hair and lace-up moccasins. "How are things in the great outdoors?"

"Fine, Casey," he said, and they shook hands. "I guess you drove over from Asheville for the big happening."

"I sure did. I didn't think I'd run into you, though. I thought you'd gone from Conso for good."

"I'm on six months' leave," Tate said.

"You're going back then?"

"Next week," Tate replied. He stuck his hands in his pockets and adopted a nonchalant air. "Say, do you know what time this thing is supposed to start?"

"At one o'clock. I've been wondering if Conso plans to send a spokesman."

"I don't know. I suppose it depends on whether or not they think the gathering is of any importance."

"Oh, this is an important get-together, all right," Casey said with a know-it-all grin. "With the Kalmia Conservation Coalition planning to announce an all-out campaign to change the zoning on Breadloaf Mountain, why wouldn't it be?"

Tate's heart sank. Perhaps the coalition had learned about Conso's plans to double the number of mobile home sites in Balsam Heights and to renege on the wilderness park.

At that point, Casey was pulled away by a camera crew, and Tate sprinted back across the street to Maggie.

"Come on, let's see what's happening," he said, taking her hand and tugging her in the direction of the platform, and as they went he explained to her what was going on.

As they approached the main body of the crowd, they saw a glamorous redhead approaching from the other direction. She caught sight of Tate and headed purposefully toward him.

"Hi, Tate. I haven't seen you in a while," she said, her eyes sparkling. She looked questioningly from him to Maggie, her gaze lingering for a moment on their entwined hands.

"Jolene, there's someone I'd like you to meet. Maggie Macintyre, this is Jolene Ott. She's head of the Kalmia Conservation Coalition."

Jolene extended her hand. "Glad to meet you, Maggie. We're always glad to enlist newcomers to our cause."

"Oh, I don't think you can call me a newcomer. My family has owned a place at the base of Flat Top Mountain ever since my ancestors settled in the 1700s. The Macintyre place?"

"Why, Maggie, of course I should have recognized your name. Your folks used to let me and my brothers and sisters fish in that little pond on your property when no one was in residence. It provided many a meal for our big family, I can tell you that."

"Jolene, are you part of this?" Tate asked, gesturing loosely at the gathered crowd.

"I'm president of the coalition and the principal speaker. I hope you're going to stick around."

"Sure," Tate said.

"Good. Uh-oh, I'd better go," Jolene said before quickly mounting the steps and taking her place behind a lectern bearing the Kalmia Conservation Coalition logo. A man fiddled with the microphone, trying to adjust it to Jolene's height. Jolene shuffled her papers and winked at someone in the crowd.

The crowd was quieting down in anticipation of the speaker, and Tate leaned over to speak directly into Maggie's ear. "Jolene is Sharon Ott's sister. You know—Rose O'Sharon, the folk singer? In fact, Jolene went away to Hollywood to live with her sister and at one time hoped to become an actress, but her career plans fell through. She came back to Scot's Cove and got interested in environmental causes. She's an effective spokesperson, as you'll see."

The microphone shrieked, and someone flicked a switch on the public address console.

"Welcome to the Rally for Reality," Jolene said, and a cheer went up from the crowd.

Tate glimpsed TV cameras rolling from a vantage point on the courthouse steps. He looked in vain for someone from the public relations department at Conso. He would have thought they'd send someone.

At that point, he was jostled by someone and spun around to see that it was Albie Fentress, his good friend who was editor and publisher of the *Scot's Cove Messenger*, the local twice-a-week newspaper.

"And we'll tell Conso that we don't need more pollution! We don't need more garbage! We don't need hordes of people sapping our limited social service resources! And we don't need higher taxes!" Jolene was saying.

"Tate Jennings! I didn't think I'd run into you here, man." said Albie in a delighted stage whisper.

"I'm taking a leave from my leave of absence," Tate whispered back.

"Leave of nonsense?"

"Stop it, Albie. You're not that hard of hearing," he said. Albie, who was in his early seventies, did wear a hearing aid, but there was no doubt in Tate's mind that Albie was joshing him a little. Maggie, who couldn't help overhearing, raised her eyebrows and looked as if she might laugh.

"And four members of the county council stand steadfastly behind the Kalmia Conservation Coalition!" Jolene said, and the people cheered.

Albie leaned closer. "Well, Tate, I know you would have at least sent someone to see what the coalition is saying about Conso," he said.

"A good rule of thumb in public relations work is to know your enemies better than you know your friends," Tate said.

"Whose rule is that?"

"Karl Shaeffer's."

"Hah!" said Albie. "As if he has any friends."

"Well, Albie, do a fair job of reporting. Karl may warm up to you eventually."

"It'll be a cold day in hell when Karl warms up to anybody. Besides, reporting isn't easy at present. My managing editor quit, and my star reporter is out with some bug. It's up to me to do the job, I guess."

"Shh," hissed a bystander, and Albie shrugged his narrow shoulders and whipped out a notebook.

Tate made himself concentrate on what Jolene was saying. "And if those folks at Conso want a fight, we'll fight! And if they want to go to court, we'll go to court! Because we don't need five hundred septic tanks on Breadloaf Mountain!" she said.

So Jolene only knew about five hundred septic tanks; she must have no idea that the number had been doubled. Conso's secret was safe, which was a relief. If this cheering crowd was any indication, all hell would break loose as soon as they got wind that the actual number of mobile home sites in Balsam Heights had been increased to a thousand and as for the park, well, he didn't even want to think about what would happen when the coalition found out that there wasn't going to be one.

Tate shot a look at Maggie. She was paying rapt attention, and so was everyone else. He shifted uneasily; the brass at Conso had seriously underestimated the fervor of these people who opposed them.

"And so, my friends, we're conducting a membership drive for the Kalmia Conservation Coalition, and we intend to pressure every county commissioner until they all see things our way, not the Conso way!" Jolene pounded the lectern in her enthusiasm.

A wild outburst of cheering and shouts of "You said it!" and "Right on!" rose from the crowd, and someone waggled a sign back and forth for the television cameras. The sign said Don't Put Breadloaf In Tin Boxes.

"What a good slogan," murmured Maggie. "I wish I'd thought of it."

It did have a certain cachet, Tate had to admit.

The cheering didn't stop even when Jolene stepped down from the speaker's platform. The group of roughnecks erupted in a fracas, which was immediately squelched by two or three self-appointed peacemakers. A straggling line of schoolchildren playing trumpets, trombones and one wheezing tuba marched around the outskirts of the crowd as volunteers handed out leaflets. Jolene herself tried to give one to Tate.

He grinned at her but waved it away. "You know my situation," Tate said. "Since I'm technically an employee of Conso, I'd better not take it."

Jolene laughed and handed the leaflet to Maggie instead. "We'll bring you into the fold yet, Tate Jennings," she said. "We're holding a coalition meeting at Pinter's store tonight. Maggie, I hope we'll see you."

"Yes," Maggie said. "Yes, Jolene, I'll be there."

Tate couldn't help it; his mouth dropped open in surprise.

HE HAD ABSOLUTELY NO luck in talking Maggie out of going to the coalition meeting.

"It looks like you're serious about hanging out with that group," Tate said that night as Maggie brushed her hair preparatory to leaving the cabin.

"Of course I am," she said, head upside down so that her voice was muffled. "The meeting is important."

Tate paced from one end of Maggie's small bedroom to the other. Before he'd started talking, he'd tried to think her out of going, tried to reach into her mind and tell her that he didn't think it was a good idea. He'd had no luck; she was blocking him again.

"I didn't think you meant it when you said you'd go," he said.

Maggie tossed her head back. "I don't say things I don't mean," she said serenely.

Tate ran a hand through his hair. "It's only our third night together here," he argued. "I thought you'd want to spend it enjoying each others' company."

Maggie's brush halted in midstroke. "Oh, Tate," she said. "I phoned Jolene earlier and she said that the meeting will only last an hour."

Tate made an empty gesture. "What am I supposed to do while you're gone?"

"Miss me terribly," Maggie said teasingly.

"Oh, I'll do that, all right. Only—"

"Only you want me to be here," she finished.

"Of course," he said lamely. It actually occurred to him that this would be a good time to tell Maggie that he loved her, and then, horrified that he could even consider using those three important words to impose his will on her, he backed off. If he ever did anything like that, he'd hate himself. Nor did he want to believe that he was capable of such manipulation. The past, he thought grimly, still had a grip on him, no matter how much he wanted to think he had changed.

Now Maggie was slipping her feet into a pair of shoes that he'd never seen before; it occurred to him that there might be a lot of things he didn't know about her. Her advocacy of environmental causes was certainly something new to him.

"Hey, I never have done anything like this before," she said, standing up and linking her arms around his neck.

Tate made himself smile down at her. "Now who's reading minds? How did you know what I was thinking?"

"I realized right away after I told Jolene that I'd be at the meeting that you wouldn't be too happy about my doing this," she said.

"I'm not."

"One of us has to, Tate. And you can't because of your position at Conso." Her eyes met his levelly.

"I hope you won't tell anyone who is a member of the coalition the things I told you in confidence, such as what Karl told me about Conso's plan to double the size of Balsam Heights and scrap the wilderness park."

"I would never do that, Tate," she said quietly.

He trusted her, or he wouldn't have told her in the first place. "I know you wouldn't. But you must realize how information such as that would add fuel to the fire as far as the coalition is concerned."

"I'll be careful. I'm only going to this meeting so I can learn more about how the coalition plans to take on the county commission. If I live here, I'll be able to vote on local issues. Tate, are you sure you won't come along?"

"You know I can't do that. I'll hook up the television set as soon as you go so I can see the Casey Nichols news report about the rally on the seven o'clock local news. Want me to tape it for you?"

"Good idea. There are blank tapes in the TV cabinet." She checked her purse for necessary items, and Tate went into the living room and began to untangle the wires attached to the back of the television set.

Maggie blew him a kiss on the way out the door, but he got up and hurried after her.

"Do you think you're going to get away with only a feeble gesture?" he asked, grabbing her from behind as she reached for the car door handle.

She turned in his arms and pressed so close that he could feel her breasts and the hard globe of her swelling abdomen against his.

"Lord, I hope not," she said fervently, and he kissed her the way she deserved to be kissed. She kissed him back, and he felt the beginnings of an arousal that was anything but feeble.

"Hurry back," he said urgently, loving her, wanting her.

"You'd better believe it," she whispered against his lips. "And when I get here, the home fires had better be burning."

Tate willed his anatomy back in line. "They already are," he said, and watched her until her car was out of sight down the long winding driveway.

Back in the house, it took him only a few minutes to figure out how to hook the television set to the cable from the rooftop antenna, and he sat back to await the local news out of Asheville. There was a report of a robbery, news of a waste spill at a hog farm, and then the earnest face of Casey Nichols popped up on the screen. Casey was taking great pains to explain the work of the Kalmia Conservation Coalition, and Tate leaned forward in his chair as the scene filmed earlier that day at the rally in front of the county courthouse unfolded in front of his eyes.

"This group of angry citizens issued a challenge to the community today," Casey said. "They say that they intend to fight the Consolidated Development Corporation over development of Scot's Cove and environs. You can be sure that—"

Tate did a double take. He was looking at a close-up of himself standing beside Maggie at the rally, and Jolene Ott was holding the recruiting brochure for the Kalmia Conservation Coalition toward him. Worst of all, he was smiling and looked as if he were accepting it. The tape had been edited to cut out the part where he waved the brochure away.

"And giving in to the Consolidated Development Corporation is not something that the Kalmia Conservation Coalition intends to do," intoned Casey Nichols, and the program cut to a commercial.

Tate leaped to his feet. He wanted to smash something. He wanted to scream at the injustice of it. He had known that Casey Nichols didn't like him, but that was no reason for that dirty double-crossing scoundrel to make him look as if he were supporting the coalition. There was no doubt in his mind that Casey had known exactly what he was doing.

First he phoned the station in Asheville and asked for Casey Nichols; he was told that Mr. Nichols wasn't in at the moment, but would he like to leave his name and phone number so that Mr. Nichols could return his call?

"No," said Tate, slamming down the phone. He drummed his fingers for a moment on the breakfast bar. He wished Maggie was there. He wished he had someone to tell how betrayed he felt. He wished he could express his anger and his fear that the powers-that-be at Conso would see that piece and think that he had taken up with the Kalmia Conservation Coalition.

Just as he was preparing to head out the door the phone rang.

"Tate?"

It was Maggie.

"They just ran the piece about the rally, Maggie. The film was edited so that it looked as if I were talking to Jolene about joining the coalition. This makes me look like a traitor to Conso, and I'm worried—"

"Tate, wait a minute. I called because there's an emergency. Your friend Albie Fentress came to cover the meeting, and halfway through it he collapsed and was taken to the hospital. I thought you'd want to know."

It took a moment for this to register. "Is he going to be okay?"

"I don't know. I'm still at the general store with some of the people who came to the meeting, and we haven't heard anything about Albie." Tate heard voices in the background.

"I'd better go over to the hospital, Maggie. Albie doesn't have any close relatives."

"Do you want me to meet you there? I hate to think of your going alone."

"Yes, if you don't mind."

"I'll leave right away."

Tate took only a moment to turn off the television and VCR before hurrying outside and jumping on his motorcycle. In a few minutes, he was roaring off toward town through a lightly falling rain.

When it rains it pours, he thought with more than a little irony, and he wondered what else could possibly happen to complicate his life.

MAGGIE RAN TO TATE as soon as she saw him striding through the door of the hospital emergency room, his hair slicked back like it was on the first day she'd met him, wet raindrops shiny on his black leather jacket.

He embraced her. "Any news of Albie?"

"They've taken him to Intensive Care. You were right about his not having any relatives. The only person anyone could think of to call was a distant cousin who lives in Virginia, and she's not well enough to come," Maggie said hurriedly.

"I'd better talk to the nurse," Tate said.

They went to the Intensive Care Unit and were briefed by not only a nurse on duty but a doctor who told them that Albie had suffered a heart attack and would likely be in Intensive Care for several days.

"Can he have visitors?"

The doctor shook his head. "Not yet."

"I'll wait here until I can talk with him," Tate said resolutely, and he and Maggie joined other well-wishers, most of whom had been at the coalition meeting, in the waiting room.

They didn't get to see Albie that night, and it was after one in the morning before they arrived back at Maggie's cabin where they fell exhausted into bed and went to sleep immediately.

Tate was up soon after dawn, and he dressed to go to the hospital without waking Maggie.

At noon, when he still hadn't seen Albie, Maggie brought him a sandwich for lunch. They ate in a small park near the hospital, holding hands afterward until Tate decided he'd better go back and see how Albie was doing.

"Has there been any fallout from Conso over that piece on the news last night?" Maggie asked as she prepared to leave the hospital, and Tate grimaced. "No, but Karl probably can't find me. He wouldn't know that I'm in town at the hospital because of Albie's heart attack, and he would be the last one to care about Albie. Karl is hardly an admirer of the *Scot's Cove Messenger.* Their editorials frequently give Conso a rough time."

"It's just as well that you haven't heard from anyone at Conso, I suppose."

"Undoubtedly."

"When will you be home tonight?" She slipped her arm around his waist, and he did the same, tucking her close.

"I'm hoping they'll let me see Albie soon, and then I'll be there as soon as I can."

"No need to rush. I'd like time to cook something good for dinner," she said. "Is there anything you'd especially like?"

"Your delicious spaghetti and you," he said.

She nuzzled his cheek. "In any particular order?"

"Surprise me," he said.

SHE WOULD SURPRISE HIM all right, Maggie thought on the way home as she stopped at the gas station to fill up. She'd greet Tate with a glass of wine at the door and invite him to drink it in a few resourceful ways. A hot bath, candlelight, making love so they'd work up an appetite, and then dinner. Or dinner first, then the hot bath, then making love, and then dessert in bed. She had pumped the gas and was trying to decide on the most exciting order of events when she literally ran into Jolene Ott coming out the gas station door as she was going in.

"Maggie, am I glad to see you! The coalition is having an informal meeting at Pinter's store right away. You won't believe what we've found out! Conso has decided to build a thousand mobile home sites on Breadloaf Mountain, not five hundred as we thought."

"Oh," Maggie said. Of course she knew this; it was what Tate had told her. It was all she could do at the moment not to tell Jolene that the land for the additional mobile home sites was going to come out of what was supposed to have been the wilderness park.

"Jolene," she said tentatively.

"What?"

But Maggie couldn't do it. She couldn't betray Tate; he trusted her.

"I—I think it's a shame about the extra mobile home sites," Maggie said.

"We all do. Anyway, this calls for immediate action. People around here are as angry as all get-out." Jolene herself was visibly upset, her cheeks flushed with anger, her eyes flashing fire.

"How did you find out about it?"

"It wasn't something that Conso wanted us to know, you can believe that, but we have ways. Just between you and me, those of us who believe in the coalition's agenda have lots of relatives, some of whom have jobs at Conso, and most of them aren't too happy about the plans for Bread-loaf Mountain. Our kinfolk may not be the upper echelon, but you'd be surprised what a clerk-typist can find out if she puts her mind to it. Anyway," Jolene continued glancing at her watch, "I hope you can come to the meeting."

"I can't tonight, Jolene. I already have plans."

"I'm sorry to hear that. I'll let you know what happens. I've got to run, Maggie. See you later."

"Bye."

Jolene hurried away, and Maggie, feeling that she'd only barely averted disaster, went inside to pay for the gas. She cared about what the coalition was trying to do, but her loyalty was with Tate.

As soon as she got home, she'd try to reach Tate at the hospital. He'd want to know that the news about the additional mobile home sites had slipped out. After all, on Monday morning, he'd be the one who had to deal with damage control, and forewarned was forearmed.

Chapter Eleven

Charlie Bearkiller came to keep Tate company at the hospital while he waited for news of Albie.

"I told Albie years ago that he'd better slow down. You'd think that newspaper was the be-all and end-all," Charlie grumbled as he and Tate lingered over cups of coffee in the hospital cafeteria.

"To Albie it is. He comes from a long line of newspaper editors and was undoubtedly born with printer's ink in his veins."

"Well, too bad he doesn't have a printing press for a heart. They might be able to fix a printing press."

"Don't give up on Albie, Charlie. He may be down, but I don't think he's out."

"They've got medicines to help him, I guess. If they don't work, we can always try the Cherokee way," Charlie said philosophically. "We have songs to be sung for making a person well, folk medicine, love charms. Thought I'd mention that last one in case you ever have a need," he said, eyeing Tate speculatively.

Tate was spared a reply when he was summoned by a nurse who said, "The doctor says you can talk to Mr. Fentress now."

Tate followed the nurse back to the Intensive Care Unit. She admitted him to a small cubicle where Albie lay in bed. Tate thought he was asleep and sent a questioning look at the nurse, who smiled encouragingly and hurried away. Feeling awkward, Tate sat down gingerly on a chair beside the bed as Albie opened his eyes. A heart monitor beeped; tubes and wires seemed connected to every part of his friend's body.

"Didn't think you'd come to see me," Albie said. He was pale but his eyes were lively, and he looked as if, with the slightest encouragement, he'd sit up and rip off all the tubes and wires.

"Are you kidding, Albie? Charlie and I have been boring each other out of our minds while we waited for you to quit napping," Tate said, keeping his tone light.

A smile touched Albie's lips. "It was some nap," he said.

"Yeah, well, you'll be back in your office at the newspaper giving Conso grief in those editorials of yours before long," Tate told him.

"Don't count on it. I'm going to have to slow down, Tate, much as I dislike the idea."

"So what does that mean? Ten-hour workdays instead of twelve?"

"It means," Albie said, displaying a hint of his old fire, "I need to hire a managing editor. Fast."

"Hire one. The *Messenger* is a fine paper. You won't have any trouble luring some discontented editor away from one of these small-town weeklies around here. The *Messenger* would be a big step up for some of those folks."

"I don't want any of them. I want you," Albie said.

"Me?" Tate was stunned.

"Sure. You. I've known ever since I read your stuff in the *Raleigh Express* all those years ago that you're a born newspaperman, Tate. Don't bother denying it."

"I happen to work for Conso, and you're their sworn enemy," Tate reminded him.

"Well, wasn't that what we were talking about yesterday at the Kalmia Conservation Coalition's rally? How the safest strategy is to know what the other guy is saying about you? I figure if I hire you away from Conso, that one-ups them."

"You're a schemer, Albie."

"I'll take that as a compliment. Are you interested, Tate?"

"Albie, I'm supposed to report back to work at Conso on Monday. That's tomorrow, in fact."

"Say you'll consider my job offer."

"It wouldn't be appropriate at this time. You realize that."

"You know, they turned my hearing aid down. I can't hear a thing."

"I'll be back to see you tomorrow. Maybe you can get it turned up by then."

"Maybe not."

"Get well, Albie. This community needs you."

"Maybe not," he said again. But when Tate left, Albie was grinning.

Charlie was in the hall, walking up and down with his hands clasped behind his back. As soon as he saw Tate, he hurried over.

"How is the old buzzard, anyway?" Charlie demanded.

"I'd say he's going to be up and out of here in no time."

"Geez, then why are we wasting our time around here? Let's go shoot a game of pool."

Tate socked Charlie on the arm. "You're on. But only for an hour or so. I've got a hot date tonight."

Charlie eyed him with interest. "Same gal you told me about before?"

"Same gal."

"I thought so," said Charlie. "Something tells me that this is pretty serious."

"I think so."

"You *think?* You mean you don't *know?*"

"I'm not sure how I'd know. Love isn't an emotion with which I've been well acquainted," Tate said dryly.

"The way you'll know is when her soul comes into the very center of your soul, never to turn away," said Charlie.

This gave Tate pause. It sounded exactly like something that Tsani had said to him during his vision, and this soul business was what Tsani had told him that he and Maggie must accomplish in order to release Tsani and Peg to the Nightland.

Tate frowned at Charlie. "Would you care to elaborate on that?" he said.

"The saying comes from the old Cherokee declaration of love. That's how the old-timers would have set the seal on commitment. You want to know the old love charms?"

"I think we'd better stick to playing pool," he told Charlie, thinking that he and Maggie had enough to think about without invoking ancient spells.

It was not, however, the kind of thing he felt comfortable saying to Charlie Bearkiller.

ARRIVING HOME, Maggie pulled her car up to the side of the cabin where she always parked it and went around to get the groceries out of the trunk. That was when she smelled bacon frying.

Bacon? Why would she smell bacon? Unless Peg Macintyre had lately taken up cooking, Maggie could think of no explanation.

But it was definitely the odor of bacon, and along with it, the unmistakable scent of frying onions wafted from the open kitchen window.

Perhaps she should have been afraid, but her first thought was that Bronwyn had decided to pay a surprise visit and was cooking liver and onions, which she dearly loved. Never mind that she, Maggie, hated liver. Never mind that she had told Bronwyn how certain strong odors such as onions upset her stomach. It would be just like Bronwyn to arrive unannounced and make herself at home by cooking her favorite meal, not remembering that such odors would present a problem for her hostess.

Maggie, carrying the bag of food, hurried up the path to the front door and let herself in. She always left the door unlocked these days; she'd been conditioned to it by Tate.

"Bronwyn?" she called expectantly.

"No," said a familiar voice, and as she lowered the bag to the kitchen counter and removed her sunglasses, she discovered that her visitor was not Bronwyn after all.

"Hi, babe," said Kip, sauntering forward casually, a self-assured smile on his face. "I heard at the general store that you've got a cabin for rent."

Maggie stared at him, scarcely able to credit his presence.

"Excuse me," she said unsteadily, "but I think I'm going to throw up."

And did, all over his brand-new Gucci loafers.

TATE WAS LATER coming home than he'd planned. He'd tried to call Maggie from the pool hall, but no one answered at her place. He suspected that she had unplugged the phone again in preparation for a night of lovemaking, which was fine with him.

It wasn't that either he or Charlie intended for him to be late, but one thing led to another and they kept thinking of things to talk about. Tate wasn't sure what time it was when he headed his motorcycle up Maggie's driveway, but it was already dark. He didn't know whether to hope Maggie had waited dinner for him or had gone to bed; stealing into her bed and cuddling her until she woke up appealed to him tonight. And then they would...

He screeched to a stop. Whose car was that? It was an unfamiliar subcompact, and it was pulled up behind the felled oak tree that Jacob Pinter's grandson was supposed to cut for firewood. Tate turned off the bike's engine and listened for a moment, but all he heard was the chirring of crickets in the shrubbery.

Nothing seemed to be amiss, and the window of Maggie's bedroom was dark. Out of habit, he looked for the robin's nest in the living room window. It wasn't there.

He supposed that the car could belong to Jacob's grandson; that the kid had stopped by during the day to chop firewood and then couldn't start the car for some reason; that he'd called somebody for a ride home and left the car until the next day. This made sense.

Tate opened the cabin's front door and flicked on the light switch. All was in order; nothing was out of place.

"Maggie? I'm home," he called. He pictured her lying in bed in the dark, waiting for him, preferably nude, preferably eager.

The bedroom door opened, and a man came out toweling his wet hair. He wore a bath towel and nothing else.

"Hi," said the man. "I'm Kip."

Tate took in the guy's state of undress; the living room light slanted through the doorway to reveal Maggie in her nightgown in the bed beyond. She looked confused, as if she'd just awakened.

"Excuse me," Tate said. "I think I've got the wrong house."

He slammed the door as he left.

PURE, BLIND SHOCK. That was what Tate felt as he gunned his bike up the mountain to his camp. He couldn't feel, he couldn't think, and he sure as hell couldn't deal with whatever was going on back at the cabin.

He'd thought Kip was out of Maggie's life. The way she had made love to him, Tate, the way she had confided in him, the way she had so readily become a part of his life—had she only been toying with his feelings? Had he fooled himself into thinking that his visions and dreams were real when they were only fantasy?

He loved her. He should have told her so during one of their sublime sessions of lovemaking when they'd felt so close and happy. He should have come back from town earlier. He should have found out what Maggie felt about him when he'd had the chance. On the other hand, maybe he already knew.

Maggie had needed someone, and he'd been there. She'd been alone and scared and pregnant. Had he been a chump all along to be there for her? Had he merely been a convenience, someone to get her over the hard times until Kip Baker decided to breeze back into her life?

He arrived at his camp, slamming on brakes with a vengeance, sending a tail of dirt flying as he skidded to a stop near his *asi*. The camp had an air of neglect even though he'd only been gone for a couple of days. He kicked at the ashes of the campfire, found that the water in the bucket was stale, went to the river and filled it. He occupied himself with these tasks that he could perform by rote, then flung himself down beside the cold ashes and tried to think.

He couldn't think. It was impossible with that picture of Maggie that was seared into his brain, the picture of her with her sheer silk nightgown pulled tight across her breasts, her hair mussed and her cheeks rosy from sleep, the picture of her with Kip.

She had said she might still love Kip, but Tate had thought that the passion and confidences that they had shared had overcome any last vestige of affection she might feel for the guy. He'd thought she loved him, Tate. What a fool he was! He should never have taken anything for granted.

Finally he lit the fire and stared into it, wishing that he had never met Maggie Macintyre.

He heard the pesky, troublesome Tsagasi laughing at him down by the river, but he paid them no mind. They would have to find someone else to torment. Kip Baker came to mind as the perfect candidate.

MAGGIE SAT FROZEN in place as Tate slammed out the door of her cabin, and his motorcycle had already roared up the mountain by the time she reached the front door.

She turned to Kip, furious with him. "What did you say to him? What did *he* say?"

Kip shrugged in that nonchalant way of his. "I introduced myself, and the guy took off like a bat out of hell."

Maggie sagged against the closed door. "He must have thought—" she began, but stopped.

Kip approached her, a quizzical smile on his face. "Must have thought what, babe?"

"Thought that you and I were in bed together," she said heavily.

Leaning toward her, a confidently seductive smile on his lips, Kip reached over and edged a finger beneath the narrow strap of her nightgown. Slowly and deliberately, he lifted it and let it fall down her arm so that the bodice slipped to expose most of one rounded breast. "Now that's the best idea I've heard all day," he said lazily, gazing at her from under half-lowered eyelids.

Furiously Maggie adjusted the strap. "Don't touch me. You'll never lay a hand on me again, Kip Baker, get that through your thick head."

"I wouldn't be so sure," he said. He wasn't taking her seriously, but then Kip never took anything seriously except his own pleasure.

"What were you doing in my room?" she said. She had become violently sick after smelling the bacon and fried potatoes with onions that Kip had decided to cook in her absence, and she had closed her bedroom door on him, put on her nightgown, and crawled into bed to await Tate. Kip had said he needed a place to spend the night; for some reason known only to himself, he had driven to Scot's Cove nonstop from some unspecified starting point. He had been driving for twenty-four straight hours and claimed that it was too late to head for Atlanta. When it came right down to it, Maggie didn't care if Kip bedded down on the couch; hopes of a romantic evening had already been squelched by her reaction to the odor of bacon and onions. She had made it clear that Kip was to leave first thing in the morning.

It took a tremendous effort to make herself pay attention to Kip's explanation of his presence in her bedroom. "There's no shower in the half bath behind the kitchen. I didn't think you'd mind if I used your bathroom. Hey, you wouldn't deny me a nice warm shower after I've driven for hours to see you, would you?" He smiled engagingly, but in that moment, she hated him. How could she have ever loved this self-centered creep?

"I could deny you anything at this moment," she said. "Get out."

"Out? You mean," and he jerked his head toward the door, *"out?"*

"Either you leave of your own volition or I will throw you out of here myself."

"Aren't I the father of your child? Don't I have rights?"

"Out," she said, heaving his duffel off the floor and tossing it out into the night. "Out," she said, picking up his loafers where he had left them and throwing them after it. "Out," she said again, placing her hands against Kip's back and propelling him toward the door.

"Can't we at least talk this over?" Kip said unbelievingly as he cleared the doorsill wearing only the towel, which had slipped dangerously low.

For an answer, she shut the door and shot the bolt loudly.

"Maggie?" Kip said, but she didn't reply. "Maggie, where am I supposed to sleep?"

She still didn't answer, and finally, after an interminable silence, she heard him cursing as he disappeared toward the dark woods.

Now that he was gone, what could she do about Tate? She had to talk to him, had to explain.

Maggie heard the same plaintive dulcimer tune that always heralded Peg Macintyre's presence and waited to see if she would appear or speak. Nothing happened, and Maggie realized that she was on her own.

But she was tired of being on her own. She wanted to be with Tate. The only trouble was, she wouldn't blame Tate one bit if after tonight he didn't want to be with her.

LOVING MAGGIE. What did it mean?

Tate, feeling the need of a spiritual experience, had built a fire in his sweat lodge. He crouched naked in the rising smoke, pouring water on the hot stones to make steam.

His song was straight out of Cherokee tradition, a lament for lost love. He didn't know if the words qualified as a love charm, but he figured they were close enough, and besides, his song came straight from his heart. The words rose with the smoke, and like the smoke, they disappeared.

Like Maggie.

MAGGIE DRESSED QUICKLY, not knowing what clothes she threw on, knowing only that she must find Tate and that he would be at his camp.

She grabbed a flashlight from the utility room and went outside.

"Maggie?"

It was Kip, who had apparently seen the beam of light from his car.

"Leave me alone," she said.

He emerged from the car. "I can't sleep in the car, it's too small."

"Stop whining, Kip. You should have thought about that before you decided to come here." She kept walking down the driveway. Thunder mumbled in the distance.

"Where are you going?"

"None of your business."

He followed her. At least he had dressed. If she wasn't so angry, she might have laughed at the way he had looked when she'd thrown him out of the cabin.

"Well, wherever you're going, I'm going, too."

She beamed her light full in his face, and he flinched.

"Cut it out, Maggie," he said. A few drops of rain had fallen, and now it started to drizzle.

"Stop following me. This doesn't concern you."

"You're heading up the mountain into a thunderstorm to God knows where and you're carrying my child. Of course it concerns me."

It didn't, but his words gave her pause. It was a long way to Tate's camp, and she could slip or fall or get lost in the woods. Kip seem determined to follow her. She knew she couldn't very well show up at Tate's camp with him in tow.

Wordlessly, she switched off the light and marched back toward the cabin.

"Couldn't you at least let me have the flashlight?" Kip asked plaintively as she reached the door.

Keeping a firm grip on it, determined that Kip wasn't going to get anything else from her, ever, she went inside the cabin and locked the door, leaving him looking after her with a hurt expression.

Maggie threw herself down on the couch and buried her face in her hands. Her life was a wreck, and it was all her own fault.

TATE PAUSED in his chanting, his throat dry and cracked. He felt a sudden whoosh of wings, and his eyes flew open to see the great white crane.

"How about the baby? Does it mean as much to you as she does?" asked the white crane without preamble. Behind the crane's mask, Tsani's eyes were anxious.

"It's not my baby," Tate said.

"*You* were no one's baby. Wouldn't you have liked it if some man had agreed to be a father to you?"

"Of course," Tate said. "I needed a father. Hell, I needed a mother, but I didn't have one who counted for much."

"Ah," said Tsani. "Here is your chance to right another wrong. This child needs you. Make yourself count for something."

"It will hardly do any good if Maggie doesn't want me."

"You don't know what she wants," Tsani reminded him.

"She apparently wants Kip."

"Kip!" said the Tsani in a disparaging tone of voice. "He's worthless."

"You think so and I think so. I'm not sure Maggie thinks so."

"It's up to you to find out. And if the child is to have a real father, that's also up to you."

"Why does it matter to you?" Tate said boldly. He wasn't sure he wanted Tsani directing his life any more.

Tsani moved closer. "I never knew my child," he said. "I lost him through my own folly. I have repented for being late on the day that I was to meet Peg and run away with her, but it isn't enough. I want to make sure that at least one baby who has no father will get a good one."

"Why me?"

"Because you are me. Don't you get it?"

"I'm beginning to wish I didn't," Tate said.

"I am ready to journey to the Nightland. We are close, my woman and I, to being together for all eternity. But before we continue, I must know if you will care for Maggie's baby."

Tate swallowed. He knew that this was an important question. Now that he had met Kip, it was brought home to him even more clearly that Maggie's child did not belong to him. And yet he had so often wished that the child had resulted from the acts of love that had made him feel so close to Maggie. Hadn't he marveled at the act itself and how extraordinarily focused he felt both during and after? Hadn't he touched the small protuberance that was the baby even as his body entered Maggie's, even as he poured himself into her, became part of her? And hadn't he known that the true miracle was the baby itself? Hadn't he wanted to feel that the baby was part of him, just as Maggie was?

Yes, as Maggie's love had grown to encompass the baby that she hadn't planned, so had his. Because he loved Maggie, therefore he loved her child. He felt, so help him, like the baby's father. And if he wasn't, it wasn't because of a lack of loving. He would give anything, anything in the world, if the baby was his. It *was* his, by virtue of love.

All these emotions ran through his mind, washed over him, and it was an entirely new experience to be able to connect with so many feelings at once. He didn't have to speak of this; he didn't have the words. But Tsani knew. "The child will have a good father in you," Tsani said softly.

Tate spoke through dry lips. "How—how can you judge?"

"I know that you have the love."

"But I don't have Maggie." In that moment, Tate thought he knew the true meaning of despair. To feel as he had always wanted to feel, to know the meaning of real love only to have it snatched away from him—this was agony, and it reached deep into his soul.

Suddenly Peg appeared, a faint apparition, and glided into Tsani's arms. In spite of his own anguish, seeing them there like that, knowing that they were together, warmed Tate's heart.

"Leave it to us," Peg said, and a dulcimer chord sounded as the two of them faded away.

Tate slept, exhausted. When he awoke, his eyes red, his mouth parched, it was dawn.

He glanced at his wristwatch, his eyes falling on the day and date feature.

Oh great, he thought wearily. *It's Monday, the day I'm supposed to report back to work at Conso.*

He dragged himself out of the sweat lodge. Somehow he'd have to pull himself together and get to his apartment in town. He wouldn't have time to get a haircut, but he knew he'd damn well better make his appearance at the Conso offices wearing nothing less than a suit and a power tie.

MAGGIE BARELY SLEPT all night, falling into a deep fitful sleep just before dawn. When she woke up, it was much later than she had intended, and she ran around the cabin eating a banana, orange juice sloshing out of her glass, as she threw on some clothes and gulped a prenatal vitamin.

A knock sounded at the door. She threw it open to see a chagrined Kip standing on her doorstep.

"What do you want?"

"To say goodbye. I'm leaving, Maggie. I won't be back."

"Good. You shouldn't have come here in the first place."

"I know that now. I wanted to say that I'm sorry for any problems I've caused you." He looked sheepish, apologetic. For a moment—only a moment—Maggie remembered that she had loved him for his little-boy quality, for his impulsiveness and his carefree attitude toward life.

"As for the baby," he went on, "I guess you know I'd make a terrible father. I've always been irresponsible, and I don't think I can change."

"Yes. Yes, Kip, I do know that. I don't expect you to be part of our lives, the baby's and mine. I don't want you to send us money or remember the baby's birthday, or... or anything."

His eyes met hers, and in them she saw relief. "Are you sure?" he said.

"Very sure."

"Okay. I hope everything goes well for you. For you and the baby, I mean."

"Thanks," Maggie said, meaning it.

"Well, goodbye, Maggie."

"Goodbye, Kip," she replied, feeling a sense of release when she realized that this was really it for their relationship. She supposed she should feel sad, but she didn't. When she saw Kip's rental car disappearing down the driveway, she knew she'd be perfectly happy if she never saw him again as long as she lived.

After she was sure Kip was really gone, she laced her hiking boots on and headed for Tate's camp. She almost ran all the way there, arriving out of breath and full of hope.

Her hope faded, however, when she saw the ashes of an abandoned campfire. A peek inside the *asi* told her nothing; she could tell he had been in the sweat lodge recently, though, by the steam still rising from the hot stones.

So he'd sought a vision; she didn't know if that was good or bad.

Probably he had gone in to work today. Tate was no fool. He'd know that the big guns would be aimed at him this morning after his impromptu appearance on TV when it had looked as if he were accepting a membership brochure from Jolene Ott. Suddenly she felt sick; last night after Kip's unsettling appearance, she had completely forgotten about letting Tate know that the Kalmia Conservation Coalition had found out about those five hundred more mobile home sites that were going to be built on Breadloaf Mountain.

How could she have forgotten something that was so important for Tate to know?

She'd better tell him. She'd call the office, talk to him, tell him about the coalition and how angry the people were.

But she couldn't. Not after last night. How could she ever face him again?

She saw Tate's headband crumpled beside the *asi;* lost in thought, she picked it up, cradling the piece of striped fabric in her hands. And then she *knew*. Tate was in trouble. She didn't know how she knew, but somehow she understood that his present difficulty was a direct result of her failure to let him know about the coalition's emergency meeting last night.

She raced back to the cabin and went straight to the phone, looked up Conso's number in the book, and called Tate's office.

"Mr. Jennings is not available at present," said the person who answered the phone. "Would you like to leave a message?"

Maggie knew that she had to be careful what she said. She didn't want to get anyone in trouble. What she had to say was meant for Tate's ears and Tate's only. And if she asked him to call her back, chances are he would ignore the message.

"No, no message," she said, and hung up the phone. Then she walked slowly and deliberately into the bedroom to put on a dress suitable for calling on someone at a place of business.

Even though she knew she was setting herself up, she would go to Tate and tell him what she knew. And after that, she'd let the chips fall where they may.

THE ANGRY MOB on the front lawn of the Conso office demanded to speak to someone important.

"Karl Shaeffer," called one of the men. "Is he in there?"

Tate rode up on his motorcycle and wheeled to a stop in his parking space. He balanced himself for a moment, his feet firmly planted on either side of the bike, before turning off the motor. The situation looked unstable. Some of the nastier Scot's Cove characters were pushing forward toward the building; others tried to restrain them.

Tate got off the bike and shouldered his way through the knot of people. A group of Conso employees, apparently reluctant to cross the line of angry demonstrators, stood silently to one side of the parking lot.

"What's happening?" Tate asked someone who was lounging against the stone wall separating the parking lot from the walkway in front of the building.

"We want the Conso brass to come out and explain why they decided to build five hundred more mobile home sites on Breadloaf Mountain," the man said.

Tate's heart sank. Maggie was the only one he told about the company's decision. He felt a white-hot stab of pure anger; she had known this was confidential information. Well, if she had betrayed him with Kip, what was to stop her from betraying him in other ways as well?

Tate climbed the steps two at a time. Through the glass door to the lobby, he saw Don Chalmers and Karl Shaeffer and a couple of vice presidents conferring in a huddle.

He threw the door open and went inside. "What's going on?" he asked.

Karl greeted him with a cold look. "Maybe *you* should tell *us*," he said with a grimace of distaste for Tate's long hair.

"Easy, Karl," said Quentin Miller, the general manager, before turning to Tate. "These people have gotten wind of our plans to expand the Balsam Heights development on Breadloaf. Apparently the Kalmia Conservation Coalition had a meeting last night that incited all the rougher elements in the group. They're demanding an explanation. And you're going to give it to them."

A meeting last night? Maggie hadn't mentioned it. But then there were other things she hadn't mentioned, too.

Tate had never expected to be hit with this problem on his first day back at work, and on top of his heartache over Maggie.

He drew a deep breath. "What would you like me to say to them?"

"Tell them the usual—more jobs, keeps the young people home—that sort of thing. Make it sound as if we have the good of the community in mind."

Tate shot an uneasy look at the crowd, which had surged closer to the glass doors. "I'm not sure that's going to be enough," he said.

"Remind them about the wilderness park. Tell them what an asset to the community the park will be," said Karl.

Tate was momentarily confused. He knew that Karl had told him that plans for the park were being—had been, in fact—scrapped. He stared at Karl. Two of the vice presidents in attendance conferred off to one side, each of them shooting troubled looks at Tate.

"It's my understanding," Tate said stiffly, "that the park is no longer in the picture."

Karl stepped forward. "It doesn't matter," he said. "Mentioning the park may be enough to calm this crowd down. No one knows about the legal loophole that will enable us to get out of deeding the park to the county except those of us present here. And we won't contradict you."

Tate expelled a deep breath. "That's not the way to deal with this group."

"I'll decide that," Karl said. There was definite menace behind his words.

Tate tried to think. If Maggie had told the people in the coalition about the five hundred extra mobile home sites being added to Balsam Heights, surely she would have mentioned in the same breath that they were going to be built on the land that had been set aside for the wilderness park. But the way Karl was talking, the demonstrators didn't know that there was going to be no park. It didn't make sense.

Outside, someone shouted something about higher taxes brought about by Conso's development of the area, and

Tate recognized one of the local thugs that he had seen at the Rally for Reality. He knew that he'd better do something to calm the crowd, and fast.

"I'll go out there and talk to them," he said. "But I won't lie."

"Tate—" Karl began, but Tate cut him off by wheeling around and walking out the door. Karl stared after him, his face a mask of anger.

"You gonna explain about Breadloaf?" someone in the crowd yelled through cupped hands as Tate took a position at the top of the stairs.

Tate smiled as pleasantly as possible and adopted a serious expression.

"I understand that you folks have some concerns about the Balsam Heights mobile home park development on Breadloaf," he said with what he hoped was the right mixture of pleasantry and seriousness.

"You bet we do," someone called.

"Yeah," cried another. "We want the truth about those five hundred more sites for mobile homes on Breadloaf Mountain."

"I understand your concern. Breadloaf Mountain is a beautiful place, and I'm sure you want to keep it that way."

A murmur of agreement ran through the crowd.

"As some of you may know, I've come back to work today after a six-month leave of absence. Your presence here has taken me by surprise, but I want to assure you that your concerns are being taken seriously by Conso management. I can't answer your questions this morning, but we will have information for you soon. I ask you to please go home. The company will be making an announcement in the near future."

"We don't want no announcements! We want the truth," said a burly man in the front row. He fingered a rock, turning it over and over in his hands.

"I understand that. But I hope you'll understand something, too. I'm not prepared at this time to talk about the matter." He hoped and prayed that no one would mention the wilderness park.

A disconsolate rumble swept the crowd.

"When will you be ready to talk?"

"Soon, I hope." Tate smiled encouragingly.

"Aw, come on, everybody, you can see he's not going to talk," said the burly fellow. He dropped the rock and moved toward the back of the group.

Tate, seeing that some of the anger had been defused, put his hands in his pockets in what he hoped was a casual manner. "I don't know anything to tell you at this point."

An uneasy silence settled over the demonstrators, broken only when one of the calmer men spoke up. "I got to get to work myself," he said. "I got no more time to waste here."

"Me, too," said another.

A few people began to wander away from the fringe, and Tate saw some of the Conso employees start to walk toward the building. He gave them an almost imperceptible nod, encouraging them to displace the crowd, which seemed to be waiting for a sign that the confrontation was over.

"When will you talk with us?" asked one still-hopeful woman.

"Someone in the public relations department will be happy to set up an appointment with the president of your group, and I believe that's Jolene Ott," Tate said.

"It is. I'll tell her," said the woman.

By this time the Conso employees were walking in the front door, and the crowd, which had barely avoided becoming unruly, had dispersed.

After watching them pile into their cars and pickups, Tate, harboring mixed feelings of certain doom, heaved a sigh of relief and went inside the building.

Karl met him at the door. "You'd better come along to my office," he told Tate, and Tate had the feeling that Karl was going to be even harder to face than the crowd.

"ALL RIGHT," Karl said, staring at Tate from under beetle brows. "If you're a member of the Kalmia Conservation Coalition, you'd better own up now."

"That's ridiculous," said Tate, glaring back at him.

"Sources tell me that your girlfriend was at their membership meeting the other night."

"I wasn't."

"You were at the Rally for Reality together. I saw it on television."

"True, we were there. We were swept up in it before we really knew what was going on. I don't see anything wrong with being there. I wasn't a participant, and Conso should have sent someone to monitor the rally so we'd know what those people are thinking. We may be able to use what I learned that day for the good of this company."

"If we were going to send someone to that rally, it certainly wouldn't have been the head of the public relations department, which you still are by virtue of this ridiculous leave policy."

"Now wait just a minute," Tate said angrily.

"I think you're the one who leaked the information about the Balsam Heights expansion to the coalition," Karl said.

Tate reeled with shock. Did Karl know that he had let Maggie in on this privileged information?

"You know I wouldn't tell company secrets to a group like that," Tate said.

"I don't know what you'll do," Karl said. "When I hired you, I never thought that you'd stop wearing clothes and run around in the woods for six months reclaiming your heritage. If you ever want to do it again in the future, I certainly hope you'll resign your position first."

Tate thought of the angry crowd demanding answers that he couldn't or wouldn't give; he thought of all he had learned during his sojourn at his camp; he thought of the simplicity of Cherokee ways; he thought of the peace he had found on Flat Top Mountain. Deep in his heart where it counted, he now thought and felt as a Cherokee; he realized it and was exulted by it.

He stood up abruptly. "You don't have to worry about what I might or might not do in the future, Karl. I quit."

He had the satisfaction of watching Karl's jaw drop as he turned on his heel and marched from the office.

"Mr. Jennings, please don't forget to pick up your mail," said Karl's administrative assistant as he strode past her desk.

"Can it," said Tate, and he kept walking.

Chapter Twelve

Maggie arrived at the Conso building and went into the lobby.

The receptionist looked at her nervously. "I'd like to see Tate Jennings, please," Maggie said.

The woman seemed to size her up. "I don't know if he's accepting appointments this morning," she said.

"Please find out."

The woman bit her lip. "It's just that if you're one of that gang that was here this morning—"

"Gang?"

"Some of the rowdier folks around here tried to make trouble earlier."

"Oh, no," Maggie said.

"You don't look like one of them."

"I'm not. I'm—" but here Maggie wavered. It was a safe bet that she wasn't anything to Tate Jennings; how could she explain to this woman why she needed to see him?

The woman smiled. "I can see you're not part of that group. If you'll have a seat, I'll ask if Mr. Jennings will see you."

Maggie sat down on a convenient chair and waited, fidgeting uneasily. She felt even more strongly now that Tate was in trouble, and in the past ten minutes, the feeling had become unbearable. And what exactly had happened here this morning to make the receptionist so wary? It must have had something to do with the meeting that Jolene had called last night. Oh, if only she had been able to warn Tate about the meeting, if only Kip hadn't shown up and ruined everything. She wanted to run to the elevator, punch buttons until she landed on the right floor, and rescue Tate from whatever situation was making him feel so angry.

Oh, God, how did she know he was angry? She heard her pulse pounding at her temples and knew she was feeling his; she felt her skin growing hot and knew his was, too. He might be able to read her thoughts, but she was experiencing his emotions as if they were her own. And it was not pleasant.

The receptionist put down the phone, a puzzled look on her face. "Mr. Jennings is no longer employed here," she said to Maggie.

At that moment, the elevator door burst open and Tate strode out. He was tugging his tie from around his neck, and his suit jacket was open. He heard what the receptionist said.

"Damn right," he said. "I don't work here any more, and I'm glad." His eyes lit on Maggie, but he didn't miss a beat. He kept walking out the door, and after a stunned moment, Maggie hurried after him, down the steps, into the parking lot.

"You were fired?" Maggie gasped as she ran up to Tate, who was stuffing his suit jacket into the carryall on his motorcycle.

"I quit," Tate said. He stared at her. She was self-conscious about the way she looked; her hair was flying every which way and her dress was twisted around so that it revealed the slight rounding of her stomach.

"You quit? Why?" Maggie asked, dumbfounded. She couldn't stop panting because she was so out of breath.

"I can't stand working here any more. I can't go on spouting the company line when I don't believe in it. And listen, Maggie, I don't appreciate your telling Jolene or other members of the coalition or whoever you told about the additional five hundred mobile home sites that Conso is going to put on Breadloaf Mountain. That was privileged information that I told you only because I trusted you. I suppose I should thank you for not telling them that there's not going to be a wilderness park. At least they didn't know that when they came marching on Conso this morning." He sounded bitter.

"What are you talking about?"

"I'm sure you know." He got on his bike and put on his sunglasses so she couldn't see his eyes.

"I didn't tell anyone. In fact, I ran into Jolene at the gas station yesterday and she told me that someone who works here—a clerk-typist, I think she said—ferreted out the information about the additional mobile home sites. I wanted to tell Jolene that there's going to be no wilderness park, but I didn't, I couldn't. I wouldn't do that to you, Tate."

"Thanks for small favors," he said. She thought he sounded as if he might believe her, at least a little.

"I don't know what I can do to make you believe me, but I never told anyone. Honestly." She was barely holding on to her composure by this time; Tate was looking at her as if she were a life form lower than plankton.

He looked away for a long moment, then back at her. "I don't know why, but I do believe you. Anyway, I'm through with Conso. The matter's moot."

"There's something you should know. I came here this morning to warn you that the coalition knew about those extra mobile home sites. I was going to tell you last night when you got home, but—'' She stopped when she saw the forbidding expression on his face.

''I don't know why you bothered about me this morning. I would have thought you'd have more interesting things to do.'' His expression was contemptuous, his eyes cold.

She swallowed. ''It wasn't what you thought with Kip, Tate,'' she said.

''The man was walking out of your bedroom, Maggie, and he wasn't wearing any more than you were.''

''You got the wrong idea. Kip was just passing through, and—''

''And so you thought you'd make him feel at home, right?''

Tears stung the back of her throat. ''Wrong, Tate, all wrong,'' she said.

''Something is wrong, all right. I thought our relationship had promise.''

''It did. It does. I was sick, Kip was frying bacon and onions when I got home, and he had come to see me, thinking I'd come crawling back to him, but I couldn't, I wouldn't, not after what he did to me, and anyway, I don't love him, and—'' She was sobbing outright now, and she didn't have a tissue. She wasn't crying only for herself, but for Tate because now she felt his pain, experienced his anguish. *Like the way I felt what Peg felt when I dreamed about Tsani's being swept over the falls,* she thought in a revelatory moment. Only this was so much more personal, so much more tragic in terms of their own relationship. Added to her own grief over Tate's misunderstanding of Kip's presence at the cabin, it was an unbearable load of sorrow.

''Here,'' Tate said, handing her his handkerchief. She blew her nose. ''And if you didn't love whatsisname, why did you go to bed with him?''

"It wasn't bed, he wanted to shower," Maggie blurted before realizing she had said the wrong thing.

Tate expelled a long breath. "Did you drop the soap, Maggie? Or have the Tsagasi decided to leave you alone? Like I have," he added.

"I—" she began, but he wouldn't let her finish.

"Go back to your lover, Maggie. I'm sure he's waiting for you with open arms." He started the bike, the noise of the engine drowning out anything that Maggie had to say.

She had managed to stop sobbing. She knew that there was no point in discussion. Tate didn't want to hear anything she had to say, and so the only thing left for her to do was to salvage some dignity from the situation. Without a word, Maggie turned her back on him and marched over to her car. She fumbled in her purse for her keys, and then she noticed the BMW's right front tire. It was flat. She heard a chime of laughter and thought, *Peg.*

And you thought all I could do was move a bird's nest in and out of the window, Peg said.

She opened the trunk and saw that the spare tire was also flat. Maggie sneaked a look at Tate. He was sitting on his motorcycle and staring at the flat tire. His eyes flicked over her, took in her slumped shoulders, her red nose, the tears welling in her eyes again.

After a moment's hesitation, he rode over to where she stood, gazing at her from behind his sunglasses. *My handsome Indian-brave, riding up on his black steed to rescue me from the massacre of my own regrets,* she thought.

His face was expressionless. "Get on," he said.

She stared at him, unsure of herself and of him.

"I said, get on. I can't leave you stranded here in this parking lot."

Maggie, not daring to hope, hesitated only briefly before slamming the trunk closed. She hiked her skirt up and straddled the bike behind him, wrapping her arms around his waist.

"Hang on tight," he warned before accelerating, and she thought, *You bet I will. Forever and ever, if you'll let me.*

For once she hoped he was reading her loud and clear.

MAGGIE HAD NO IDEA where Tate was taking her, and she didn't care. At least he was taking her with him. That was all that mattered.

She was surprised when he stopped the motorcycle in front of the *Scot's Cove Messenger* office, a neat brick building in the middle of town.

Slowly she got off the bike. "What are we doing here?"

"We have a paper to get out. Come along, Maggie. We're going to put your writing skills to work."

"But—" she began, but Tate only grabbed her hand and hauled her along with him.

He seemed to know the people who worked there, and she met the receptionist, the reporter, the ad salesman, and the print shop staff all in one grand sweep of the office.

Tate called the group around him and in short order had informed them that he was their new boss, that they were going to put out a paper that Albie Fentress could be proud of, and that they were all going to work their behinds off to do it. Furthermore, if anyone didn't like the idea, that person could leave and not come back.

No one left.

Maggie had worked on a daily campus paper while she was in college, and she knew the fundamentals of a good news story. Tate assigned her to a vacant desk, and soon she had her hands full with the backlog of work.

Tate was self-assured and knowledgeable, and, sensing how important it was to him not to let Albie down, Maggie did as she was told. She was eager to help Tate, and not only

out of her own guilt. She knew after ten minutes in the
Messenger office with him that there were other compelling
reasons why he had quit his job at Conso. He was a newspaperman through and through, and she didn't need a sixth
sense to know it. Tate had clearly found his niche.

Later when he called her into the office that he was using, the one with the words *Managing Editor* lettered on the
door, and asked her to write a feature about the Kalmia
Conservation Coalition, she agreed without a murmur.

"What slant should the article about the coalition have?"
she asked him.

He spared her a shrewd look. "Write it any way you like,"
he said, and Maggie sat down at the computer monitor on
her desk and pounded out a hard-hitting article about the
coalition and its purpose. She didn't pull any punches, either; she made sure that she set forth the aims of the orga-
nization, its objective of changing the zoning on Breadloaf
Mountain, and after a phone call to Jolene Ott, quoted her
copiously. When Maggie finished, she felt drained. She took
her feature to Tate, wary of his reaction.

When Tate read what she had written, he was elated.
"This is exactly what we want," he said.

"Top management at Conso isn't going to like it very
much."

"I couldn't care less what they think," Tate said
brusquely.

Because Albie had been out for days and because during
that time, the staff of the newspaper had had no direction,
it took longer than they had anticipated to finish what
needed to be done for the next issue of the *Messenger* to be
on the stands in the morning. But they did it. One by one
members of the staff departed, tired but elated with the
pleasure of a job well-done.

Finally, after everyone had left, Tate called Maggie into his office. Under the bright fluorescent lights, he looked tired, and his shirt was disheveled. Several empty foam cups littered his desk; one had spilled coffee across a stack of papers.

"Could I talk you into something to eat?" he said.

You could talk me into anything, Maggie thought. Aloud she said, "Sure. The kiddo and I are pretty hungry."

He almost smiled at that, but not quite.

The only restaurant open at that late hour was a bar that served sandwiches, and the raucous shouts coming from inside convinced them that the atmosphere there would be anything but restful. As they were deciding to leave, Jacob Pinter walked out. He beamed when he saw Maggie.

"I sent a prospective tenant to see you yesterday," he said. "Guess he didn't like your place."

Maggie avoided looking at Tate, but she felt a flush starting in her neck and working its way upward just the same.

"I guess he didn't," she said, not immune to the irony.

"The fellow stopped by my store this morning. Asked for medicine for chigger bites. Seems he camped out in the woods up there on the mountain and picked up a few. That's a city slicker for you. Well, guess I better be on my way. My wife don't like me to be out this late." He grinned at them and ambled off in the direction of the parking lot.

Maggie avoided Tate's eyes.

"Chiggers, huh? Maybe the Tsagasi are on my side after all," said Tate. Maggie cast him a sidelong look, waiting for him to crack a smile, but he didn't. She didn't know what to say, but at least Jacob, bless him, had confirmed that she and Kip hadn't spent the night together.

Whatever his thoughts on the matter, Tate wasn't lingering on them. "We'll go to my place, heat up a can of soup.

It doesn't sound too appetizing, but it's the best I can offer," he said as they got back on the motorcycle.

Maggie was beyond caring what she ate; given half a chance, she would have laid her cheek against Tate's broad back and fallen asleep as they rode. She felt the tension in Tate's muscles and gripped him even more tightly. Was he aware of her holding him? Did he realize that she wanted nothing so much as to hold him like this all night long? By the time Tate stopped his motorcycle in the garage of the modest apartment building where he lived when he was in town, Maggie was wondering if he was still capable of knowing her thoughts or if he had tuned her out.

"Come on," he said when she stood hesitantly beside the bike. He led her up a narrow inside staircase and opened the door on a large room with a view of the town spread out below.

"What a great view," she murmured. The building stood on a low hill, and from here she could see Flat Top Mountain. Through a door on one side of the living room, she saw a small den occupied by a desk and bookshelves filled with books and basketball trophies, and through another door, she saw a bedroom. She turned her eyes away from the king-size bed, not wanting Tate to know that she had noticed it.

"Do you want chicken noodle soup or beef barley?" Tate called from the kitchen.

"I don't care. Either is fine," Maggie said distractedly.

Tate appeared at the kitchen door, hands braced on the frame. "I asked you what you wanted. Don't make me do the choosing."

"Chicken noodle," she said.

"That's better," he told her, and she thought he smiled before disappearing again.

"Would you like some help?" she called after him.

"Nope. Relax. You worked hard today." She heard him using the can opener, dumping the soup into a pan.

Not knowing what else to do, Maggie sat down on the couch, apprehensive about what would happen next. Tate had said some terrible things to her back in the parking lot at Conso this morning, and she still had no idea if their relationship had a future.

When the soup was hot, Tate brought a tray and set it on the coffee table. Without a word, he handed Maggie a bowl. Instead of sitting down beside her, he pulled a floor cushion over to the couch and sat on it, leaning against the couch arm.

Maggie didn't know whether to start a conversation or to wait until Tate did. He looked as tired as she was; his hair was tangled, and he had deep circles under his eyes. So did she, probably. Once she had finished the soup and a few crackers that Tate also provided, she felt her eyelids growing heavier and heavier.

"Maggie," Tate said, and her eyes flew open. "You did a fine job helping me with the paper. Thank you."

"I was glad to help," she said, forcing herself awake. She hesitated, then plunged ahead. She was curious to know what Tate planned for his future, although it had seemed obvious as they worked on the newspaper. But for him to switch from his PR job at Conso to what was sure to be an adversarial role at the *Scot's Cove Messenger* was a complete about-face.

"Do you really intend to be the managing editor of the *Messenger*?" she asked.

Tate shifted his position so that he was looking at her. "Yes," he said. "Albie offered me the job when I talked with him at the hospital, and I wanted to take it, but there was the problem of what I should do about my position at Conso. Then, when Karl was attacking me for what he per-

ceived as my involvement with the Kalmia Conservation
Coalition, it all became clear in my mind. I walked out, and
I'm never going to regret it."

"I'm glad, Tate. No job is worth compromising your integrity."

He stared at her for a long moment. There was something hard in his gaze, and she had a moment of forebod-
ing.

"No man is worth compromising your integrity, either,"
he said. "That's why I was surprised to find Kip at the
cabin."

She blinked rapidly. "Nothing happened. After what Jacob Pinter said, you must believe me."

"I always wanted to believe you, but Maggie, when I saw
Kip walking out of your bedroom, all my old confused
feelings came back, and it was like the many times in my
childhood when I'd thought somebody loved me and then
found out that their version of love amounted to a way of
manipulating me so I'd do what they wanted. Can you
blame me for thinking that you had used me?"

"I can't blame you for anything, Tate. You didn't do
anything wrong. You were programmed by your past to see
things a certain way, and you're having a hard time getting
around it."

"You understand," he said unbelievingly.

"Yes," she said, her voice a mere whisper.

Then, without knowing quite how it happened, she was
in his arms, listening to his heart beating beneath his shirt.
She absorbed the reality of him, loving him, willing his heart
to be open to what she had to say. She pulled away, but only
far enough so that she could see his face.

"I threw Kip out last night, Tate. I never want to see him
again," she said. Quickly she related how Kip had wanted

to take a shower and how she had awakened only when she heard Tate walk in the front door.

He gazed deep into her eyes; she felt as if he were looking into her very soul. "I do believe you. But Maggie, Kip Baker meant a lot to you for a long time. You're pregnant with his child."

Maggie would have given anything if her baby had not been Kip's. Holding Tate's gaze with her own, she took his hands in hers and placed them gently on either side of her abdomen. "I'm carrying another man's child. It's true. But I think of my baby as yours, Tate, yours and mine, by virtue of the love I've felt for you every time we made love. I never felt this way about Kip, never had this depth of feeling for anyone in my life, and Kip certainly doesn't love my child and never will. I wish that my child had been fathered by you, Tate Jennings, because in my heart you are the father of my baby and always will be."

Slowly Tate moved his hands to cup the precious lump that was the baby. A warmth spread through her, starting in her abdomen and spreading to her chest, thighs, face. She felt his tenderness; it embraced her and the baby, and his love filled her up, made her complete.

"I wish the baby was mine, too," he said. "Then I would have some claim on you."

Her eyes were wet; she blinked back the tears. "You already do," she said.

"I don't want to find happiness and have it yanked away from me again. I'm afraid, Maggie."

"What would make you believe that what we feel for each other is real, Tate?"

"'When your soul comes into the very center of my soul, never to turn away,'" he quoted. These, as he recalled, had been Charlie's words exactly.

"Such a beautiful thought," Maggie murmured.

"It's not original," Tate said, and he went on to tell her how he had first heard about this mingling of souls from Tsani in his vision.

"Tsani said that he and Peg can't go together to the Nightland until we correct the mistakes of the past. From what I can figure out, that won't happen until our souls blend and become one. I'm not sure how that happens," he said wryly.

You know, said Peg's voice, and suddenly, she did.

"We have to let down all the barriers," she said, the words pouring out without her thinking about them. "We can no longer think of ourselves as separate. And we're not, Tate. I've always known that you can tell what I'm thinking, and lately—lately I feel what you're feeling. We're thinking and feeling as one person, Tate. I *know* this."

Tate stared at her. "Maggie. Is this true?"

She gazed at him steadily. "You know it is," she said.

"You learned to block my mind from your thoughts. There have been times when I couldn't get through."

"Not any more. Not now that you've learned to feel your emotions. We're the only ones who can keep ourselves separate and apart, no one else can do it, we have to work at coming together. Oh, Tate, I don't want to be apart from you in any way. I used to think that if our bodies were one in making love, that was all we needed. But there's more, so much more. Do you understand?"

"I think I do. I certainly feel that I'm standing on the edge of something wonderful and beautiful," Tate said.

"So am I. And I don't want it to pass me by."

"Then let's jump into it. Together," Tate said, cupping his hands around her face.

She looked deep into his eyes and saw how much he loved her. All her doubts melted away; Tate was right for her and for the baby. Only moments ago, she had been so tired that all she could think about was sleep. Now she felt energized, pulsing with excitement about the future, about her life, about love.

She knew the secret. Suddenly everything that she had learned on the mountain became clear. Love was not one-dimensional, a joining of bodies. It was a unique blending of the mental, the emotional, the spiritual and the physical. Maybe there were even more dimensions to love than she and Tate had even dreamed—just as there were more dimensions to reality than they had suspected before Peg and Tsani had entered their lives.

Make this new knowledge work for you, Peg told her, and Maggie closed her eyes, summoning the infinite power of love into her most profound consciousness, willing herself to transmit that limitless love to Tate and to the baby and to every human being who came into her sphere of influence forever after.

"Maggie?"

When Tate spoke her name, Maggie opened her eyes and saw that they were surrounded by a golden glow, and in that moment it seemed to expand to include the whole world, the universe, galaxies. She felt happy, joyous, loving.

Tate touched her face, touched her hair, touched her breasts. He felt the wonder of that moment, too; she knew he did, and with growing understanding, she lifted her lips for his kiss. His mouth, so sensual, so seductive, captured hers, and she remembered how it felt to have that mouth upon her throat, her breasts, her belly. Her head spun, her mind reeled, and she felt his mind trying to get in tune with hers. She had been blocking it, blocking him, but now, open to love, she let him in. As she did, she felt his love for her radiating from him in great rushing waves of emotion.

Time and space evaporated, and in the place where she was she saw and felt and knew only Tate, who was somehow naked, his kisses inflaming her desire. She tunneled her hands through his unruly hair, heard him whispering her name, discarded her clothes in movements as light as air. As she sank beneath him, felt his body enter hers, she was floating, drifting, lost on a cloud of sensation. She heard her voice, but was it hers? It sounded unfamiliar in her ears, and dulcimer music was everywhere, and silvery laughter and the beating of white wings. And when she looked up at Tate, into his eyes, she saw the essence of the man inside and knew him as the lover she had lost so long ago at the waterfall, and he had returned for her, and they were going to have their baby, and she smiled into his soul, felt it rise out of him and wrap her in love, and she entered into it without hesitation, leaping across the chasm of doubt without fear.

"Margaret!" he cried, and in that luminous moment of merging she knew that old wrongs had been righted, old sorrows laid to rest. All that was left was the future, stretching before them bright and beautiful, her soul within his, his soul within hers, a future of love forever and ever.

"I love you, Maggie," he said.

"I love you, Tate," she replied, wondering how she could have ever found those words difficult to say, and then the heavens opened and smiled above her.

She heard another rush of wings, felt Peg's release and Tsani's triumph, and before she fell asleep in Tate's arms, she knew that she had somehow, for the space of a split second, touched eternity.

"GET MARRIED!" said Bronwyn, aghast.

"If he ever asks me," Maggie said. It was six weeks after the day that Tate quit his job at Conso; also six weeks after the night when she and Tate had released Peg and Tsani to the Nightland by admitting their love for each other.

"I thought that after Kip, you didn't want anything to do with men. I thought you could never trust anyone again."

"Call it a lover's leap," said Maggie. "A huge leap of faith and trust and love."

Bronwyn seemed to digest this. "Does this mean that you won't ever come back to Atlanta?"

"'Fraid so," Maggie said, licking her ice-cream spoon. She had finally gotten around to trying ice cream and pickles to see if it was a good combination; the answer was no, if the pickles were kosher dill and the ice cream peppermint. She made a mental note to try another flavor of ice cream next time. She wrote Butter Brickle on the pad of paper by the phone; underneath, she wrote, Gherkins.

"What about your job?"

"Am I not writing scintillating ad copy every day for MMB&O? Is it not being efficiently submitted by fax? Are you not completely happy with my work?"

"Well, sure, but I suppose this means we're going to continue working long-distance."

"I like the arrangement, and besides, Tate can't leave his job at the *Messenger*. Albie's doing fine, but he's only going to work mornings from now on, and Tate has to pick up the slack."

"Is there any chance that you're going to become a newspaper reporter, too?" From the tone of Bronwyn's voice, you would have thought that this was a fate worse than death.

"No, not a chance. And Tate isn't a mere reporter. He is managing editor, thank you very much. He's making waves, too. After his in-depth coverage of the Kalmia Conservation Coalition and what is now being called the Monday Morning March on Conso, the coalition has so much support that Conso can't ignore it any more. Jolene Ott has actually met with the company president and they're discussing those five hundred extra mobile home sites on Breadloaf, Jolene is optimistic that she can talk the company into modifying their plans. The coalition has exposed Conso's plans to scrap the wilderness park, the *Messenger* has run outraged editorials about it, and now the state legislature is getting involved. Tate is elated.''

"Ho hum," said Bronwyn pointedly. "I can't imagine why you think this is interesting to me."

"I didn't. I wanted to tell you how Tate and I are making a difference here, that's all." She heard the sound of Tate's motorcycle racing up the driveway and craned her neck for a view of him. She was always happy when she saw him at the end of the day, and it seemed sometimes that she lived for the moment when he walked through the door, hair bouncing around his shoulders, and kissed her.

"I hope I don't have to come for a visit," Bronwyn said with a martyred air. "Please tell me you're all right."

"Couldn't you come for a visit even if I'm fine? I miss you, Bronwyn."

At that moment, Tate walked in the door, tossed a copy of the latest *Scot's Cove Messenger* on the counter, and gave Maggie a big loud smack on the cheek.

"What was that?" asked Bronwyn.

"Tate kissing me," Maggie said.

"Who is that?" Tate asked.

"Bronwyn. I'm trying to talk her into coming for a visit. When would you suggest she come?"

"How about for our wedding?" Tate poured himself some iced tea from a pitcher in the refrigerator and eyed Maggie over the top of his glass.

Maggie stared at him.

"We'd better get married, don't you think? Before the kiddo thinks he doesn't have a dad?" Tate's eyes were sparkling.

"I think," Maggie said into the phone, "that I've just received a proposal of marriage."

Tate took the phone away from her. "She did. Will you come, Bronwyn?"

"When is it?" Maggie could hear the words from two feet away.

Tate studied Maggie, taking in her openmouthed astonishment, her blond hair caught up into a haphazard ponytail, the loose white dress shirt, formerly his, that she wore over light blue leggings to accommodate the kiddo.

"Saturday," he said.

"We're getting married on Saturday?" Maggie shrieked.

"At four in the afternoon. Right here on Flat Top Mountain," he informed her.

"You'd better let me talk to Maggie," Bronwyn said.

"I don't think she's capable of speech right now," Tate replied.

"I...I—" Maggie stammered. She jumped up and down, threw her arms around Tate, and kissed him on the mouth.

"What was that?" Bronwyn asked.

"Maggie kissing me."

"Do you two always kiss on the phone?"

"Usually we kiss on the lips. Maggie, don't. Maggie, stop. Maggie, don't stop," said Tate.

Maggie relieved Tate of the receiver. "I think we'd better hang up now," she said hastily to Bronwyn. "We obviously have a lot to talk about."

"Wait a minute! Aren't you interested in an RSVP?"

"Will you be here?"

"Will I! Nothing less than your wedding could ever get me to Scot's Cove again, Maggie. It had better be good. What should I wear?"

Maggie covered the mouthpiece with her hand. "Bronwyn wants to know what she should wear."

"Anything," Tate said.

"Anything," Maggie repeated into the phone.

"What are you going to wear? What's he going to wear? No, don't tell me. If he's going to be wearing a loincloth, I really don't want to know."

Maggie giggled. "I'll probably be wearing something in maternity wear. The kiddo is getting bigger every day."

"Great," Bronwyn said without any discernible enthusiasm. "What would you like for a wedding gift?"

"We have everything we need for the house. How about a present for the baby? A crib, a high chair—"

"I'll give you a silver teething ring from Tiffany's," Bronwyn said. "Monogrammed."

Inwardly, Maggie groaned. Leave it to Bronwyn to suggest something totally impractical.

"I think it's about time you hang up and tell me whether you accept my proposal," suggested Tate.

"I have to hang up now, Bronwyn," Maggie said, and she did.

She and Tate gazed at each other, their faces wreathed in smiles.

"I take it you've accepted," he said, folding her into his arms.

"Yes, a thousand times yes," she replied.

He rested his chin on the top of her head. "I started thinking about Peg and Tsani going off to the Nightland together, and I thought that they shouldn't be the only ones who live happily ever after. Besides, I want the kiddo to have my name. I want to be a good daddy, the best daddy in the world, and the way to prove my good intentions is to marry the kiddo's mommy."

"I love you, Tate. It seems like I always loved you, even when I didn't know you."

"But you did know me. A long time ago. When I was Tsani and you were Peg."

"This time, the legend has a happy ending," she said, gazing deep into his dark eyes.

"And we are going to have a happy beginning," he declared before kissing her.

When they pulled apart, Maggie looked down at her stomach. "I think we also have a happy middle," she exclaimed in surprise. "I think the baby just moved."

He placed his hands on her abdomen. "I can't feel a thing," he said.

"Kiss me again," she commanded. "That's what started him kicking before."

He kissed her, but nothing happened. "Come on, kiddo," he coaxed against her lips. He kissed her again, and again, nothing.

"The only thing I'm feeling is a mad consuming passion for you," he said, and she laughed delightedly.

He swung her up in his arms and bore her away to the bedroom, kissing her all the way to the bed, and soon the only sound was of a clock's ticking. But that wasn't all that Maggie heard. From somewhere floated a bit of silvery laughter, and behind it, she could barely discern a chord played on a mountain dulcimer.

Epilogue

Maggie decreed that their child would not make his worldly debut in a hospital; instead, the long-awaited kiddo would enter the world via natural childbirth in the cabin on Flat Top Mountain where scores of Macintyres had been born before.

And so it happened that a small nervous group gathered in the living room of the ancestral home to lend their support to Tate and Maggie as Maggie labored to bring forth their child behind the closed door of the bedroom. Above the old double bed hung the finished quilt, which was serving as a wall hanging until Maggie donated it to the museum. The quilt's final square had been added only a month ago; it showed Peg and Tsani together against a dark background sprinkled with stars, which was Maggie's idea of what the Nightland must look like.

"Push, Maggie," Tate said, his arms encircling her as he held her up in the bed, and Maggie gathered every ounce of energy within her and pushed. "Push, push, push," Tate repeated until she collapsed against him, beads of perspiration standing out on her forehead. It didn't seem fair that the thrill of childbirth wore off after about ten minutes of hard labor.

"Don't you have some Cherokee magic that will help?" Maggie implored the nurse-midwife, Judy Bearkiller, who was Charlie Bearkiller's sister-in-law.

Judy smoothed Maggie's damp brow. "You want me to try the old way?"

"Old way, new way, I don't care as long as it works," Maggie said.

Judy took a yellowish liquid from her bag and poured it into a cup.

"Wait a minute, what's that?" Tate said.

"We call it yellow root," she said.

"Do I have to drink it?" Maggie eyed the stuff balefully; it seemed to her that too much was being required of her. Push, breathe, push, breathe. She'd had enough. She wanted her baby, and she wanted it now.

"Not yet. I will show you."

Judy stood behind Maggie and blew some of the liquid onto the top of Maggie's head, singing in the Cherokee language. Then she blew more of the liquid onto Maggie's breast and sang another verse. Finally she handed Maggie the rest of the liquid in the cup. "Now you drink it," she said. "It is supposed to make your baby jump down."

"Jump down?" said Tate, thinking that there had already been more than enough leaping in this family to last several lifetimes.

"Be born," explained Judy.

Maggie drank uncomplainingly and in a matter of moments was seized with a huge contraction and then another. Tate cradled her close, crooning encouragement into her ear.

"The baby is coming," Judy announced dramatically.

A few more contractions, and Maggie felt the baby's head. Another contraction, and the body was born. Another, and the midwife uttered a jubilant cry.

"A boy," she said. "A fine healthy boy."

Tate kissed Maggie's cheek. Her eyes sought his. "I love you, Maggie," he said softly, and thankfully she clutched his hand. She knew she could never have done this without him. Finally she closed her eyes, wanting nothing so much as to sink into a state of peaceful exhaustion.

Tate held his son in his arms, admiring the downy yellow fluff on the baby's head, which was pure Maggie, and the dimpled cheeks, and the chubby face. Finally, although he was still marveling, the impatient midwife reclaimed the baby and shooed Tate out of the room so that she could attend to Maggie and the baby in peace.

A jubilant Tate emerged into a living room full of people, all sitting on the edge of their chairs as this episode of high drama required.

"Is it a bow or a meal sifter?" demanded Charlie Bear-killer.

Tate was nonplussed. "It's a—a kiddo," he finished lamely.

"A boy is a bow, a girl is a meal sifter. So, which is it?"

"A bow. A boy. A fine, healthy boy.

"Is Maggie okay?" Bronwyn asked.

"Maggie is wonderful." He couldn't begin to tell them how wonderful she had been, how her strength had impressed him, how her bravery had inspired him.

"She must be so happy," said Jolene.

"*I* am so happy," Tate assured her.

"I hope this doesn't mean that the paper is going to be out late tomorrow," said Albie in a gruff tone.

"No, but I'm thinking of putting my son's birth announcement in the front page headline," Tate said with a straight face.

"What is his name?"

"Mac. Short for Macintyre."

"I like it," said Bronwyn, surprising him. Bronwyn hardly ever liked anything.

A series of anxious questions about mother and son followed, and before long Judy Bearkiller opened the bedroom door and beckoned.

Maggie, propped up on pillows, her son nestled in her arms, looked euphoric. She held out one hand to Tate, who clasped it between his immediately. They smiled at each other, exchanging a glance of intimate congratulation. Then they both smiled at their friends.

"This is our son, Macintyre Jennings," Maggie said, and everyone clapped spontaneously.

Before long, their friends trooped into the living room, leaving Maggie and Tate alone with their wide-eyed and alert baby. As Tate settled close to Maggie on the bed, they heard the popping of a champagne cork on the other side of the door, and their son yawned.

"I think he's bored," said Maggie. "Things aren't lively enough around here for him."

"Wait until the Tsagasi start chasing him."

"That doesn't worry me somehow. The Tsagasi were good for you, weren't they?"

"Everything is good for me. For the first time in my life, I have a real home, a family and a job I love. I've never been so happy, Maggie."

"The only way I could be happier is if I had a couple more kiddos just like this one," Maggie said.

"You've got to be kidding," Tate said. After her hard labor, he couldn't believe that Maggie would be willing to go through the whole process again.

"Not kidding. Kiddo-ing," she said solemnly. "Wait until I'm well, and I'll prove how much I want another baby. A girl this time. Maybe we'll call her Peg. Or Meg. I'll have to think about it. Tate, get down the family Bible. We have an entry to make.''

Tate took the tattered book from its shelf in the wardrobe and opened it to the page listing births.

''You write it, Tate,'' Maggie said, and so he wrote in his firm strong hand, ''To Margaret Macintyre Jennings and Tate Jennings, a son, Macintyre Jennings.'' Underneath, he inscribed the date.

Maggie read what Tate had written and smiled her approval. ''I think Tsani and Peg would be pleased,'' she said.

Tate closed the Bible and set it aside. Then he kissed the top of his son's head.

''You know what I was thinking while I was in labor?'' Maggie asked dreamily.

''Probably how miserable you were and how much you wanted to get it over with.''

''Bingo. You can still read my mind. But the other thing was that I was so glad that you were holding me. Knowing that you were there for me every bit of the way made the experience of childbirth even more special. I can never tell you how much it meant to me.''

''It's I who should be thanking you. For making me part of your life. For showing me how to love. And for giving me a son. I want to hold you—both of you—forever. To belong to you. To know that you want me and need me—''

''And love you. Forever.''

She lifted her lips for his kiss. He kissed her lingeringly, lovingly.

''I think I hear the music, Tate,'' she said against his lips. ''Dulcimer music.''

''I hear it, too,'' he said, and for a moment, only a moment, they saw the vague outline of Peg and Tsani standing at the foot of the bed with their arms around each other. They looked blissful and radiant and somehow at peace.

Thank you, said Tsani. *We love you,* said Peg, and she smilingly blew a kiss in their direction. Then, still in each other's arms, they faded away into the night.

He's at home in denim; she's bathed in diamonds...
Her tastes run to peanut butter; his to pâté...
They're bound to be together

for Richer, for Poorer

We're delighted to bring you more of the kinds of stories
you love in FOR RICHER, FOR POORER—where lovers
are drawn by passion...but separated by price!

In June watch for:

#634 *REBEL WITH A CAUSE*
By Kim Hansen

Don't miss any of the
FOR RICHER, FOR POORER
books—only from

HARLEQUIN®
AMERICAN ◆ ROMANCE®

BRIDE'S BAY RESORT

UNLOCK THE DOOR TO GREAT ROMANCE
AT BRIDE'S BAY RESORT

Join Harlequin's new across-the-lines series, set
in an exclusive hotel on an island off the coast of
South Carolina.

Seven of your favorite authors will bring you exciting stories
about fascinating heroes and heroines discovering love at
Bride's Bay Resort.

Look for these fabulous stories coming to a store near you
beginning in January 1996.

Harlequin American Romance #613 in January
Matchmaking Baby by Cathy Gillen Thacker

Harlequin Presents #1794 in February
Indiscretions by Robyn Donald

Harlequin Intrigue #362 in March
Love and Lies by Dawn Stewardson

Harlequin Romance #3404 in April
Make Believe Engagement by Day Leclaire

Harlequin Temptation #588 in May
Stranger in the Night by Roseanne Williams

Harlequin Superromance #695 in June
Married to a Stranger by Connie Bennett

Harlequin Historicals #324 in July
Dulcie's Gift by Ruth Langan

Visit Bride's Bay Resort each month wherever
Harlequin books are sold.

HARLEQUIN ®

BBAYG

HARLEQUIN® AMERICAN ROMANCE®

*With only forty-eight hours to lasso their mates—
it's a stampede...to the altar!*

WILD WEST Weddings

by Cathy Gillen Thacker

Looking down from above, Montana maven
Max McKendrick wants to make sure his heirs get
something money can't buy—true love! And if his two
nephews and niece want to inherit their piece of his
sprawling Silver Spur ranch then they'll have to wed the
spouse of *his* choice—within forty-eight hours!

Don't miss any of the Wild West Weddings titles!

#625 THE COWBOY'S BRIDE (April)

#629 THE RANCH STUD (May)

#633 THE MAVERICK MARRIAGE (June)

Bestselling authors

ELAINE COFFMAN
RUTH LANGAN

and

MARY McBRIDE

Together in one fabulous collection!

OUTLAW Brides

Available in June wherever Harlequin
books are sold.

HARLEQUIN ®

OUTB

HARLEQUIN®

Don't miss these Harlequin favorites by some of our most distinguished authors!
And now, you can receive a discount by ordering two or more titles!

HT #25645	THREE GROOMS AND A WIFE		
	by JoAnn Ross	$3.25 U.S./$3.75 CAN.	☐
HT #25648	JESSIE'S LAWMAN		
	by Kristine Rolofson	$3.25 U.S./$3.75 CAN.	☐
HP #11725	THE WRONG KIND OF WIFE		
	by Roberta Leigh	$3.25 U.S./$3.75 CAN.	☐
HP #11755	TIGER EYES by Robyn Donald	$3.25 U.S./$3.75 CAN.	☐
HR #03362	THE BABY BUSINESS by Rebecca Winters	$2.99 U.S./$3.50 CAN.	☐
HR #03375	THE BABY CAPER by Emma Goldrick	$2.99 U.S./$3.50 CAN.	☐
HS #70638	THE SECRET YEARS by Margot Dalton	$3.75 U.S./$4.25 CAN.	☐
HS #70655	PEACEKEEPER by Marisa Carroll	$3.75 U.S./$4.25 CAN.	☐
HI #22280	MIDNIGHT RIDER by Laura Pender	$2.99 U.S./$3.50 CAN.	☐
HI #22235	BEAUTY VS THE BEAST by M.J. Rogers	$3.50 U.S./$3.99 CAN.	☐
HAR #16531	TEDDY BEAR HEIR by Elda Minger	$3.50 U.S./$3.99 CAN.	☐
HAR #16596	COUNTERFEIT HUSBAND		
	by Linda Randall Wisdom	$3.50 U.S./$3.99 CAN.	☐
HH #28795	PIECES OF SKY by Marianne Willman	$3.99 U.S./$4.50 CAN.	☐
HH #28855	SWEET SURRENDER by Julie Tetel	$4.50 U.S./$4.99 CAN.	☐

(limited quantities available on certain titles)

	AMOUNT	$
DEDUCT:	**10% DISCOUNT FOR 2+ BOOKS**	$
ADD:	**POSTAGE & HANDLING**	$
	($1.00 for one book, 50¢ for each additional)	
	APPLICABLE TAXES**	$_____
	TOTAL PAYABLE	$_____
	(check or money order—please do not send cash)	

To order, complete this form and send it, along with a check or money order for the total above, payable to Harlequin Books, to: **In the U.S.:** 3010 Walden Avenue, P.O. Box 9047, Buffalo, NY 14269-9047; **In Canada:** P.O. Box 613, Fort Erie, Ontario, L2A 5X3.

Name: _____

Address: _____ City: _____

State/Prov.: _____ Zip/Postal Code: _____

**New York residents remit applicable sales taxes.
 Canadian residents remit applicable GST and provincial taxes.

HBACK-AJ3